DISHONORED®
THE VEILED TERROR

ADAM CHRISTOPHER

TITAN BOOKS

DISHONORED: THE VEILED TERROR

Print edition ISBN: 9781789090376
E-book edition ISBN: 9781789090383

Published by Titan Books
A division of Titan Publishing Group Ltd
144 Southwark Street, London SE1 0UP

First edition: September 2018
10 9 8 7 6 5 4 3 2 1

Editorial Consultants:
Harvey Smith
Paris Nourmohammadi

Special thanks to Harvey Smith, Brittany Quinn,
and everyone at Arkane Studios.

A CIP catalogue record for this title is available from the British Library.

Printed and bound by CPI Group (UK) Ltd, Croydon CR0 4YY

DISHONORED®

THE VEILED TERROR

The night is cold and the air is heavy with moisture, just like it always is in this rat-infested city. No matter the time of year. No matter the season. Winter or summer; Month of Hearths, Month of Clans, Months of shit-stained Darkness—Dunwall, capital of the Empire of the Isles, the great and gray metropolis, largest city in the world, is cold and it is wet and it is miserable and life in it for those who call the streets their home is as hard as it is short.

This is a fact the girl knows only too well. Sometimes she can't remember how long she has been on the streets, can't remember anything more than flashes of her previous life, the life before the cold and the wet and the surviving.

Sometimes all she remembers about the life that was hers, once, a long time ago, are flashes of memory: an image of her mother, her features sharp and malnourished, her manner always cruel, always angry, her only true and constant companion the bottle of foul-smelling liquor that cost more than it would to feed herself and her young daughter for a week. Her voice as hard as her bony fists, the skin across the knuckles tearing red time and time again as she splits her child's cheek. Time and time again.

The memories aren't hers. She keeps telling herself that. They are a story, told around the guttering fire in the old whale oil drum at the back of the dark alleyway, a story that could have been told by any of those wretches, young or old, who gather around the smoky, stinking flames for warmth night after night after night.

But that memory is a truth. What is the lie is that she cannot remember. She knows this. She remembers it all.

No matter how hard she tries.

She is still a child, but only just—and she has seen more than any child should see. And there are others—the girl can count at least two more living on the streets of Dunwall who are her age. And then there are the gangs—the Hatters, the Bottle Street Gang. Some of them are the same age, or thereabouts, as she, but many are older, having survived the city by joining with others to fight against it.

It is a good plan. One day she hopes to catch their eye with her own particular skills. One day she hopes to find a home among them, perhaps even friends. The others, the ones who light the fires and huddle together and try to stay alive just one more night... well, they are not friends. Stories are shared but names rarely are, and the tales of past deeds are likely tall indeed, woven merely to earn a place at the fire and another night in the relative safety of company. Everyone is too focused on surviving to take any real interest, and anyway, the past is irrelevant.

All that matters is the here and the now.

All that matters is surviving. Each night is a battle to be won, sometimes quite literally.

Nights like tonight.

The three men are not in uniform but they all wear

hooded tunics, and she can see the remnants of the earlier rainfall clinging in beads to the boiled wool of their cloaks. They looked like boys from the City Watch, and perhaps that is what they are. But tonight they are waiting. She can sense it. There is murder in the air, the potential for violence singing like arcane electricity through the night, as they wait in the alleyway and watch the bar on the street corner ahead.

Despite the hour, it isn't dark. Far from it. With the passing of the rain the clouds have parted and the moon is full, bathing the city in a silvery monochrome.

She keeps to her hiding place as she watches the men. She is good at that, good at using the jumbled angles of this ancient city to make herself unseen, day or night. It's a skill she had to learn, but also one that seemed natural, innate. Perhaps it was an unknown product of her upbringing, the need to hide from her mother evolving into an instinct from an early age without her even realizing. Or perhaps she was born with it, this gift for stealth and secrecy and subterfuge. A gift that has served her well on the streets of Dunwall these last few years.

She peers at the men across the street. She has been looking for them, even if she doesn't want to admit this to herself, because if she did, she would also be forced to admit that she has no idea what she is going to do now she's found them. But she watches. The men talk in low voices, teeth flashing and eyes glittering beneath their hoods.

Are these the ones? Were they the ones who stood by as that letch leered at Deirdre, his companion yelling, calling them wharf roaches? Were they the ones who watched, who grinned, as the fur-collared shit from Serkonos swung his silver-topped cane, cracking Deirdre's skull like an egg, while his companion just laughed, and laughed, and laughed?

She wills herself to confront the memory, the horror of that night echoing loudly in her head. There had been the pair of dandies from Serkonos, and three officers of the City Watch, their patrol leading them to the scene of the crime.

Except it wasn't a crime. Not in Dunwall, where the murder of a street urchin in front of officers of the law could be bought off with a few coin and a sly wink.

As the patrol moved along, the dandy with the stick stood rocking on his heels, admiring his handiwork with a sneer she would never forget. His companion's mirth didn't die; he merely offered to buy his brother a new cane. Then the brother turned, and looked at the other girl—looked at her—and the leer returned all too quickly to his face.

He was soft. He died easily. The splintered end of one of the wooden gazelles that had decorated his coach made for an admirable weapon, especially effective when embedded in his eye.

The dead man's brother dropped to his knees, trying to help his kin. She wanted to kill him too, but his cries for help would soon bring others, so she took her one chance.

She ran, leaving Deirdre. She had to. But she didn't run far. She had to come back, to get Deirdre. She told herself that, even though she knew it was impossible.

She looped back around the cobbled streets, vanishing into shadows, until she was back at the scene. The dandy and his dead brother were still there. So was Deirdre. The patrol of the City Watch who had witnessed her lover's murder had also returned, and were talking to the coachman.

She watched them. She memorized their faces, their voices.

One day, they would pay. One day, her time—and theirs—would come.

Tonight is the night.

Yes, these are the ones. Yes, she has found them.

She pads forward on the rain-slick cobbles, the noise from the tavern masking her movements. She reaches for the knife at her belt, and then—

Her foot catches in a divot in the street. She falls, her hands and feet sliding underneath her as she struggles to get purchase.

One of the men turns toward her, and says something. His companions laugh, but she can't make out the words over the roaring of blood in her ears. Her heart thuds in her chest, strong enough to burst out.

He turns away. She hasn't been seen; the fold of the man's hood obscures his peripheral vision.

She stands and takes a breath. Maybe this isn't the right moment. Maybe this isn't the right night. It is three against one and she needs to be sure of her mission.

She runs to the alley. She climbs the thick iron drainpipes that crowd the wall, moving up onto the roof with effortless ease.

And then she sees him.

Black hood. Black mask. The knife gleaming in his hands. He is as still as a gargoyle and crouches on the edge of a nearby roof in much the same pose.

He jumps.

One of the men laughs, and then his laugh is cut short as his throat is sliced open from behind. Hot blood spurts out in front of him as his head is yanked backward, spraying his two companions. The attacker pushes the body sideways and turns his attention to the other two.

They don't stand a chance.

She watches as he gets to work. He is efficient, and the only sound she can hear is the snick of his blade and the gurgling of throats freshly cut. A moment later there are three bodies cooling on the cobbles and a man wiping his blade with a rag, which he then tosses onto the corpses.

Who is he? And where has he come from? She moves forward, edging toward the edge of the roof, leaning out across it. Dunwall is full of gangs, but she hasn't seen the like of him before. She is familiar with death at the end of a blade, but the way he struck, the way he handled his weapon, it—

She sucks in a breath. He has turned around, is looking at her. The moonlight is reflected in the two round goggle eyes, and as he breathes she watches the can-like beak of his mask rise and fall, rise and fall. What she can see of his hair is dark, and at the edge of his mask is a scar.

And then—

And then he is gone.

She stands tall. Looks around. She is alone on the rooftop and the three dead men are alone on the street, although she knows they will not be alone for long. High above, clouds scud across the full moon, the disc bright enough to make her squint. She looks away.

And she sees him. He is running across a rooftop on the other side of the street. With no alleyway on that side, he must have climbed up the sheer side of the building.

An impossible feat.

One she believes the masked man is entirely capable of.

She wants to know more.

She wastes no time. She races after him, skirting the

street, jumping from building to building, all the while keeping him within sight. His agility and his speed are impressive, and there is no way she can even catch him, not from here.

She makes a decision.

She doubles back to the alley. She rattles down the pipes, races across the street—leaping over the three dead men—and makes for a side road. She is behind him now, and by a long way. But she refuses to give up.

She will never give up.

Another left, another alleyway, this one bounded by warehouses, the walls crawling with a complex lattice of steel ladders and stairs. An easy enough path. She only hopes she is not too late.

She climbs. The steel platforms rattle under her feet, but there is nobody around, and she doesn't care anyway.

She has to reach him. Has to.

Because what she had a glimpse of was…

Was what? She doesn't know. Doesn't know who he was. Doesn't know what she will do when she finds him. She is a witness to murder, and she knows what happens to witnesses.

Just look at the three dead City Watchmen on the street somewhere behind her.

But the stranger. There was something about him. Something she could see.

He is…

He is a way out. He is an escape.

She can sense it. The man in the mask had a purpose, a reason for being there, a rationale for killing those men.

Perhaps the same rationale she had.

Seeing him had stirred something inside her. A desire—a need—for a purpose. Not just revenge, but something more. Something... bigger.

The rooftops of the warehouses are flat expanses that shine wetly, the water that has gathered on them inches thick. She splashes forward, pausing only to get her breath, her eyes all the while scanning the surroundings for any sign, any movement.

Her breath steams around her face. Her muscles ache. Her head spins.

She is too late. There is nothing. She is alone on the roofs as the city sleeps beneath her.

The man in the mask has gone.

The factory roofs are interrupted at intervals by tall chimneys, their bricks black and slimy. She walks forward, almost staggering, clutching at the nearest for support. Her energy is suddenly gone, evaporating into the night air like the residue of the rainfall around her.

She has lost him. It hits her, hard, and she can't explain why, not really. But part of her knows. Because for just a few seconds, she had a glimpse of something else.

Another life. Another future.

A future she might have had.

As her breathing slows, she slides down the chimney and slumps onto the rooftop. She closes her eyes, feeling the pricking heat behind the lids. She holds her breath, begins to count, tells herself to forget and that life, such as it is, goes on. The three men she wanted dead are just that, and she is safe, because she didn't do it.

Somehow, that doesn't make her feel any better.

And then she opens her eyes and she sees him, a few hundred yards ahead, crouched on the edge of the rooftop, looking at something below.

He pushes himself off into open air and vanishes from sight.

*

She finds him, at last. Their chase has taken what feels like hours, dawn breaking as she trails him to what is, apparently, his final destination, perhaps a hideout, a base. There, across the street, he jumps from a rooftop to a balcony and then slips inside the shattered window of a broken building.

This part of Dunwall, if not actually in ruins, is fast approaching that state, abandoned to the rats. It is not a part of the city she would normally venture into. Dunwall is a dangerous place, especially for one such as she, but this district is something else entirely.

This district is deadly.

Despite this, she doesn't hesitate to follow him, taking the same path as she jumps down to the balcony and steps through the window.

The room inside is gloomy and damp. The carpet is rotting underneath lopsided, broken desks stacked high with moldering papers. An office of some kind, once upon a time.

She pauses, listens, hears nothing. The door ahead of her is open. She moves toward it and steps into a disintegrating hallway. She checks around her, then picks a direction and walks.

The rest of the building is in the same condition. Whatever business was run from here, it was a significant one. The hallways are hung with many large paintings, all warped, like the wood-paneled walls, by the incessant damp. A creeping wave of black fungus is eating the walls.

The building may be empty, but there are signs of life. Some of the rooms have been cleared out, filled with camp beds arranged in rows; others, converted into storerooms, are stacked with crates and barrels.

Her stomach rumbles as she looks over the contents of the room. There is food here, and plenty of it. Enough food, she thinks, for a small army.

She hesitates. Would anything be missed? The place seems empty—well, empty apart from her and the masked man, who lurked somewhere—but she decides it isn't worth the risk, or the time.

She has to find her quarry. Has to.

She turns away from the room and returns to the passageway. She follows a stairwell down to more rooms on the lower floor of the building. The spaces here are larger; several offices have been knocked through to form one large rectangular chamber. There are several mannequins arranged around the room, mounted on swiveling stands, their arms stretched out to hold square wooden panels. Some of the panels have a bull's-eye painted on them, and there are similar target marks painted onto the foreheads and chests of the dummies.

On a long, low trestle set up against one wall, she counts four crossbows—three small, single-handed models, and a larger version—laid out, ready for use. Beside the crossbows are a handful of bolts and a short dagger in a scabbard.

It was a training room. Perhaps she had been right about the army.

It wasn't a sound that told her he was standing behind her. It was a feeling, a sensation of presence, the empty room suddenly occupied by someone other than herself.

She turns around. She watches as he pulls off the mask, grabbing it by the can-shaped respirator. His short hair is slicked back. The heavy scar runs down the right side of his face from forehead to jaw. His eyes are bright but cold.

She stands tall. She doesn't break his gaze. She doesn't make a sound.

"You followed me," he says. "Found this place, and now you're not begging or running for your life."

She lifts her chin, and takes a step forward. "There is nowhere to run," she says, "and I'm not very attached to it, to tell the—"

The words die in her throat. The man reaches toward her, palm up, waiting for her to take his hand, to join him. Except…

Except he is not the man she followed. Gone is the hooded jacket, the heavy gloves, the thick belts crisscrossing the barrel chest. The man who now stands before her is small and slim, his hair black and shiny, the bangs jagged over his forehead. His face is lit by a blue light that comes from nowhere.

His eyes are a bottomless, unfathomable black.

He laughs. She falls to her knees. Behind him, the room dissolves and she can see the infinite smoky nothing orbiting the world of hard, metallic rock on which he stands.

She knows him; she knows this place.

The Outsider stands in the Void, offering his hand.

"Our business is not yet finished, Billie Lurk," he says.

She feels the creeping cold before she hears the crackling, the sound of splintering wood, of ice splitting on the surface of a lake.

Billie looks down, and watches as the black metallic stone shifts underneath her, moving up her legs, enclosing them, transforming her flesh and bone into the stuff of the Void itself. The rock moves up her body, inch by inch.

She reaches out to the Outsider, but her hand and arm are already made of Void stone.

She screams, and the world goes dark. The only thing she can hear is the Outsider's laugh.

1

DUNWALL, GRISTOL
4th Day, Month of Wind, 1853

Billie Lurk woke with a start, her heart pounding in her chest, her breath steaming in the cold air of the small room she—temporarily, at least—called home.

She sat up, and shoved the blankets off her. Despite the chill air, she was too hot, her skin slick with an oily sweat. As her heart rate settled, she rubbed her face and blew out her cheeks.

The dream, *again*.

She lay back and closed her eyes, stretching her muscles, which were stiff and sore from another night on the hard mattress. The memory—the *immediacy*—of the dream began to fade, and she began to relax.

It was the same each morning, and had been for weeks now. She'd lost count of the number of times she had awoken suddenly, yanked out of her nightmare in a kind of blind terror that, thankfully, abated as soon as she came to her senses.

The dream. Okay… no, it wasn't, strictly speaking, the *same* dream every time. But there was a sort of formula, a pattern to them—the dreams pulled on long-buried memories, throwing her back into her past, showing her slices of her personal history she would rather not revisit. But each time, events in the dream began just as she remembered them: same people, same places, same snatches of conversation—although she knew not to rely on those parts.

And, each time, just where she didn't expect it, something would change. The memory twisted, events in her past unraveling into nightmares.

Nightmares featuring one central character.

The Outsider.

Billie sighed, and flung the rest of the blankets off the bed before swinging her legs over the side. She leaned her elbows on her thighs for a moment, and stared at the bare floorboards as she counted, just to be sure she really was awake, just to be sure the Outsider didn't appear right there in front of her, in a puff of smoke, laughing as he always did in the dream. She knew she was awake because her right arm, the one that wasn't flesh and blood but instead a twisted collection of Void-stone shards held together by some arcane magic, started to ache with a bone-deep chill—which was ironic, considering there was no bone in the limb. But ache it always did after the dreams, and Billie knew that the increasingly intense throbbing pain would soon be joined by a headache, one that started behind the thing in her head that wasn't her own eye, but which was a sliver of one that had belonged to some divinity long since departed.

She took a breath and stood. The morning air was cold—in fact, the room was freezing, but she had little choice in her lodgings. She didn't know how long she was going to stay in Dunwall, but what little money she had left she had to guard closely. The corner room in the attic of a tavern in one of the less salubrious neighborhoods of Dunwall was pure luxury compared to some of the places she had once called home. Here, she had a roof over her head and a narrow single bed and a rickety, lopsided table beneath a small leaded window that didn't close properly. Billie ducked her head under the sharp angle of the ceiling that jutted down beside the bed and pushed the window open. The stiff hinge protested with a harsh squeal, and the cold morning air wafted in over her skin. It felt warmer than the chill in her arm, and she angled her shoulder, taking a moment to enjoy the sensation.

Yes, the dreams were different each time. And she didn't normally dwell on them—bad dreams were a part of life now, not just for her, but for everyone, right across the Empire of the Isles—but this one was… well, it was *different* different.

This one was the first time she had dreamed of Daud.

The Knife of Dunwall. Leader of the Whalers. The man who had saved her, so many, many years ago, granting her a new life, one she had enjoyed before she very nearly threw it all away—only to be saved by him a second time.

Daud, her mentor. Her friend.

He was dead now, of course. It had been a year now, more or less, but this was the first time she had dreamed of him. She didn't know whether she should be grateful for that or not. Because since the death of Daud, and the fall of the Outsider, dreams were not the same. They were dangerous things, powerful enough to drive a person out of their mind. That she had gotten off so lightly was something she didn't take for granted, although she knew it was probably because of the Green Lady she habitually took now. Word of the effectiveness of the herb had spread, and the price had been rising steadily over the last few months. Another expense Billie had to be very careful with.

As for the other man in the dream—well, he was there, each and every night. Billie didn't know if other people dreamed of the Outsider. It was hard to know, now, given that the nightmares, so widely reported in the days and weeks that had followed Billie's journey into the Void, had faded from public interest. When everybody was plagued with the same disease, nobody wanted to read about it.

Billie thought that was fair enough.

And she also knew that dreams were dreams and that Daud was dead and the Outsider was gone, and that he wasn't coming back, no matter what he said to her each and every night while she slept.

Billie leaned out of the window, breathing in the fresh air. Finally, she began to feel the cold, but as she reached to close the window, the clouds parted and a shard of morning sun pierced the gloom of the city, spotlighting her small corner of it. For a moment, Billie closed her eyes and enjoyed the warmth on her face and pretended she was someone else, somewhere else. Her headache began to ease, and as she absently flexed her magical right arm, the dull ache began to leave it too.

Then she opened her eyes, squinting into the light. The city of Dunwall stretched out in front of her, the densely packed, angled slate roofs shining from the night's rain. It was, she had to admit, remarkably pretty, and as she leaned farther out and inhaled deeply, she smelled earth and stone, and she smelled water and…

Billie grimaced, and then she pulled back into the room and laughed, one hand pressed firmly against her nose.

Oh, yes, *that* was the Dunwall she remembered.

Then the laughter died in her throat and she stood by the window, staring out at the view, and she wondered how long the beautiful, ugly, sparkling, fragrant city had left to live.

2

DRAPERS WARD, DUNWALL
4th Day, Month of Wind, 1853

One month. That was how long Billie had been back in Dunwall, and after a year on the road, it already felt like a lifetime. But it also felt like a homecoming, and—for now, anyway—she enjoyed the relative stability. The capital of the Empire was where she had done most of her growing up, where she had learned the skills needed to survive. After so long away, she had to admit that she had felt Dunwall calling to her.

Standing in the doorway of the Lucky Merchant pub, the down-at-heel tavern that she was calling home, Billie wrapped the heavy Tyvian greatcoat around her and did up the double row of buttons almost to the neck, before pulling the huge collar up around her ears. The wet mornings in the city were cold, and the sun always seemed to take an age to warm the granite and slate of the place. And besides, Billie hadn't really felt warm—properly, comfortably warm—since…

Well, not since that day, when she entered the Void and changed… *everything*.

From the pocket of the greatcoat, she took a large eyepatch of black leather and slipped it over her head, adjusting it so it covered the Sliver of the Eye of the Dead God that was still embedded in her right eye socket. Since the fall of the Outsider, the Sliver hadn't fallen silent, exactly, but the powers it once granted had faded, the magic sleeping, slow to stir when she called upon it, so she didn't. Having the arcane object in her skull didn't impede her at all—she could still see perfectly well with it—and, even without the eyepatch, it didn't attract the same kind of attention it used to, not since a small proportion of the population had started to modify their own bodies, desperate to find a way to stop the dreams. In her travels over the last year, she had seen men with the shattered fragments of bone charms pierced through their skin like fish hooks, seen women with weird tattoos covering their faces, as if the hieroglyphs—most likely random shapes half-remembered from runes, their protective properties a fiction created by the backstreet artists who offered to ink their unwitting client's skin for a healthy weight of coin—would protect them from their night terrors. Among the more aristocratic classes, there had even been a fashion for embedding gemstones in the skin, the shiny, cut facets of emerald and ruby arranged in geometric patterns over the cheeks, arms, hands.

Billie found some modifications more repulsive than others, but she also used it to her advantage, the Sliver going mostly unnoticed during her travels. Although sometimes it attracted comment, usually from those carrying their own strange marks, who took the glowing red gem in her eye socket as a more extreme—and therefore more interesting—modification. But today, she could do without any attention and without the distraction, particularly where she was heading. The mission was hard enough, and Billie needed the anonymity more than anything, at least for now.

Mission. *Mission.*

Billie rolled the word around inside her head as she

walked through the city. Was it really a mission? True enough, she had come back to Dunwall with a specific purpose in mind, but calling it a mission seemed a little... well, it seemed a little pretentious. *Daud would have called it a mission,* she thought, chuckling into the collar of her greatcoat.

Ah, Daud. Hardly a day had passed since the fall of the Outsider that hadn't brought him to mind. She took solace in that. It was as if he was with her, by her side as she traveled the Isles. She remembered the tales of his life after his exile from Dunwall on the orders of the Royal Protector, Corvo Attano—the stories he told of his years of wandering, searching for some kind of meaning and purpose to a life he now found... unmoored. He'd found that purpose. It was one that consumed him, *became* him, leading him on a quest of his own, where eventually he would find his way back to Karnaca. There Billie had found him, freed him, helped him. The master and the apprentice, together again, on one final mission, one last time.

Billie marched on down the streets of Dunwall. Here she was, on her own mission. She wondered if she was just repeating the cycle of exile, journey, return, following the same path Daud had taken, not because she had found a purpose of her own but because it was the only thing she really knew.

No, that wasn't it. She really *did* have a mission, she told herself as she crossed into Drapers Ward. It was still early, the city only just starting to wake up, but already the merchant stores that lined the streets of this area were bustling with activity as shops were opened, blinds were raised, and barrels and carts were wheeled out onto the cobbles, the finest wares available in Dunwall showcased for all to peruse. Billie passed two neighboring shops, both with aproned workers outside furiously scrubbing in silent competition to see whose doorstep was the cleanest. Nobody paid Billie the slightest bit of attention. The streets were quiet but far from empty, and she walked with purpose, collar high, head down, hands thrust into the pockets of the greatcoat acquired on her last trip to the frozen northern Isles. If the merchants and traders of Drapers Ward had suffered a bad night of terrors, none of them showed it. Perhaps, like Billie, they had all discovered the benefits of chewing Green Lady.

Of course, not everybody could afford the herb, and even if they could, it didn't always work. For Billie, it dulled the dreams but also dulled her mind, and while she wasn't entirely sure that was ideal, it was better than succumbing fully to the night terrors. For those who hadn't found some kind of balm, herbal or otherwise, she couldn't imagine how they functioned.

Because the dreams were getting worse. Billie had wondered, at first, whether the effects of Green Lady were simply fading as her body became tolerant of the herb. But she had spent a month now listening to the chatter in the pubs and shops of Dunwall, eavesdropping on tales told by sailors fresh off the ships that docked at the many ports that lined the Wrenhaven River, reading the newspapers—especially those imported from Morley and Tyvia, where the editors were looser with their language than the Dunwall press. It seemed that, indeed, the situation was getting worse, not better.

It had started almost as soon as Billie had returned from the Void. Stepping back into the world felt… different. It wasn't anything you could see—the sea and the sky and the ground were all still where they were supposed to be. She remembered the sense of relief she felt when the world was still where it was supposed to be. But after a while, she realized that something *had* changed.

It was just a feeling, nothing more, but Billie knew she was different—existing apart from the world, somehow, through no fault of her own—so she trusted her instincts. For some weeks after her return, Billie stayed in Karnaca, and each night she slept like she had never slept before.

And then the dreams started. They didn't worry her, not at first. She had been a dreamer all her life, and nightmares were not unusual. But the dreams she'd had before were nothing more than a consequence of the life she had led, most likely. An inconvenience that occasionally woke her but which was soon forgotten.

When the screams started, she knew something was wrong.

But the screams were not hers. They were coming from somewhere else, drifting in through the windows she kept open on the hot and humid Karnacan nights. And they were not the screams of violence, the shouts and cries and wails that were paired with pain and torment, sounds associated with acts of crime, or, conversely, the heavy hand of the Grand Serkonan Guard. Billie had lived her kind of life long enough to know those kinds of screams only too well.

These were screams of fear, the sound of a pure, primal terror. The first night, as she jerked up in bed, heart pounding, ripped from a nightmare of her own, she had thought they were just a part of her own dream world. But on the second night, she heard them when she was awake, and then she heard them again and again, night after night, as she sat by the window, watching Karnaca.

It seemed that nearly everybody in the city was dreaming, their nightmares becoming night *terrors*, the visions so real, so awful, that they sent people running out from their homes and into the streets. After a few more nights, Billie had stayed up, waiting for the cacophony, and had then gone out to investigate, but all she found were dazed residents of the city wandering around in the dark, meeting fellow dreamers, exchanging bewildered conversations, some even breaking down in each other's arms. Soon, the Grand Guard began increasing their night patrols, doing their best to guide confused people back to their residences. Billie trailed the patrols, listening to their conversations, and from them she learned that Karnaca was not the only city affected by the terrors of the night. It was, at least according to rumors if not official reports, happening all over the Empire, from Tyvia to Morley, from Gristol to Serkonos.

So, yes, something had happened. The world *had* changed, and Billie knew it was, if not her fault, exactly, then a very real consequence of her actions.

The Outsider was gone, and the world had changed.

That was when the Sliver of the Eye of the Dead God began to burn. It was subtle at first, an irritation Billie had hardly even noticed, but over the next days and weeks, the pain slowly grew, eventually becoming so bad, so intense, it felt as though her head was being crushed in a vise. The pain came and went, but she never knew when it would be at its worst, although drawing on the power of the Sliver certainly didn't help, and even then she didn't know whether the artifact's fading, erratic abilities would be available for her use.

Chewing Green Lady seemed to help, although to take the edge off the pain as well as dull the dreams meant she was chewing rather a lot of it. But it was better to be functional, at least, rather than spending days in dark rooms, wishing the pain away, trying not to fall asleep in case the night terrors came, unchecked.

But her supply of the herb was running low, and before

she could return to her mission, she had to restock. Fortunately, Dunwall was one of the best places to get it.

Because if you wanted something that wasn't sold by the normal kind of merchant, something illicit, illegal, but above all *rare*—say, a pouch of Green Lady—Billie knew just where to go.

Checking her direction, Billie tugged at the collar of her greatcoat, adjusted the eyepatch over the Sliver, and headed toward Wyrmwood Way.

3

THE STREETS OF DUNWALL

4th Day, Month of Wind, 1853

It was only a matter of minutes before Billie knew she was being followed. She headed south, across Kaldwin Bridge, then turned west, making for Patterson Street. The walk to Wyrmwood Way was a long one, but it felt good to be moving, giving her body at least some kind of mild exercise, the cool morning air easing the dull throb in her head.

And besides, she wanted to learn more about whoever it was on her trail.

By the time she hit the southern side of the river, she had learned just one thing: the person following her wasn't very good at it. In fact, his attempt at tracking her was so farcical Billie was tempted to stop and introduce herself.

The man was wrapped in a heavy gray cloak that, while decorated with exquisite black embroidery on the sleeves, had clearly seen better days, the once almost regal garment now tatty and worn, the embroidery coming away from the velvety fabric in several flapping pieces. The cloak had a huge hood pulled down so far that it must have been exceedingly difficult for the man to see anything other than his feet and a small patch of road, let alone the person he was following. He was by far the most conspicuous person out on the streets; she could see as she glanced behind her that he had caught the eye of not just herself but many of the citizens around, and even officers of the City Watch.

It was ridiculous, and Billie's temper began to fray. She stopped at intervals, pretending to either check direction or look into store windows as she passed along a merchant row; each time, the cloaked figure would dart into an alleyway or turn his back to her, as though the voluptuous cloak would render him somehow invisible in the middle of the street. As soon as Billie resumed her march, her tail sprang into action, once again following her far too closely.

Billie didn't know who he was, didn't know why he was following her, didn't care about either of those things. Strange things had happened in the world in the last year, and more than a few citizens of the Empire had been touched by events in some way. Billie wondered whether the man's vast hood concealed some kind of body modification, or perhaps he had been chewing a little too much of his own kind of herb lately.

Her anger faded, replaced with amusement. He was an interesting distraction. She was in no danger, and after a while she ignored him. Then, as she drew closer to Wyrmwood Way, the ache in her head began to increase, and her attention returned to the task at hand: namely, the acquisition of a good few ounces of Green Lady. As she approached Darrellson Street, the long thoroughfare that acted as the unofficial northern border of the Wyrmwood district, Billie felt the weight of the coin in her coat pocket. Normally, she would have had more than enough to see her through the next few weeks—but how long exactly now depended on the current price the black marketeers of Dunwall were charging.

At Darrellson Street, the foot traffic thinned noticeably.

She passed a trio of guards from the City Watch standing beneath a lamp post, having reached the end of their patrol route and unwilling to proceed any farther. She felt the men's eyes on her as she crossed the invisible boundary and found herself on Wyrmwood Way.

Head down, collar up, Billie moved briskly down the street. Of course, while Wyrmwood Way was a somewhat… *unusual* street, there was no particular danger here on the outskirts of the district. Indeed, she wasn't the only person venturing into this territory. The City Watch might not patrol anywhere beyond Darrellson, but, despite the early hour, there were several more adventurous citizens perusing the wares on display outside the lopsided buildings that lined the street.

But what she needed wasn't to be found on Wyrmwood Way itself. She had to go deeper into the district. To Mandragora Street, where there was an apothecary's store Billie had used before.

A few minutes later, as she turned into that street, the store just ahead on her right, Billie paused and looked around. The person following her in the ridiculous cloak had vanished, probably too nervous to enter a district known for its villainy.

Billie smiled. That would have included her. Once.

She walked down the street, and entered the store.

The apothecary of Mandragora Street was a single, square shop, the walls of which were lined with shelves stacked with tins, jars, and bottles in hundreds of shapes, sizes, and colors, while down the center of the main space, two more large shelves ran, piled with more of the same. At the far end of the room, opposite the door, was a serving counter, which also acted as a barrier designed to prevent customer access to the more expensive—and potent—wares locked behind leaded glass doors in the cabinet beyond.

Billie was not the only customer. At the counter, the apothecary—a bearded man with barrel chest and tree-trunk arms, who looked like he should be roughing people up in the name of the Dead Eels Gang despite the dirty long white coat he was wearing—was talking to a younger, and far smaller, man dressed in drab, gray clothing that was almost in rags. Even from the doorway, Billie could smell the small man's reek, despite the heady mix of aromas that permeated the room from the apothecary's stock.

The apothecary glanced over his customer's shoulder at Billie as she entered. As he gave a sniff of disinterest, she saw he had a body modification of his own, a curved, hook-like sliver of whale ivory pierced through the flesh of his right cheek. The skin around the puncture looked red and angry. As he returned his attention to the first customer, Billie scooted around one of the shelves in the center of the room, keeping out of sight of the counter.

When shopping in Wyrmwood district, you tended to give other patrons their privacy.

Billie pursed her lips and scanned the shelves around her, but what she wanted wasn't on display, wasn't even in the locked cases behind the counter. Green Lady was an altogether more unusual commodity than the impressive collection of potions, herbs, salves, tonics, and powders on display in the main part of the store. She would have to wait to ask the apothecary himself, try to strike some kind of deal for a good supply… preferably with nobody else in the store.

Except the first customer didn't seem to have any intention of leaving. Billie folded her arms and frowned, her back to the pair as she eavesdropped on the conversation she had walked in on.

"Now listen, and listen good," said the apothecary. "I'm not giving you any more Addermire's, and that's final." His voice was calm and level, but with enough force behind it to give his words the authority his customer clearly hadn't yet been able to accept.

Silently, Billie turned and leaned out from behind the shelves, so she could see what was happening.

"Look, Jacko," said the customer, one hand reaching toward the apothecary, "please, you have to listen to me. Jacko, you have to. All I need is *one* more vial. Just one, and I'll be out of your hair for good, I promise, Jacko, I really promise, I do."

Jacko stood back and folded his thick arms across his chest. He scowled, and gave a slight shake of the head.

"I'm sorry, Mr. Woodrow, but there's nothing I can—"

"Jacko! Come on now, Jacko! See me right, won't you?"

The apothecary sighed and unfolded his arms, before leaning on the counter in a way that Billie could see was supposed to be intimidating, if only his customer wasn't so utterly desperate. The small man did twitch, just a little, but whether this was due to the rapidly deteriorating attitude of the apothecary or something else entirely, Billie wasn't sure—although she would have put coin on the latter. There was certainly something wrong with him.

"Now, you listen to me, Hayward," said Jacko, his voice now a low rumble from his vast chest. "*Listen*. I've been good to you. You know I have. I know your troubles. And I've tried to help. But you have to understand that my business doesn't normally run to charity. Just because I knew your mother and helped her when your father got sick, doesn't mean I can keep you supplied with Addermire Solution. They don't make it anymore. What stock I've got left is a precious commodity, one I have to protect."

"I'll pay!" Woodrow spluttered, his hands diving into his tattered clothing. "Jacko, I can pay… I just…" He paused, looking down at himself as his roving hands failed to come up with any coin. He jerked his head up and leaned on the counter, bringing his face just about level with Jacko's chin. "I know a place!" he said, far too quickly. "I'll level with you, Jacko. I know a place, hidden, it is, where there's some of the Abbey's platinum. It's a… secret. It's not far. I just… I just need a little time to get it. You know how it is. And maybe… and maybe you can just give me some Addermire before I go, just a little bit, just so as I can get there and come back all the quicker, right, Jacko? Right? Jacko, tell me I'm right, will you?"

Jacko sighed, then in one swift movement he grabbed Woodrow by the front of his tattered jacket, lifting the man clear off the floor and yanking him across the serving counter on his stomach.

"Don't you come to me with that story again, boy!" roared Jacko. "That's the second time you've tried it, not that your addled mind would remember! You know as well as I do that any treasure or coin the High Overseer had squirreled away was confiscated by the Empress after she dissolved the Abbey of the Everyman."

"No, no, not all of it, Jacko, not all of it," said Woodrow, trying his best to speak as the apothecary's fists tightened at his neck. "Listen, Jacko, me and some of the other Overseers, we—"

Jacko wrenched the man further across the counter. Woodrow cried out in surprise and kicked with one leg, his knee knocking a set of brass tins off the top of the serving bench. They hit the floor with a clatter and spilled open, sending a fine, dark green ash fanning out across the flagstones.

Jacko snarled. "No, *you* listen to *me*, Hayward. There are no Overseers anymore, my son. You know that better than I do. And there's no more Addermire Solution for you now, neither. So either you leave and you don't come back, or I break your legs and you can go crawling to your friends and tell them that Jacko's patience has run clean out, got it, lad?"

Billie watched the scene unfold with interest. So, the customer claimed he was an Overseer. Billie *hrmmed* quietly to herself.

Of course, there was no such thing as an Overseer. Not anymore. That was something else that had changed after the Outsider had fallen, something far more concrete than strange dreams and visions. Just days after Billie had returned from the Void, she began to hear rumors about strange happenings at the Abbey of the Everyman. Billie ignored the reports at first, but over time they became more and more outlandish, culminating with the bizarre story that the High Overseer had become moonstruck and, having called a meeting with high-ranking officials of both the Abbey and the Sisters of the Oracular Order, killed more than a dozen of his brothers and sisters—including the High Oracle herself—before being finally overpowered.

That was a year ago. Since then, there had been no official news, no announcements or proclamations, but Billie had pieced the story together and traced events back, and had found that it was true that, just after the fall of the Outsider, neither the High Overseer nor the High Oracle had been seen in public again.

The Abbey of the Everyman lasted only another six months after that, when, without warning, Empress Emily Kaldwin abolished the institution. An entire battalion of soldiers from Whitecliff was ordered into the Abbey in Dunwall in a symbolic show of force, occupying the building while it was stripped of valuables. Most of the Overseers simply fled. Those who tried to put up a defense were killed or locked up in Coldridge Prison, where they remained to this day. There were other rumors, too, that the High Overseer was *not* dead, that he had been kept hidden in the Abbey, his mind broken, and that he was now locked in Coldridge in an iron straightjacket.

Billie wasn't quite sure about *that* story.

But at least the Overseers hadn't suffered the same fate as the Sisters of the Oracular Order. While the Abbey had been dissolved and the post of Overseer abolished, the men—those who hadn't resisted the Imperial army, anyway—had been allowed to go free. The Sisterhood was actually *hunted*—across the Isles, their chapels were stormed, most of the Sisters themselves burned at the stake on sight.

But according to Billie's sources, this wasn't Emily's doing. The order of the Empress had been the same for the Abbey and for the Order, as the two were merely branches of the same institution. But something had happened to the soldiers sent to turn out the Sisterhood, and what should have been a firm but lawful suppression turned into massacres, all over the Isles, as chapels were torn down and the Sisters killed. The news was shocking, although the silence from the Empress was, for Billie, perhaps even more so. Billie had never heard quite what happened to those soldiers to make them go rogue. Some said they had seen horrors beyond imagining within the walls of the chapels, things which had driven them berserk. Others said a cabal of military commanders with a vicious streak and a secret agenda against the Sisterhood had been responsible.

Whatever the case, the Sisters of the Oracular Order were no more.

Meanwhile, the strange behavior of those Overseers who had hidden themselves across the Isles, fearful of persecution, had steadily worsened. Billie suspected it was the same dreams that plagued everyone—but because they were former Overseers, who had obsessed over the arcane, they were probably preconditioned to be among the worst affected. They fought amongst each other in the street, becoming rabid, insensible, and highly dangerous. Those the City Watch didn't round up found darker corners to hide in, turning their broken minds to low-grade sorceries in an effort to regain their status—and their sanity.

Hayward Woodrow, at least, seemed one of the more cogent former Overseers that Billie had encountered. That he was even still alive spoke of some skill at self-preservation, something you needed at least some of your wits to manage.

At the apothecary counter, Jacko and Woodrow seemed to have reached an impasse. Dangling over the counter, his ragged clothing bunched up around him, the emaciated Woodrow was no match physically for the muscular bulk of the apothecary. Jacko was clearly well suited to his job—his store contained many rare, valuable, and highly illicit items, and he would have had to deal with far worse than Woodrow on a fairly regular basis. Billie cursed herself for walking in on this encounter. She liked to think she was a patient person, but the pounding in her head was getting worse, and she could only hope it wouldn't distract her from making the best deal possible for some Green Lady.

Jacko snarled again, but he released his grip on Woodrow. The young man slid back to his side of the counter, lost his balance, and fell heavily onto his bony backside. Jacko resumed his folded-arms pose behind the counter and looked at the man down the length of his nose, a sneer on his mouth.

"Now get your skinny ass out of my shop, and crawl back to whatever black muckhole you came from. And you can tell your friends that Jacko's emporium is closed for business from now on, okay?"

Woodrow shuffled backward on his hands until he hit the shelf behind him, making him jolt with apparent fright. Billie could see he was shaking more than ever. That he wanted—*needed*—Addermire Solution so badly hinted strongly that he was addicted to the stuff. Perhaps that was what had kept his mind together for so long. No wonder he was desperate.

As was she. Perhaps she was addicted to Green Lady. The herb wasn't particularly dangerous, or even that strong—Billie had no idea how much you'd have to take to suffer the kind of withdrawal that Woodrow was clearly going through—but yes, she felt the same almost irrational desire for the substance. But here, seeing Woodrow, dressed in rags, shivering on the floor, she vowed to herself that would never let herself sink so low. She was strong. She was in control.

And what Jacko had said was right—Addermire Solution wasn't made anymore. As far as she knew, nobody was making that kind of restorative elixir.

Billie was tired of waiting. She had work to do, and the scene in the apothecary's was nothing but an annoying distraction. She stepped around the shelving and walked toward the counter, ignoring Woodrow, ready to barter with Jacko for her own particular needs.

That was when Woodrow leapt to his feet. From the depths of his cloak he produced a crude knife, the blade a rough, triangular shard of black metal, the surface dented, almost undulating, while the grip was just some greasy bandages wrapped around the haft.

"Back! Get back!" he yelled, waving the knife in front of him.

Billie watched him, watched the knife… and felt a stabbing pain in her head as the Sliver suddenly seemed to catch fire, burning like a coal in her eye socket. She hissed in agony, and fell back against the counter. As she looked over at Woodrow, she saw his strange blade leave a smeary trail of red and blue in the air as he swung it, like two superimposed afterimages of the weapon, flashing in Billie's vision.

Billie focused on her breathing. She'd seen something like that before—several times, in fact: hollows, soft spots where the Void leaked into the world, giving her glimpses of… *other* things. She also knew that neither Woodrow nor Jacko knew the colored streaks were there. Only she could see them, thanks to the Sliver.

Woodrow's weapon was no ordinary knife. It was linked to the Void—directly.

Jacko raised an eyebrow, and glanced at Billie as she recovered herself. Then he sighed and turned back to Woodrow. Even with the knife, he was going to be absolutely no match for the apothecary unless he got very, very lucky.

Then again, Billie thought, the man was desperate. He was an addict, and he needed his fix, and he wasn't going to get it.

That made him far more dangerous and unpredictable. In Woodrow's mind, he had nothing to lose.

And who knew what powers his strange knife possessed?

Billie blinked away the colors, and took a careful step sideways. Woodrow watched her. He swept the bright blade of the knife from side to side, cutting the empty air between himself and his two opponents. Behind the serving counter, Jacko was rolling his shoulders, ready to deal with this new level of annoyance from a problem customer. The key, Billie understood, was to get Woodrow out in one piece. This section of Wyrmwood district was close to the relative safety of Dunwall proper, and while it was a little rough and tumble, venturing into the stores and markets that occupied this end of Mandragora Street was hardly considered a dangerous pastime. Indeed, enough of Dunwall's reputable citizenry gave this part of the district their custom that it was in the interests of the businesses here—legitimate or otherwise—to keep the area clear of crime and violence. In fact, it was up to them entirely, given that the City Watch refused to patrol here.

Or, to put it another way, a drug-addicted former Overseer threatening people with a weird knife was bad for business.

Woodrow seemed unsure what to do next. It was clear that his desperation for Addermire Solution had driven any kind of logical decision-making out of his head. But even armed as he was, he couldn't take out Jacko—and he certainly couldn't take out both him *and* Billie.

Could he? Billie watched the knife again, wondering what it was and where it had come from. Almost without conscious thought, she flexed the fingers of her black shard arm, ready to summon her own Void-touched weapon into being.

Then she stopped herself, and fast. The power of her arm, like her eye, had become unpredictable, unreliable. Summoning the Twin-bladed Knife would either bring the weapon into her hand or send a bolt of pain shooting through her body, so intense that she would be lucky if she woke up before the week was out.

Now was not the time to experiment. She would have

to rely on her natural abilities, as she had done for nearly a year, to help the apothecary, if she was to get what she had come for. Behind her, she heard Jacko crack his knuckles.

Time was up.

The apothecary walked over to one side of the serving counter and swung a hinged portion of it up, stepping through as he did so. At this, Woodrow jerked into life, pressing himself against the shelf behind him, knife held in his outstretched arm. As the countertop banged shut, he jumped in fright, the sudden movement sending the shelves rocking, dislodging a few tins, which bounced harmlessly on the flagstones. Two large glass jars shattered, sending their contents—some kind of light, dried flower—puffing up into the air, filling the store with a cloying, sweet smell of decay.

"All right, all right, you've really done it this time, my son," said Jacko, rolling the sleeves of his white coat up, revealing a set of dark, complex tattoos covering both his forearms. The designs might just be decorative, or perhaps they were a set of ancient runeshapes which he believed would protect him and his business. "I've had enough for one morning. I've a business to run, and now you really do owe me for damages incurred."

Jacko took a step forward, and Woodrow swung with the knife, the blade flaring in Billie's eye. There was still at least two yards between the two men, and the action did nothing to arrest Jacko's progress as he marched forward, ready to throw the errant customer bodily out of the store.

That was when Woodrow let out a sound that was somewhere between a scream of rage and one of grief. He stood tall and turned the knife on himself, slashing the blade down his chest before tearing the remains of his jacket off, exposing his white chest. Then he adjusted his grip on the knife's makeshift handle and stabbed the point just under his collarbone. Crying out with the effort, he began carving lines into his flesh.

Jacko paused, brow knitted in confusion. He stepped back, just as Billie moved forward to help him. They looked at each other in confusion, then Jacko turned back to Woodrow.

"You will *not* bloody well bleed all over my floor too!" said Jacko, shaking his head, his huge hands curling into fists. "You little piece of excreta, I'll bottle your liver and sell it for gout, you little—"

Jacko froze. Billie stared at him, wondering what the problem was, and then saw the muscles in the apothecary's neck were rigid, the tendons standing out like cables, as he shook, frozen in place.

Just then, the Sliver flared again, the burning pain spreading out over her whole face. Billie gasped as the pain took hold. Through the roaring of the blood in her ears, she heard something else.

"*Yram da haal, yram da haelt, tilb mal, yram, yram.*"

Woodrow's face twitched and his eyes rolled back into his head. He repeated the strange words, even as he kept working the tip of his blade in his flesh. Billie focused once more, concentrated, and staggered forward toward Jacko. He rocked on his heels as she grabbed him, but didn't otherwise move as she used his body as an anchor, pulling herself around toward Woodrow. Her lungs heaved as her vision was once more clouded with the red and blue images coming off Woodrow's blade.

The crash that followed helped clear her head. Recovering, at least partially, Billie looked over her shoulder and saw that Jacko had toppled over like a felled tree. His stiffened neck muscles had, fortunately, stopped him from being brained on the flagstones, but as Billie watched he began convulsing, his eyes wide, a white foam bubbling at the corners of his mouth.

Woodrow had slid down to the floor, his back against the shelf, blood pouring down his chest and his arm. He was still holding onto the knife, but the blade had stopped moving, the tip stuck in a cut just below his ribcage. Around him, his blood had mixed with the spilled dried flowers and was congealing into a dark, sticky mess.

Billie took a step forward, and then another, but it was hard. Another nightmare brought to life, the endless battle against an invisible force. She could see Woodrow's lips move as he continued to mumble.

"*Eco, lazar, lapolay, yram. Eco, lazar, lapolay, yram.*"

Billie had no idea what language he was speaking, and she didn't rightly care. It was clearly an incantation of some kind, some crude, nascent manipulation of Void energy—helped by his knife?—that was actually managing to have an effect on the world.

An effect that was getting stronger. The sweat broke out on Billie's forehead as her struggle to reach Woodrow became harder and harder. The shelf behind him was shaking violently of its own volition, and from behind her she heard a series of loud cracks as the glass cases by the serving counter began to split open.

She had seen sorcery before. It had to be connected to the knife. Billie was grateful she was strong enough to resist.

For now, anyway.

She gritted her teeth and found a low growl developing somewhere deep in her chest. The scream that followed surprised even her, as she leapt through the air toward the former Overseer. Woodrow, locked into a trance, didn't see her coming.

As soon as their bodies connected, the effects of the man's incantation broke. For the briefest of moments

Billie felt suspended in time, at just the point where her raised forearm connected with Woodrow's chin. Then the moment passed, and Billie landed on Woodrow, the young man crumpling onto the flagstones with Billie on top of him. Immediately, Woodrow began to twitch beneath her, his spasms increasingly violent. Billie pressed down on him, willing the seizure to stop. After a few moments, Woodrow's body relaxed, the fit passing. He sighed, his head lolling to one side, as he fell unconscious.

"Stone me!"

Billie climbed off the young man and turned around to see Jacko approaching. The apothecary rubbed the back of his head with one hand, the other wiping the flecks of foam from his lips, but the big man looked otherwise no worse for wear. He stood over Woodrow, looking down at the man's twisted body.

"I'll tell you," said Jacko, "I've had my fair share of scum come through those doors, but none of them ever carved themselves up in my shop just because I refused to extend any more credit." He sighed, and peered down at the former Overseer. "Here, he's not dead, is he?"

Billie shook her head. "No, only unconscious."

"More's the pity," said Jacko. He carefully knelt down next to the slumbering body, trying his best to keep out of the mess of dried flowers and blood on the floor. He peered at the knife, Woodrow's fingers still loosely curled around the grip. "Odd sort of blade," said Jacko. "Looks homemade, like he chipped it out of stone." He shrugged. "I would have thought metal would have been better. Even someone living in the gutters could find a piece of old scrap around to make a shiv out of."

In Billie's vision, the knife still bled a red and blue aura. It made the Sliver sing in her head.

It *was* stone. Jacko was right; she could see it now. A

shard of stone, chipped into a rudimentary but perfectly serviceable blade.

She had a feeling she knew exactly what kind of stone it was.

"I think it might be an artifact," she said. "Something connected to the Void."

Jacko turned his head over his shoulder to look at Billie. His lips were pursed, but his eyes were wide with interest. "You reckon so?"

Billie shrugged. "He was getting the power from somewhere. That was no ordinary sorcery."

"That it wasn't," said Jacko, rubbing the back of his head again. He began peeling Woodrow's fingers off the knife. "Still, there's no accounting for stupidity. If he was so desperate for Addermire's he could just have paid me with this." The knife freed, Jacko examined it, turning it over carefully in his hands. "There's a good trade in artifacts these days." He held it up. "Nice. Very nice."

Billie glanced down at Woodrow. The young man was still bleeding, the pool growing beside his body. "How long has he been a customer?"

Jacko was still admiring his new acquisition. "Mmm? Oh, a few months now," he said. "The amount of Addermire Solution he got through, I figured he was buying on behalf of a whole group of them. Y'know, more Overseers. He never said, but I didn't ask any questions and his money was as good as anybody's. And trust me, I wasn't complaining. Addermire Solution is, shall we say, a rare vintage indeed, with a price to match."

Billie frowned. "Bought using money stolen from the Abbey, I presume?"

Jacko just shrugged. "What do I care? Coin is coin. Platinum is platinum. Although with the Abbey dissolved, trade in their ingots is outlawed, so you have to be careful with them." He jerked a thumb over his shoulder, indicating the back of the shop. "But I have my own crucible. Can never get it hot enough to completely melt the things, but enough to soften it so as I can stamp it into new molds." He turned the knife over in his hand, then used it to point at Woodrow. "Except then he ran out of it."

"And you gave him credit?" That didn't sound like the usual kind of business practice for a storekeeper in Wyrmwood, even one at the more polished, if not quite respectable, edge of the district.

"Well," said Jacko, spreading his hands, "he was a good customer and all. I'd made a tasty profit from him, and he said he had more money. I wasn't going to turn off that particular stream of revenue, know what I mean?"

"Except he didn't come back with any more money," said Billie.

"Ah, no, that he did not. And yes, perhaps I was stupid. I didn't see him for a while, and then he started coming in, and he was begging now. At first he seemed to understand what 'no' meant, but each time he came in, he got more and more desperate. I mean, look at the state of him! He never looked that bad. Bloody addicted to that stuff, I reckon."

Jacko turned and stepped back behind the counter, inspecting the cracked glass of the cabinets.

"Bloody hell, what a palaver." He whistled through his teeth. "Still, he's paid for the damages." Jacko tossed the knife end over end in one hand, then he stopped and looked back over his shoulder. "Here, is he still bleeding over my bleeding floor?"

"He is."

"Well now," said Jacko, bending down to retrieve something from beneath the counter. He emerged a moment later, holding a bundle of crepe bandage and a handful of colored cleaning cloths. "I suppose I should patch him up before I throw him out. A customer bleeding on the doorstep is not a good look, and I do still happen to be an apothecary." He paused. "Here, thanks for the help, lady. I'm assuming you came by for something in particular. Give us a hand again and maybe I can arrange a bit of a discount."

With that, he tossed the bundle to Billie. She caught it, then sighed, and knelt on the ground and began to unwind the bandages.

As she worked, she thought back to the incantation—and she thought about the knife. It was an artifact, certainly, but not an ancient one. Woodrow had made it himself, carving a knife out of a shard of stone—very unusual stone.

Void stone.

Billie got to work dressing Woodrow's wound. She was happy for Jacko to keep the knife—this was his shop, after all—but that didn't stop her wondering how Woodrow had got the stone.

Perhaps things were far worse than she'd feared.

4

WYRMWOOD DISTRICT, DUNWALL
4th Day, Month of Wind, 1853

The world was ending. If anything, Billie was now more sure of that than she had been even an hour earlier, having just witnessed Woodrow's primitive, but effective, supernatural manipulations. That, and the fact that he'd had in his possession a piece of Void stone large enough to make a knife, meant that things were not just *bad*—they were getting worse.

Billie left the apothecary's store with a small pouch of Green Lady and a much lighter purse of coin. The discount Jacko had ended up offering, even as Billie helped him throw Woodrow's bandaged form into the alleyway out the back of the store, didn't add up to much, but Billie had found the unexpected information she had gathered to be worth the trip on its own.

As she headed north from Wyrmwood Way, back toward the mighty Wrenhaven River, Billie refocused her attention on her mission, the reason she was in Dunwall in the first place. She had been here a month and had achieved little; now, a chance encounter in the apothecary's store had given her the final piece of the puzzle, and she had enough information to act.

Because there was something far worse going on in the world than a plague of nightmares and the resurgence of strange sorceries. These were just symptoms of something much larger.

The world was being pulled apart.

It had started shortly before the dissolution of the Abbey of the Everyman, and Billie had her suspicions that the two events may well have been connected. Because what arcane rituals had the High Overseer and the High Oracle enacted within the walls of that sacred building, in their attempt to repair the damage that Billie herself had done? The Outsider had fallen, and had left a vacuum in his place. For the Abbey and the Sisterhood, their very existence depended upon that black-eyed bastard.

What lengths would they go to in their efforts to replace him? To restore a new divinity to the Void?

It was nothing more than a suspicion, but Billie was willing to put a fair amount of weight behind it. Because it was just before the Empress announced the Dissolution that the first Void rifts appeared.

Billie had seen the first one in Tyvia, out on the tundra, as she made the arduous trek between Meya and Pradym, chasing a rumor. At first, she thought it was an uncharted glacier, but as she got closer, she realized the huge wall that cut across the snowy wasteland wasn't made of Tyvia's famous blue ice—in fact, it wasn't a solid wall at all. Instead, it shimmered like a jagged curtain of light, undulating through the landscape. It stretched up as far as she could see, and seemed to extend from horizon to horizon. It was impossible to see through it, although it didn't seem to be quite opaque.

It was similar in some ways to the Void hollows Billie had seen, but the sheer scale of the phenomenon was beyond anything she had ever experienced, and while it *wasn't* a hollow—there was nothing to see beyond it or through it, just deeper and deeper layers of wavering, shattered blue light—Billie had enough experience of the arcane and of the Void itself to recognize it for what it was.

It was a crack. A fissure in the very fabric of reality—a rift between this world and the Void. The fall of the Outsider had somehow pulled the two parallel dimensions apart, the barrier between them sliding like a fault line.

The rift was beautiful. It danced in Billie's eyes, the Sliver burning hot in her head, clouding her vision with red and blue sparks until she could barely see the real world. She had fallen to her knees, then, as the pain coursed over her body. She had closed her eyes, concentrating, pushing the power of the Sliver out of her mind as she struggled to focus on what was here, now, all around her. Snow. Ice. Rocks. The world, the real world.

That was when she heard it. A faint vibration, a buzz like a whale oil tank. She looked up, her vision now clear, and she saw that the rift was actually *moving* toward her. The progress was infinitely small—just a few millimeters in the space of a minute or so. At that rate, it would take months, if not years, to reach civilization.

But it would reach it eventually.

That was when Billie realized how much danger the world was in. It hadn't just been changed by the fall of the Outsider; it had been damaged—physically.

Billie turned around and headed back to Meya. From there, she traveled by sea to northern Gristol. By the time she arrived, people were already talking about it, retelling the stories of travelers and traders who had encountered weird glowing cracks in the sky, holes in the world. Most were as big as your hand. Some were as big as a house.

Billie knew they could get a great deal bigger than that.

Billie headed south, chasing reports, seeking out stories. She found more Void rifts, although none as large or as devastating as the one out on the Tyvian ice. But as time went on, the stories grew. Eventually, the newspapers picked them up; but the sensationalized reports had been countered by official statements from the Academy of Natural Philosophy in Dunwall, which insisted the Void rifts were a natural atmospheric phenomenon.

Then Alba happened.

Reports were sketchy, the truth impossible to verify, but Billie managed to piece something together.

The city, in southern Morley, had been struck by a rift, one so large that it had, literally, torn the city in two. And it was enough to set off a powder keg, disturbing the delicate balance of power between that country's joint rulers, the Queen and the King. A civil war had broken out, lasting exactly three days before a ceasefire was called, the opposing wife and husband having apparently settled their differences. But by then, most of Alba had been reduced to rubble, the casualties numbering in the thousands.

That was late last year. Billie hadn't seen the city herself since then, although she had traveled to northern Morley, attempting to map at least part of the Tyvian rift as it stretched eastwards across the Isles. And she had found it, the giant wall having progressed several miles south of its previous latitude.

It was only a matter of time before it swept down across the whole world, destroying everything in its path.

To be fair, the authorities had taken notice after Alba. The Empress had mobilized her battalions at Whitecliff, although Billie had encountered only a few troops on her travels, guarding some of the larger rifts that had sprung up over Gristol, often cooperating with local militias and town guards.

But really, they were powerless to do anything, and they knew it.

Which was precisely why Billie had come back to Dunwall. She had seen the effects of the Void rifts with her own eyes. She knew the dangers. But, despite her knowledge, this wasn't a problem she could solve. If she wanted to save the world, she needed to get help. She needed Emily Kaldwin, Empress of the Isles, seasoned adventurer, and dedicated friend.

Except Emily wasn't in the city. No sooner had she arrived in Dunwall than Billie made her way to the Tower, her free entry and audience with the Empress guaranteed. Time was of the essence, and she had much to discuss with her old friend.

The Tower guard admitted her without delay. The Imperial court received her immediately. Only it was a court without an Empress. Billie discovered, to her dismay, that Emily and her father, the Royal Protector Corvo Attano, had left on an official journey north, a diplomatic mission to Wei-Ghon. They were not due back for weeks.

Billie left Dunwall Tower reciting favorite curse words learned from several different languages.

For the next few weeks, Billie *had* tried to make contact with Emily, but Wei-Ghon was at the northernmost edge of the Empire, and communication was slow and difficult. In the meantime, her headaches grew, along with her appetite for Green Lady, until eventually Billie realized there was only one other place in the world she could possibly go to for help.

The Academy of Natural Philosophy.

5

ACADEMY OF NATURAL PHILOSOPHY, OXBLOOD WAY, DUNWALL

4th Day, Month of Wind, 1853

The Academy of Natural Philosophy stood proudly at the edge of Dunwall, resplendent with perpendicular columns and Gothic arches. In the center of the Academy square stood the famous bronze statue of its founder, Erasmus Kulik, and it was here Billie paused to suck the last residue of Green Lady from her teeth before clearing her throat and heading up the sweeping scallop-shaped stone stairs that led inside. She adjusted the eyepatch over the Sliver. She didn't want it, or her arm, to distract the attention of the people she was going to meet.

Hoping to meet. That she could get into the building was a given—while the Academy was restricted to members and pupils, Billie's long association with the institute's most famous son, Anton Sokolov, guaranteed her access. But while getting in the door was one thing, meeting the academicians was another matter entirely. Even if she secured an audience, she wasn't exactly sure how prepared they would be to listen. It was the Academy, after all, which had put so much effort into dismissing the ever-increasing reports of the Void rifts as harmless meteorological phenomena.

On her way over from Mandragora Street, Billie hadn't

seen any sign of the strange man in the tatty velvet cloak. Perhaps more than ever, the city was full of all kinds of people, the strange and the desperate alike. The man had most likely just been a vagrant, one lucky enough to have acquired the castoff robe of a high-class citizen, and had either been following her out of moonstruck curiosity, or had just been heading in the same direction.

Billie put the matter out of her mind as she pushed open the great doors of the Academy and stepped into its hallowed halls.

The entrance hall of the Academy was designed to impress, Billie reflected as she moved through the cavernous stone space, the vaulted ceiling soaring three, four stories high over her head. The chamber was roughly elliptical, with a massive staircase directly opposite, splitting at a gallery on the first level before sweeping up on the left and right. On the sides of the hall, narrower, but no less impressive, staircases headed straight up, disappearing into darkened corridors.

The center of the hall was dominated by an enormous skeleton, suspended by wire from the ceiling—the bones of a leviathan, one of the giant deep dwellers. The beast's remains were truly gargantuan—although still dwarfed by the dimensions of the hall—the thing larger than a set of heavy rail cars, and hanging high enough that students and academicians could walk clean underneath it. Indeed, as Billie moved toward the rear of the hall, a trio of natural philosophers trotted down the stairs on the left, their long black academic gowns trailing, and crossed beneath the whale bones, before heading up to the stairs on the right. They were in hushed conversation, leather-bound journals tucked firmly under their arms, and they paid Billie no heed.

The grand staircase was flanked by two glass-fronted offices. One was unmanned; behind the counter of the other sat a rotund man in a pale gray gown, his attention entirely focused on a heavy book balanced on a wooden reading frame in front of him. He wore tiny round glasses with thin gold wire frames.

Billie thought she might as well start with him. As she got closer, she saw more clutter on his desk—a typewriter, a stack of desk files, and a brass plaque that proclaimed his position as the Head Porter.

Billie had no idea what that meant, but she took the fact that he was sitting in what seemed to be the Academy reception to be an indication he would know who she needed to speak to. But when she got to the counter, the little man didn't even look up from his book. Billie sighed, stood tall, and tapped on the glass.

"Yes?" He still didn't look up. In fact, even as he spoke, he licked a finger and turned a page of his book.

"I need to speak to the..." Billie faltered. Who did she need to speak to? The only natural philosopher she had actually known was Sokolov himself, and he was long gone. What had his position been at the Academy? The... head? Principal? Master? Billie realized she had no idea of how the Academy was organized. She needed someone in authority, but she wasn't sure asking for the "boss" was going to get her very far.

Sensing her hesitation, the Porter looked up from his book, then peeled off his wire-rimmed glasses, which had been so tight they left bright red marks on his face. He leaned up a little from the counter, his eyes flicked up and down Billie's body with clear disapproval.

"Are you a student, Miss...?"

"No, I am—"

The Porter sat back down and returned his attention to

his book. "If you wish to apply for tutorship, the office of the registrar does not open until the fourth day of the Month of Harvest." Without looking away from the page, the Porter half-turned his body and began blindly shuffling through some of the papers by his elbow. "If you would care to—"

"Listen," said Billie, "I need to speak to someone in charge here."

The Porter either wasn't listening or was deliberately ignoring her; Billie suspected a little of both. He wasn't a particularly old man, at least not physically, but Billie wondered how the sheltered life within the Academy might age a person's mind.

"—complete an interview request form, stating your particulars and your fields of interest, then it *may* be possible to apply for an application to be invited to attend a pre-screening interview sometime next year and—"

"Hey!"

The Porter jumped in his seat, his glasses dropping off his face. He looked at her through his window with his jaw slack and his mouth in an O of surprise.

"Well, *really*, miss! I'll have to ask you to—"

Billie slammed her magical hand against the glass. As the Porter watched, a thin rime of frost began to form on the glass around her fingers, and the sleeve of her coat dropped, revealing the twisting, floating shards of Void stone that formed her arm.

So much for not attracting attention.

"My name," she said, slowly, carefully, "is Billie Lurk, and I need to talk to somebody in charge. Right. *Now.*"

The Porter stared at her, his jaw flapping, before he practically fell off his stool and rushed off, nodding and muttering to himself.

Billie relaxed. So far, so good.

She hoped, anyway.

6

ACADEMY OF NATURAL PHILOSOPHY, OXBLOOD WAY, DUNWALL

4th Day, Month of Wind, 1853

Billie didn't have to wait long. The Porter returned within a few minutes, trailing two academicians, who strode with some purpose into the hall. After some awkward introductions—yes, she really had been a friend of Anton Sokolov; yes, she really did expect that to count for something; yes, she really did have important news to share; yes, she really did need their help—she was led into the Academy's council chamber.

Three hours later, she was still there. And in that time, she could hardly believe what she was hearing.

The high ceiling was set with stained glass, which cast a rainbow of colors across the octagonal chamber. Billie stood at one of the sides of a huge eight-sided oak table that filled the room. Around the table sat seven natural philosophers, each wearing a heavier academic gown in charcoal gray, with black banding on the sleeves. Three men, four women, experts in their fields, the most senior and most respected natural philosophers in the whole of the Isles—and all highly annoyed at having been pulled from their research or teaching duties by this strange interloper, all resentful of the intrusion and the favor owed to Billie, thanks to her connection with their most illustrious member, Sokolov.

She shifted on her feet, feeling the heat rise in her face as the seven cowards before her unwittingly stoked her temper. They looked at her like she was nothing more than one of their specimens to study. That was probably the whole point—the table had eight sides but only seven chairs. Whoever was summoned to appear before the council was supposed to feel uncomfortable. But Billie had been in far worse situations than having to stand for three hours. She could stand there for another three or another thirty if it meant getting the help she needed.

Except she knew she wouldn't. As it turned out, getting into the Academy was the easy part. Getting information, answers, *anything* at all out of the Academy council was another matter altogether.

Simply put, these shits didn't believe a word she said.

Billie ground her molars as the members of the council muttered to each other, shaking their heads. The Head of the Academy, Professor Finch, stared at her with naked contempt from his ornate chair opposite. Clean-shaven and hollow-cheeked, with long gray hair swept back, he scowled at Billie, but his eyes did occasionally dart around the table as he listened to the debate.

Right about now, she was ready to leap across that same table and choke the life out of the old man.

"But there is no evidence of any instability whatsoever," said a young woman—Professor Burton—immediately on Billie's left, interrupting her murderous thoughts. Burton had cropped blonde hair and was at least two decades younger than most of the other members of the council. Whatever her position was, it was clearly important, the way the silence fell on the table as all eyes turned to her as she spoke up.

"Go on," said Finch. He leaned on the table with one elbow and stroked his chin as he watched her.

"As the council knows," said Burton, "this Academy has natural philosophers in the field all over the Empire. There are geological survey teams in Tyvia, geographers in Morley. There are historians combing through every Abbey chapterhouse in Gristol, and forensic folklorists cataloguing everything that survives from the burned archives of the Sisters of the Oracular Order in Baleton." She paused, and turned in her chair to look up at Billie. "With all due respect, Miss Lurk—" she said the name with a scowl; Billie turned her ire on the woman and wondered just how long it took for someone to die when burned at the stake "—we have had no reports from any of our staff of these 'Void rifts,' as you describe them, nor is there any sign that anything untoward is happening, whether in cities like Dunwall or Karnaca, or at the edges of the Empire, as you claim."

Billie felt the muscles in her body tense. She folded her arms tightly, trying to hold in her frustration.

"I told you what I saw in Tyvia," she said, focusing on the words, willing herself to remain calm even though she was repeating information she had given several times already. "The northern tundra had been torn apart by a rift. The whole continent was cut in half. Northern Morley is the same."

One of the others at the table—a fossil by the name of Cromer, entirely hairless except for a perfectly square patch of beard on his chin—shrugged.

"A natural phenomenon, my dear lady," he said, not actually looking at Billie but at somewhere over her shoulder. "The Tyvian glaciers are famous for their unusual effects upon the local weather."

"And in Mor—?"

"May I suggest a further survey, Professor," an elderly lady, Professor Reed, broke in, "to chart ice flow along the southern coast of Tyvia?"

"A superlative suggestion, Professor!" This was Morozov, a man of similar age to Professor Burton, his face round and soft, his gown stretched out over his sizeable stomach. "We could also perhaps map the fish populations to the southwest of Wei-Ghon. I have long had a theory about the migration of the Serkonan river mullet during their spawning phase, whereby I believe they adapt to salt water and…"

Billie took a step back slowly from the table as the seven leaders of the Academy—the greatest natural philosophers of the age—began to rigorously discuss the merits of mounting an ocean survey.

It had been no good. She had made her case. She had described the Void rifts, only for them to be discounted as freak weather effects, seasonal changes, interesting astronomical and atmospheric phenomenon worthy only of mention before quickly discounting them as unimportant. She described how parts of Tyvia, Gristol, and Morley had been physically damaged by the rifts, how the rifts seemed to be moving, how eventually they would destroy everything in their path. This was dismissed as a fantasy, with more than a little suggestion that, despite her association with Anton Sokolov, Billie Lurk was to be politely entertained, but not trusted.

And Alba. What about Alba?

Nothing, was what. An internal matter for the Queen and King of Morley. Whatever short war had taken place there, it was nothing to do with the Void rifts and it most certainly was nothing to do with the Academy.

When she tried to talk about the dreams and nightmares plaguing the Isles—twice—she was curtly interrupted and told not to discuss such arcane frippery within the walls of the Academy.

Of course. She should have known. The finest minds

in the entire Empire, uninterested in the workings of the world, willfully blind to the evidence she had presented. The Academy liked to think it stood apart somehow from the world it was dedicated to studying. So far, nothing of what she had presented directly affected them, so why would they care? How many of the seven seated around the table had been troubled by dreams and visions? Or did they all chew Green Lady like she did, dulling their senses, muting their dreams?

Their ignorance was as blissful as it was—Billie had to admit—expected. This was why it was plan B, why she had sought Emily's help above all others. Here, standing in front of the Academy council, it was even more obvious that Billie wasn't one of them. She was a scoundrel, a criminal, an assassin—a murderer. It was only Sokolov's name that allowed her the audience. She was lucky they hadn't called the City Watch to take her away.

Billie wasn't entirely sure that still wasn't going to happen.

Let them try.

She looked around the table. Once again she was superfluous to requirements, the seven academicians now busy arguing about what size anchor their hypothetical survey ship should use.

She'd had enough. Billie stepped up to the table.

"*Listen!*" She slammed her black-shard fist onto the ancient woodwork, immediately feeling the blaze of power coursing through the magical limb. Beneath her stone-like hand, a sheen of frost once more spread out, forming tiny, wicked shards that stood up from the table. A second later the oak split, the crack traveling up the table toward Professor Finch. He watched, his eyes wide, and as the fissure reached the edge of the table in front of him he cried out and flung himself backward, upending the heavy chair and falling with a thud to the floor.

The other natural philosophers froze in position, staring first at their incapacitated senior, then at their uninvited guest. Billie looked at each of them, her lip curling in a snarl.

"You're just all lucky I'm going to let you out of this room alive," she said, her voice nothing more than a quiet whisper. As Finch's hand, then face, appeared over the edge of the table, she hissed and opened her fist, dragging her Void-stone fingers across the table, the surface peeling off like the skin of a fruit. "I came here for help. I've seen things I don't understand. Things I think are dangerous. The world is coming apart at the seams, and it's not only affecting the land, and the sea, and the air, but the people too. The Abbey of the Everyman is gone, but I've seen what happened to the Overseers—those who survived. The rifts are destroying the world, while the dreams are destroying our minds."

The natural philosophers glanced variously at each other and at the table, unwilling to acknowledge the truth, unwilling to admit the facts. Billie could see it in their faces. Finch, meanwhile, had managed to get to his feet. Billie turned her gaze on him and he took a step backward, his throat bobbing as he swallowed in fear. He stepped back again until his back hit the wall.

"Or maybe it's nothing," she continued, her gaze fixed firmly on Finch. "Perhaps it's a conjunction of the stars. Perhaps it's a change in the weather. The world moves in cycles, in seasons, and maybe that's all it is. And trust me, I hope you are right."

Billie stood back, relaxing her hand. At least she had their full attention now.

"But if I'm right, then we're in danger—all of us. Maybe we can solve things. Maybe we can fix things. That's why I came here. I've seen what's happening, but I don't know what to do—only that if we don't do something, and soon, it's going to get worse. There will come a time when you won't be able to ignore what's happening, no matter how afraid it makes you."

Silence. The seconds grew long, then Finch reached behind him and pulled on a thick velvet rope that hung on the wall. Somewhere far away a bell sounded.

"I think we have heard enough," he said. Behind Billie, the doors to the council chamber opened. She glanced over her shoulder and saw the portly form of the Porter standing in the doorway.

"Yes, Professor?"

"You can show our visitor out, Porter."

"At once, Professor."

The Porter stood to one side, and gestured to the open door. Billie looked at him, then looked around the council again.

"It really frightens you that much?" she asked.

Professor Finch clasped his hands in front of his gown and lowered his head, looking at Billie down the length of his not insubstantial nose. He cleared his throat in an effort to regain some level of authority.

"We owed Anton Sokolov a great many things," he said, his voice perhaps not carrying as much gravitas as he had clearly hoped, "but you can now consider that debt paid in full. It is time for you to leave, and I suggest you do not come back."

Billie's head throbbed. The effects of the Green Lady were fading. Her vision crackled with the blue-red halo as behind her eyepatch, the Sliver saw a little beyond the veil of the real world, and her magical arm ached with the familiar, creeping cold.

Then she turned on her heel and marched out of the room.

That was it. Mission failure.

She was on her own.

7

ACADEMY OF NATURAL PHILOSOPHY, OXBLOOD WAY, DUNWALL

4th Day, Month of Wind, 1853

After so many hours wasted inside the Academy, the sudden daylight in the square outside the massive building was a shock to Billie. She stood at the top of the main stairs, feeling the eyes of the Porter boring into her back, but she was in no hurry to move. That they hadn't called the City Watch was telling. They were frightened of her, but didn't want to cause a scene. And now her head ached, the dazzling light was strongly tinted in red and blue no matter how much she tried to ignore the view of the world as seen through the Sliver, and to top it off she was tired and hungry.

And angry. What had she expected to happen, really? Yes, she'd been friends with Anton Sokolov. She had helped him. Saved his life. They were from opposite ends of society, forced together by circumstances far from their own choosing, but there was no doubt in Billie's mind about the bond they had formed.

A bond that, clearly, Professor Finch and his mummified cronies didn't put much value on.

Billie looked back. The Porter was still standing by the great oak doors of the Academy, hands clasped firmly in front of his gown, his lips pursed together as he stared at her. She shook her head, and he turned with a sniff and disappeared back inside.

Asses, the lot of them.

The square lurched a little in her vision, the edges sparking red. The Sliver of the Eye of the Dead God was being… difficult. More than usual. She reached into her coat and felt for the pouch of Green Lady again.

"I would think you've had more than enough of that today already, young lady!"

Billie looked up. Standing in the square, beneath the statue of Erasmus Kulik, was an old man with collar-length white hair swept back from his forehead. He was wearing a tattered charcoal-gray cloak with black bands on the arms. He lifted his hand, the gown falling away to reveal a bony white arm.

"Nasty stuff, that particular plant," he said. "Sold as Green Lady here, but another variant is known as the Black Weed of Karnaca, as I'm sure you know. The nomenclature varies, but the stuff is all the same. My favorite is the name they call it by in eastern Morley—Fool's Fancy. Fool's Fancy! Sounds right to me. Nasty stuff. Addictive, dulls the senses—"

"And makes old fools like you tolerable."

Billie trotted down the steps, approaching the stranger at a pace. For his part, he didn't move, although he did pull his arm back and clutch the edge of his gown, lifting his chin defiantly as she approached. When she was close enough, she saw he was shaking, just a little.

"I'd ask how it was any of your business," she said, "and also why you were following me this morning, before I gutted you like a hagfish, but I've wasted enough time today already."

She brushed past the old man—not enough to knock him over, but with enough force to, hopefully, give him the message to stay well away—but she hadn't gone a handful of steps before he called out to her again.

"It is my business, young lady," he said, "quite simply because I believe you."

She stopped in her tracks. She didn't turn around.

"You are quite right," said the stranger. "Your observations keen, your deductions astute."

Billie cocked her head. "Right about what?"

"Oh, most things. The rifts. The dreams. And how it all started, of course."

Billie turned slowly on her heel. She set a steely look on the man and walked back toward him. Again, he didn't move, although, if anything, he now looked more scared of her than he had before, a sharp contrast to the confident bluster in his voice.

She looked him up and down. He was old, perhaps in his seventh decade or beyond—certainly older than Sokolov had been when she had known him. Thin, wiry, clean-shaven but with patches of whisker on his neck that he had missed. His white hair had a yellowish tinge and was in need of a wash, as did his cloak—which Billie now saw was the formal academic gown of a senior natural philosopher, the same as those worn by the members of the Academy council she had just met with.

The two stood facing each other for a few moments, then the man cleared his throat and looked around, finishing with a glance over his shoulder back toward the Academy. Billie followed his gaze, but the doors were still closed and there was nobody about.

"Well, I suppose—"

Billie grabbed the man by the throat and dug her fingers in. She lifted him under the jaw—he was small and light and old, but she had no intention of decapitating him outside the Academy—until he was forced to balance on his toes.

"Who are you?" asked Billie.

"Gah!" The man gurgled, his bony hands clutching at the sleeve of Billie's greatcoat—the sleeve hiding her black shard arm.

Billie hissed between her teeth and let the man go. He dropped to his feet but didn't fall over. Instead, he coughed twice, then straightened his back and took on an air of faded authority as though nothing had just happened. Adjusting his gown, and gripping the lapels with two skeletal fists, he lifted his chin to Billie—who stood a good six inches taller than him.

"My name is Dribner. Withnail Hugh Bruce Dribner, Professor Emeritus of the Academy of Natural Philosophy, at your service."

Dribner gave a deep bow, sweeping his moth-eaten cap off his head as he did so.

Billie looked down at him, and frowned. "*You're* a professor?"

Dribner looked up, before he straightened up. "Well, *Emeritus*, but yes, young lady, a professor indeed—"

"Emeritus?"

"Ah… indeed."

"Meaning, you're retired?"

Dribner pursed his lips. "Well, some may adhere to such a definition. Personally, I prefer to call it a temporary sabbatical."

Billie felt her eyebrow moving up of its own accord. "Don't tell me, it wasn't voluntary?"

The retired professor peered up at Billie, then looked around again, before stiffening. Glancing over his head, Billie saw that the Porter had reappeared outside the doors of the Academy and was watching them.

"I suggest we decamp to my laboratory at once," said Dribner, pulling at Billie's coat while watching the Porter, any sign of fear now gone. "I feel we have much to discuss."

"You're telling me you have a laboratory?"

Dribner turned around. "I believe that is just what I said, young lady! Do pay attention, please!" He made to move off, but Billie caught his gown. It slid around his body a good deal before he noticed.

"What do you know about what's happening?"

"Young lady, I know a very great deal. About the Void, about the Outsider—and about what became of him." He tugged his clothing free from Billie's grip. "Now, if you will come with me, perhaps I can provide some of the answers that those buffoons in there refused to furnish." He jerked his thumb back toward the main building.

Billie released the gown. Dribner nodded appreciatively, readjusted his clothing, and smoothed his hair down, then, with a final glance at the scowling figure of the Porter, gripped his lapels once more and marched across the square.

"This way!" he called over his shoulder.

Billie watched him for a moment, then sighed, and followed.

What did she have to lose?

8

DRIBNER'S LABORATORY, ACADEMY OF NATURAL PHILOSOPHY, DUNWALL

4th Day, Month of Wind, 1853

As she followed the little man who claimed to be a former professor of the Academy of Natural Philosophy, Billie argued with herself about whether it was a waste of time or not. Dribner was a strange fellow, and Billie wasn't entirely sure what to make of him, or his position. Professor Emeritus? She wondered if he'd awarded the title to himself, given his implication that he had been, well, *forced* into retirement.

And where, exactly, was this supposed laboratory? Surely not within the bounds of the Academy itself? If he was fired, or retired, or on sabbatical, would he really still be working at the very institution he was no longer, technically, a full member of?

Dribner led Billie on a circuitous route around the huge Academy building, back to Oxblood Way, then down a series of side streets until finally they looped back around into the cloisters that formed the rear of the Academy campus. He walked with purpose between the sunlit columns with Billie close behind, and none of the academicians or students they passed stopped them.

Then Dribner turned and led her through a tall, arched doorway back into the building itself. The passageway was short and hairpinned into an overgrown garden parallel to the cloisters, although clearly far less frequented. There was a path through the unkempt lawn that led to a narrow, crumbling stone staircase. Dribner trotted down the steps, and when Billie caught up with him he was fussing at a rusted iron grille secured by a multitude of padlocks of different shapes and sizes looped through the gate from top to bottom, each apparently opened by a different key from a huge ring he had unearthed from somewhere in his gown.

It was almost laughable, but for some reason, Billie wanted to know what he had to say. He was an old man, and she wondered if he had known Sokolov. Was he a former colleague, perhaps? Sokolov had never mentioned his peers—with characteristic arrogance, he had only ever been interested in his own work.

Given the behavior of the Academy council members, perhaps he was just like everyone else here, in that respect. Did that include Dribner? It seemed likely. He had an air of superiority about him, although tempered by the hard times on which he had apparently fallen.

He finally opened the gate and waved her through. As they walked down a long stone corridor, the walls slick with slime, into what must have been one of the oldest parts of the Academy, two things in Billie's mind kept her following the strange little man down the narrowing corridors.

The first was that *he* had found *her*, not the other way around. He had been following her, seeking her out. While she had been in Dunwall for all of a month, the first time she had seen him had been this morning. But he clearly knew who she was—and more importantly, *why* she was here—and he wanted to talk. Perhaps there was far more to him than met the eye.

Second, he claimed to believe her—although so far she hadn't said anything to him about what she'd seen. She wondered if he had been listening outside the council chamber as the seven members of the council pointlessly debated nothing at all. Had he somehow slipped past the withering gaze of the Porter? That seemed likely. From what little she had learned of him, Dribner seemed like an independent spirit, able to move about the Academy without much difficulty.

More and more like Sokolov, she thought.

Deep in the bowels of the building, the passageway ended in a black oak door behind another iron gate, the space illuminated by the bright but dappled daylight that fell through what looked like drainage grates over their heads. The door had a single, huge lock, and it took Dribner so long to twist the large key in it that Billie wondered if she should offer some help. But then the mechanism clunked home, and he took hold of the door's giant ring handle. He paused, and glanced over his shoulder, his lips pursed.

"I must insist that you consume none of your Fool's Fancy in my laboratory," he said.

Billie shrugged, but then she felt the growing pressure between her temples, the Sliver lighting up in her skull. Almost at once, her vision flashed red and she nearly staggered, supporting herself in the narrow passageway with her magical arm. As soon as it touched the wall, the pale stonework frosted over.

Dribner glanced at it. "Yes, I suspect things like that will happen. It will be worse once you are inside the laboratory, but I must insist, on no account take any Fool's Fancy. It is imperative I have you at full, well, *capacity*, shall we say, for what I need to show you."

Billie said nothing, but she nodded. She felt a little ill,

her head beginning to pound, like it did whenever she was near…

Near a Void rift.

Dribner sniffed. "Prepare yourself," he said, turning back to the door. "Personally, I find the experience somewhat invigorating, but then I don't have an arcane artifact in my head, now, do I?"

Then he twisted the ring handle with both hands. There was another heavy sound as the mechanism disengaged from the ancient wall, and with all his strength he pushed the portal open.

Billie's head spun, her vision flashing with red and blue afterimages. Gritting her teeth against the pounding in her head, she pushed herself along the wall to step into the chamber beyond. As she crossed the threshold, she yanked her eyepatch off, as if that would make the burning pain go away.

The room was circular, built from the same ubiquitous brick and limestone as the rest of the Academy, but here the walls were dark with damp and mildew. At the cardinal points, reinforced iron pillars stretched up to the low ceiling, and in the space between the pillars and the chamber walls were crammed workbenches and cupboards, every surface stacked with equipment—glassware, retorts, frames, burners, crucibles. Loose paper leaned precariously on pyramids of books. Magnifying lenses, pens and pencils, measuring devices, and drawing instruments littered the surfaces. In one corner there was a pile of five empty whale oil tanks, and three full ones were rather more carefully arranged beneath a table, with another installed in a power unit set into the wall. There were no windows, and no other door, and while the pale blue glow of the full whale oil tanks was reasonably bright, they were not the main source of the light in the room.

Billie was right. In the center of the chamber was a Void rift.

She stared at it, feeling herself so powerfully drawn to it that she forced herself to take a step back, planting her feet firmly on the stone floor. Next to her, Dribner nodded.

"Yes, it has a certain effect, doesn't it?" he said, closing the door. He circled the room, walking behind the pillars as he checked over various pieces of equipment. Billie remained by the door, transfixed by the rift.

It was small, and it hung in the air well clear of the walls, floor and ceiling. It undulated, a shimmering curtain of blue light, roughly rectangular in shape but with a flickering, flame-like edge that glowed red.

It was beautiful, this hole in the world. As Billie stared at it, the vision provided by the Sliver of the Eye of the Dead God began to take over, rendering the rift in monochrome red, the intensity increasing the more she looked. When she turned away to look for Dribner, the intensity faded immediately, but she felt an almost physical pull back toward the rift as the Sliver was drawn to it. Like the other rifts she had seen, it had some of the characteristics of a Void hollow, but with nothing visible on the other side.

Dribner appeared from behind one of the pillars, chuckling. He pointed at the rift.

"I had surmised something like that would happen," he said. He tapped his cheek with a finger. "That artifact in your head, it is drawn to it, isn't it? My theory is quite obviously correct. That object is more part of the Void than the real world—consequently, you are too, and you are drawn to it." He chuckled again. "A fortunate and rather useful situation, I think. Yes, very useful."

Billie shook her head. She turned back to the rift, and just as Dribner said, she felt the pull of the Sliver again.

"How did you know the rift was here?" she asked.

"Ah, now, there we must thank our mutual friend, the renowned Anton Sokolov."

"So you did know Sokolov?"

Dribner frowned at her. "What? Know Sokolov? Why, of course I did! What would ever make you think otherwise? Good gracious, young lady, have you not been paying the slightest bit of attention? Really, the youth of today."

Billie's eyebrow went up again at his outburst, and she watched as the old man continued muttering to himself as he moved around the underground laboratory. On one side of the chamber, a series of large wheeled frames sat, folded against the wall, and now he began to pull them around, unfolding from each an array of jointed arms and clamps. Billie stepped back to give him room, keeping her hands to herself, declining to offer any assistance. She had no idea what he was doing, but given his tetchiness, there was no doubt that an offer of help would just irritate him further and cause even more delays.

Billie watched him in silence for a few moments. Once he seemed to have calmed down, she spoke.

"So the Academy lets you run your own experiments, down here?"

"They do."

"Even though you have, ah… retired?"

Dribner shrugged as he wheeled one of the stands around. "My family has had a long connection with the Academy. My great-grandfather even contributed a rather large proportion of his not inconsiderable fortune to the endowment of the Chair which the illustrious Professor Finch now occupies. They wouldn't dare throw me out!"

After a few more minutes, Dribner had arranged the stands around the rift, encircling it completely in the complex metal framework. After adjusting the clamped arms so they were all pointing at the rift, he then spent even longer installing other instruments in place. Billie watched as he pulled items that looked like spyglasses, others that looked like large magnifying lenses, out of a variety of boxes and set them up in the clamps. He took out a coil of leads, connected various plugs to various inputs, then handed two heavier cables to Billie.

"If you would be so kind as to connect this," he said, not looking at her, his eyes roving over his instrumentation.

Billie took the cables over to the whale oil tank installed on the wall and connected them to the ports, sliding the tank cover closed as she did so. Then she turned around to survey Dribner's work from the other side of the room.

The Void rift was now surrounded by instruments, all connected by one set of cables to the old wheeled console, and by the other cables to the whale oil tank. Dribner was behind the console, his hands flying over the switches and levers, his ancient face illuminated by the glow of the rift and the lights that flashed on the controls under his fingertips.

Billie folded her arms and leaned against one of the iron pillars as she watched, trying to make herself comfortable. Whatever Dribner was up to, he wasn't a man to be hurried.

Eventually, apparently satisfied, Dribner threw a lever with a flourish. Underneath the console, installed on the lower shelf of the wheeled trolley, was a large squat box that looked very much like an audiograph machine, without the horn. A chattering sound emanated from the box, and a moment later Billie saw the edge of a punch card begin to appear through the slot in the top of the box. It emerged slowly, then began to spool out onto the floor, the card covered with a dense pattern of holes.

Dribner glanced down at the card, then he leaned on

the console, elbows locked, and looked up at Billie.

"I expect you have a lot of questions, young lady," he said.

Billie said nothing.

"Of course, you are impressed by my application of natural philosophy to the matter at hand," said Dribner. He held his chin high. "As well you should be. The work I am carrying out here is a direct continuation of the researches of Sokolov himself. Unlike those amateurs above us—" he rolled his eyes to the ceiling and gave a *huff* before continuing "—I believe that the world is in great danger, and that we must do everything we can to put things right."

Billie pushed herself off the pillar, and moved over to stand by Dribner at the console. Maybe the old man wasn't moonstruck after all. "I tried to tell them, but they didn't believe a word I said," she said. "You heard it all?"

"I did indeed. Oafs, the lot of them. Bring back the rat plague, that's what I say." He cleared his throat. "Anyway, ah, yes, I was in a little… vestibule, a place I often use for quiet contemplation and a place where I know nobody can find me—it neighbors the council chamber, you see—and I overhead your arguments. Compelling they were, too. The fall of the Outsider has caused a… movement, shall we say, between the Void and our world. The Void itself has become unmoored, and the two realms are being pulled apart, the consequences of which will be devastating."

Billie nodded. "I've already seen the damage created by the rifts, and I've seen what the dreams are doing to people."

"Indeed, two phenomena with the same cause. And the situation will continue to worsen, until both the Empire of the Isles—the *body*, shall we say—and the citizens thereof—the mind—are rent asunder!"

Billie glanced over Dribner's complex arrangement of equipment. The punch card machine continued to chatter by their feet.

"You've been researching the rifts, here?"

"I discovered this one just a few months ago," he said. "I had heard about the rift in Tyvia, which you saw for yourself—it has at least been reported in some of the more obscure regional newspapers. Here in my own modest laboratory, I was continuing Sokolov's work. Before he left, he entrusted me with his notes, and his collection, to ensure that someone would carry on without him."

Dribner moved over to one of the workstations against the wall and pulled down a thick book from the shelf. Dribner began leafing through it, and Billie leaned over to look. It was a bound set of handwritten notes, written by Sokolov himself.

She recognized the handwriting, but not the words. "Sokolov wrote his notes in another language? What is it? I don't recognize the script."

"It's not a language, as such," said Dribner. "It is a code. It seems the others in the Academy took something of a dim view of his later work—especially once Finch became head. They never got on, those two. I think that was one of the reasons Sokolov never returned to the Academy, not properly, anyway. But although Finch and the others discouraged his research, he continued, using a code—the key to which he entrusted to me, to ensure that I, and only I, would be able to read his notes and continue the work."

Billie looked over the pages. The code was a mix of words and numbers and symbols that looked more like mathematics than language. Certainly indecipherable without a key.

"Finch was afraid, wasn't he?" Billie glanced up at

Dribner. The old man's face was lit from the console below, the effect deepening the shadows on his already gaunt face. "He still is," she added. "Afraid of magic and the arcane."

Dribner snorted. "Finch is a fool. And you are right, he is afraid." He flipped the book over, and began leafing through it from the back. Here, Billie saw, were a set of diagrams of objects she knew only too well—bone charms and runes. They were highly accurate sketches, and were accompanied by more notes in the complex code.

"Sokolov became obsessed with the Outsider and his magic. He managed to gather a number of objects the Abbey of the Everyman would have called 'heretical.'" Dribner paused, and laughed. "With no Abbey and no Overseers, who can now say what is heretical or not?"

Billie reached over to the book and flipped through the pages herself, scanning the catalogue of objects.

"Sokolov collected artifacts?"

"Charms, runes. Most came from a collection of a man called Norcross, I believe, who had a private museum somewhere in central Gristol. There was a fire, a year ago now, maybe. Norcross was killed, and most of his collection went up in smoke, but Sokolov used his extensive contacts to retrieve at least part of what was left. He believed there were more artifacts that survived the fire, which had been taken from the ruins and moved by person or persons unknown to Morley."

"Okay," said Billie. "So what did Sokolov learn from his share?"

Dribner leafed back through the book. "Well, a few things, some interesting, some not. I confess, I have yet to fully decode all of his notes, and it is possible there is a volume or two missing. But, regardless, based on earlier research, Sokolov had developed a system of instrumentation with which he could measure the supernatural, as it were." Dribner gestured to the console and to the frames surrounding the rift. "I have continued its development, with certain modifications, as you can see."

Billie began to understand. "So, by using the instruments to measure the supernatural, you can actually measure the rift?"

Dribner's lips moved as though he were re-running her words through his mind before coming up with an answer. Then his eyes widened, and he nodded.

"An astute mind. Said it myself. Very astute."

"And what did you discover?"

Dribner pointed at the rift. "That you are correct, the rifts are moving as the Void slides away from the world. Or perhaps 'moving' isn't the right word. 'Shearing' would be a better term. As the Void shears away, it damages the world, and that damage will only increase over time. Not only that, the rifts are *linked*. They are not discrete events, but they are all the *same* event, all parts of the whole. Eventually, the rifts will almost certainly join together, and that will be the end of everything."

Billie whistled through her teeth. "So how do we stop it? How long do we have?"

Dribner flapped his arms in frustration. "The latter point, I have yet to determine. As to how we stop it—that is where you come in."

"Me?"

"Yes, you, young lady. You are unique. The Outsider has fallen, and he has taken his magic with him. Oh, there are *other* magics, certainly—oh yes, I saw the fuss that young Overseer made at the apothecary's—but as one divinity falls, so others compete to take its place. With the Outsider gone, those who carry his mark are no longer linked to him, and they have no power." Dribner stabbed a finger at Billie. "But you... *you* are different. You were never marked, yet you are linked to the Void—more so than any who carried the Outsider's Mark. That makes you useful for the task we face."

Billie folded her arms, and stepped closer to the rift. It shimmered behind Dribner's instruments, a blazing, silent fire. As she stared into it, she felt the pull on the Sliver, and the pounding in her head began to sound once again.

"But," said Dribner from behind her, "I must insist you give up on your Fool's Fancy. It may be painful, but you need to let the parts of you that are part of the Void be drawn fully to it. That herb dulls not only your senses, but also your tether to the Void. If you are to be of any use, you must clear your mind entirely. Only then will the full potential of your connection be useful to us."

She turned back to Dribner, the sensation fading. "Very well. So, if I'm linked to the Void, and can sense the presence of the Void rifts, what do you want me to do? You want me to find something, don't you?"

Dribner grinned at her, then raised his hands in the air so the sleeves of his gown fell away. Then he plunged his hands back down to the console and pulled a couple of levers with a theatrical flourish.

At once the subterranean chamber was filled with the hum of power. Billie felt the Sliver burn in her head, but despite the discomfort, she turned to the rift—without Green Lady, this was something she was going to have to get used to.

Some of the lenses and spyglass apparatus that surrounded the rift were now glowing with power as beams of smoky white light were projected into the rift. Beneath Dribner's console, the punch card machine chattered as it began to spit data out at a much faster rate than before.

"The rifts are the result of the separation of the Void from the world," said Dribner, raising his voice over the buzz of his equipment. "But their movement and enlargement are not."

Billie's face creased in confusion. "*What?*"

Dribner gestured to his console. "It seems I am not the only one probing these phenomena. Someone else is experimenting, and it is their meddling that is causing the rifts to destabilize, threatening us all. More than that, I believe their actions are deliberate."

"You think they are *actively* damaging the rifts—the rift?" Billie blinked, the Sliver of the Eye of the Dead God like a red-hot poker stabbing into her brain. She gritted her teeth, concentrating, as she focused on Dribner. The old man's face spun a little in her vision, but his expression was firm.

"I believe so, yes," he said. "For what purpose, I can't say. But what I can say is that if we are to save the world from certain and total destruction, we must find this other party and put a stop to their experiments."

Billie frowned and shook her head. "I don't understand. I thought you said Sokolov's work was unique?"

"Young lady! It is, it is! Don't get me wrong. But it is possible that others have achieved something similar in parallel." Dribner raised his arms again, and turned his body to the room. "A significant portion of my work here was only made possible thanks to the acquisition of the Norcross collection. But I also think Sokolov was right when he said that some of that collection was taken by parties unknown. It is possible—indeed, it is *likely*—that, whomsoever they are, they have found their own way of using the artifacts, although for a far darker purpose, if my data are correct."

Billie's mind was racing. This was... well, unexpected, to say the least. But maybe Dribner was right. If there was anyone who could stop this, it was her.

"Okay," she said. "I need to find these 'parties unknown', and put a stop to their activities. Fine. But where are they? Didn't you say Sokolov thought the artifacts were taken to Morley? Do we know where in Morley?"

"I did hope you would be able to tell me that, young lady." Dribner pointed at the rift. "I have increased the power flow, allowing my instruments to probe deeper into the rift. The rifts are connected to each other, and you are connected to the Void, thus I had theorized that you would be able to sense the connections, and possibly locate the source of the interference."

Billie turned to the rift. Immediately, the Sliver began to burn. She clenched her fists by her side. She almost asked the old man what she had to do, but—

She knew. It was as Dribner said—as she was part of the Void, so the Void was part of her. And the rift was where the Void and the world intersected.

Just like a Void hollow.

Billie took a deep breath, and then another, puffing out her cheeks. She focused, letting the view of the world through her human eye fade, until she was just using the power of the Sliver. A moment later, her vision spun into a blue haze, the rift dancing in front of her in brilliant flashing yellow.

But the center of the rift itself was clear. It was distorted, as if she was looking through smoked glass, but there was something there.

It was a city, she realized, although it was too indistinct to be recognizable. Most of the buildings looked like ruined shells, except for one, a tall tower capped by a spherical roof, standing on a hill. Above it was another structure, a dark, curved object, far too large to be any kind of man-made structure.

"Can you see anything?" came Dribner's voice from a thousand miles away.

Billie concentrated. Already the vision through the rift-hollow was fading. Then the world snapped back into normal colors and the Sliver pinged in her skull, sending a pulse of white-hot pain coursing across the top of her head and down her spine. Billie staggered back against the console.

The old man turned the power back down, and the humming in the room faded, although Billie's head was ringing like a bell. Dribner peered at her.

"Well?"

Billie looked up, her head beginning to clear. "I'm not sure. I saw what looked like a city."

"Yes?"

"A city in ruins."

"Oh."

"There was a tower, with a round top."

"Ah!"

Billie stood up from the console and rolled her neck, wincing as it clicked painfully. "You know where that is?"

Dribner clapped his hands. "Indeed I do, young lady. I believe you saw Alba! That tower will be the Royal Observatory. A unique building in the Isles."

Billie forced herself to look back at the rift. It hung there, suspended between the instruments. There was nothing to see in its rippling blue light, but Billie was also pleased to note that the Sliver wasn't getting as hot as it had been. Maybe she *could* control it, use it, as Dribner said, now she knew for sure that the rifts and the hollows were very similar phenomena.

"Alba," said Billie. She looked back over her shoulder. "That explains the ruins. The city was wrecked by the Three-Day War."

"Ah, yes, that is the case. An unfortunate circumstance for our neighbors. But the city is being rebuilt—in fact, that makes your task easier."

"It does?"

"Oh yes. The city has almost recovered—it's as big a port as it was before the war, perhaps even bigger—but there is still a lot of reconstruction going on. Not only will you be able to secure passage with relative ease, your presence will go unnoticed. People from all over the Isles are streaming to the place to find work. Civil wars are, apparently, rather good for business. Well, their aftermaths are, anyway."

Billie nodded. Alba. Yes, Dribner was right. She'd been there a handful of times, and remembered the tower of Royal Morley Observatory, although she didn't think it had been on a hill. Then again, her vision through the rift had not been crystal clear—there had been the huge, curved shadow looming, for instance. It seemed that whatever—whoever—was interfering with the rifts was probably interfering with her vision through it.

"Okay, looks like I need to go to Morley and take a look. But if the destabilization is deliberate, it could be dangerous—we don't know who we're up against. I'd like your help, but I don't think it would safe for you to travel with me."

Dribner drew himself up again into his proud academic pose, chin up, gown clutched in his bony hands. "Young lady! Why, the very thought! I have no intention of abandoning my work. The very suggestion, the *very suggestion*!" He looked at the floor and shook his head.

Billie sighed at the strange man. He had more in common with his fellow natural philosophers in the Academy over their heads than he knew.

"I'll go to Alba," said Billie, "and see what I can do. If I can stop whatever is going on, I will. If not, I'll gather as much information as I can and bring it back." She waved at the array of equipment in the laboratory. "Maybe then you can do something more with this setup."

"A capital suggestion, young lady. Capital." He lifted his chin and grinned at her. "I knew you were the right person for the job."

Billie almost laughed. "I think you mean the *only* person."

Dribner's smile dropped, and he cleared his throat. "Yes, well, I can't stop to talk all day. I have work to do. And so do you, young lady, so do you."

The pair shook hands, and as he returned his attention to the console, Billie retraced her route out of the subterranean laboratory and back up to street level.

How things had changed. Meeting Dribner had been a huge help—in fact, it was more than she could ever have thought possible. Not only did the old man seem to know what was going on, together they had a solid plan for what to do next. He'd confirmed her fears, but had introduced a dangerous, terrifying new aspect.

The destabilization was deliberate. The movement and spread of the rifts was no natural phenomenon.

Someone was doing it on purpose. Why, neither she nor Dribner knew. But that someone had to be stopped, or the world would be destroyed.

9

ALBA, MORLEY

17th Day, Month of Darkness, 1853

The journey from Dunwall to Alba was a full forty days by ship, and Billie spent nearly all of that time pacing the deck of the cargo clipper, frustrated by the time it was taking to continue her mission when the future of the world was at stake.

She laughed at that. Her mission. Oh yes, she'd found one, all right—true enough, she had considered herself to be focused on her task prior to arriving in Dunwall, but after meeting with Dribner and understanding the situation, she felt a new clarity of purpose.

All she had to do was save the world.

Easy.

Dribner had been right about another thing, too—Alba's need for labor and materials. After leaving his laboratory, Billie had secured passage on the *Western Hunter*, a passenger steam clipper that had been converted into a light cargo freighter, the captain seeing a larger profit shipping materials to the rebuilding city than taking people. He'd made an exception for her, once she'd offered him enough coin—more than she could afford.

Alba was the largest city on the southern coast of Morley, and thanks to its relative proximity to Dunwall, was a major port—indeed, it was somewhat larger than

Morley's capital, Wynnedown, which, situated as it was on the northeastern coast, was far removed from the main trading routes. As the *Western Hunter* approached the city, they were met by a pilot boat and guided to their berth through a myriad of other vessels that crowded the harbor. Billie was the first off the vessel and headed into the city, impressed by what she saw.

It seemed war *was* good for business.

She couldn't remember the last time she'd been in Alba, but regardless, the place was almost unrecognizable. While the port area looked largely unscathed, the remainder of the city seemed to be divided between reconstruction and devastation, new buildings and repair work sitting alongside crumbling ruins and cleared lots—it seemed that Dribner had somewhat overestimated the amount of rebuilding that had been done. For a war that had lasted a mere three days, Billie could only imagine the barrage that the town must have suffered to have caused such widespread damage. While she knew about the war—it was hard to escape news of it, no matter where she had traveled in the Isles—she didn't know, and had little interest in, the politics of the conflict. Morley's system of government—joint rule by a queen and a king, united in marriage not through love, but power play—seemed a little archaic to her.

Billie walked deeper into the city, pleasantly surprised to find the weather far more agreeable than that in Dunwall, despite the time of year, the perpetual gloom of the Empire's capital replaced by cold but clear skies, giving her a perfect view of the two objects that now dominated Alba's skyline. She'd seen both from the deck of the *Western Hunter*, and had spent hours staring at them almost as soon as they had come into view. Here in the city, they were even more overwhelming—and she knew now what the big curved shadow she had seen through the rift in Dunwall was.

It was part of a giant bridge, a causeway of truly monumental scale that soared high above the city, at least a thousand feet in the air. It looked for all the world like an iron bridge for electric rail cars, the kind common all over the Isles, but enlarged to such a degree it looked faintly ridiculous, like a child's toy somehow dropped on top of the city. The causeway was still under construction, and unsteady-looking scaffolding stretched up to it; hundreds of workers crawled over every surface, while dozens of heavy block-and-tackle were being used to winch up more girders and ironwork to the upper levels. The causeway ended abruptly at its highest point, midway over the city, while the back half of it curved gently down, disappearing as it plunged into the second of Alba's great wonders: a Void rift. It meant that the causeway seemed to hover almost impossibly above the city—anchored in an inaccessible other world.

The Sliver of the Eye of the Dead God grew hotter the more she looked at the causeway. The rift was similar to the one that crossed the Tyvian tundra, although here it was much larger, rising up into the clear sky until it faded from view. It looked almost as if it were dividing the entire city in two, cutting clean through the gigantic curve of the causeway.

Billie could only stare in awe as she walked around a city that was bustling with people—citizens getting on with their lives, visitors earning their coin by helping to rebuild. The whole place felt alive, every street busy, as though this was just another large, prosperous city in the Empire… just one that was sliced in half by a mysterious, arcane phenomenon that nobody apparently paid any heed to, in case it drove them out of their minds. The locals she recognized from their blonde hair and trim, conservative clothing. Outsiders were easy to spot, with their rather more assorted clothing, together with a fair amount of tattoos, piercings, and other arcane body modifications. For the moment, Billie kept her eyepatch on, but she didn't feel out of place at all.

After a couple of hours' wandering, Billie paused in a town square, allowing herself a moment of observation and planning. She bought some food from a market stall and sat on a bench with her back to the causeway, enjoying for a moment the sudden release of pressure inside her skull as the Sliver faced away from the rift. She ate slowly and watched people for a while.

As she had thought, there were two other kinds of people about, different to the regular citizenry.

The first were the Royal Morley Constabulary—the local equivalent of the Dunwall City Watch, although here they had authority across the whole country, and could be found in every city, town, and village on the island. They were dressed in forest-green jackets with white leather bandoliers, white pants tucked into high black boots, and peaked caps, the crowns of which were bright scarlet. They came and went in patrols of two or three.

The other group, she didn't recognize. Their uniforms were black and devoid of any insignia or other distinguishing mark. Their jackets had high collars, with buttons running from chin to waist that were hidden behind a folded seam of cloth. Their pants were black and their boots were black and the sharp garrison caps they all wore were black.

Whoever they were, they looked military. Billie racked her brain, trying to identify the uniforms, but she couldn't come up with anything. As far as she knew, the Royal Morley Constabulary also doubled as this country's armed forces. But it was more than likely that one of the consequences of the Three-Day War had been an expansion, probably a reorganization, of the military in Morley. The presence of so many of the black-uniformed guards was perhaps to be expected—and it made no difference to Billie. She didn't intend to get involved with local affairs if she could help it.

Billie turned on the bench to face the rift, but her attention was drawn back to the causeway. How impossibly huge it was. It was certainly a fascinating sight.

And not just because of the scale of the operation. There was also the fact that the causeway intersected with the rift itself. Despite that, work seemed to be continuing, which was in itself surprising. The sheer amount of physical labor engaged on the project boggled the mind, and she couldn't guess what the causeway was actually for.

But she was determined to find out.

10

LEVIATHAN CAUSEWAY, ALBA
17th Day, Month of Darkness, 1853

The early dusk was beginning to fall by the time Billie reached the area immediately surrounding the base of the causeway, the daylight fading with surprising swiftness at these northern latitudes. This close to the site, where it had suffered most from the war, the nature of the city had changed rather dramatically. The once proud stone architecture of Morley's grandest city had been reduced first to rubble, and then to empty lots as the demolition teams had gone to work, leveling entire blocks to prepare the ground for what had yet to be built. Between these lots, the old cobbled streets were still mostly intact, an echo of the past now suddenly out of place, although still well used by the construction gangs and their carts and other vehicles, which formed the steady traffic that Billie did her best to blend in with.

From here, Billie could see the other object from her rift vision—the tower of the Royal Morley Observatory, the golden dome of which rose above what little skyline was left here, silhouetted against the gently undulating wall of the huge rift behind it. Somehow, the tower had survived, possibly the only piece of recognizable architecture left in this quarter.

As Billie made her way onwards, she saw the empty lots

and cleared building sites were starting to be filled with other things—prefabricated huts and shacks that stood on temporary foundations of wooden pallets, and between them, stacks of building materials: wood, iron, stone, brick, gravel. Some of the materials seemed to match the scale of the great causeway, with impossibly large iron girders stacked in ordered towers, portable cranes hard at work transferring them to the loading beds of electric rail cars, which zipped from here to the causeway site on temporary tracks that had been laid over the cobbled streets.

By now, there were no ordinary citizens about. This was the realm of the laborer, nearly every man and woman dressed in dusty work clothes as they carried out their tasks. The rest were the black-uniformed guards. Although nobody seemed to have noticed Billie, or had paid her any particular attention if they did, she was aware she stood out. If she was going to get right up to the causeway construction—right up to the rift itself—she was going to have to blend in a great deal better.

After another half-hour of walking—the site now a dense township of the prefab buildings, the roads almost too busy with construction traffic—Billie stopped. She could go no farther—at least, not as she was.

Ahead of her, the road was closed off by a large double gate set into a high iron wall. A handful of black-uniformed men were loitering by the gate, and they glanced in Billie's direction as she read the sign that arched over the closed portal.

LEVIATHAN COMPANY
CAUSEWAY PROJECT SECTOR 2 GATE A
NO ADMITTANCE WITHOUT PASS

Leviathan Company—the organization, Billie guessed,

that the black-uniformed men worked for. They did seem to be patrolling the streets and watching the workers, more like guards than supervisors.

By now the men at the gate were all scrutinizing her, their conversation over. Billie gave them what she hoped was a friendly nod, then turned on her heel and headed back the way she had come.

If she was going to get through the gate, she needed a pass.

Billie headed back down the cobbled street, then turned down a side road and followed the line of the iron wall until she reached a more built-up zone of the city, where there were several original stone buildings still standing among the temporary structures of the Leviathan Company. Among them was a tavern, the Golden Tulip, which was the only structure with any signs of life, the rest of the area apparently shut up for the night.

The tavern was small and heaving, and the air was hot and full of noise, every man and woman in the place enjoying the warmth and the company after a hard day's work. Billie walked in and vanished immediately into the crowd. It took her a good few moments to squeeze her way to the bar. As she pushed past the other patrons, she saw they were all workers. There were no black uniforms in sight.

The woman behind the bar had her long gray hair in a tight plait that was wound into a circle on the top of her head, her skin the same deep brown as Billie's. She nodded at her new customer as she chewed a wad of tobacco. Billie pushed the sudden craving for Green Lady from her mind and ordered a rum, before moving along the bar to find a corner slightly less crushed with drinkers. Once installed, she leaned back against the polished wood and sipped her drink, all the while aware of the pull of the Sliver of the Eye of the Dead God, dragging her focus in the direction of Alba's huge Void rift.

The rift—with the causeway running right through it. If anyone was conducting experiments, destabilizing the rift deliberately, that seemed like a good place to start looking. And to do that, she had to get on the other side of the iron wall. And to do *that*, she needed two things.

A disguise.

A pass.

Thinking through her options, Billie continued to sip her drink and watch the crowd. The patrons came and went, mostly in large groups, perhaps corresponding to the end of shifts at the construction site. The iron wall was still some distance from the causeway itself, so it seemed likely that some, if not all, of the workers here had the requisite pass to get through the gate and to their work section.

Billie began to eye up likely targets.

"Here for the sign-up, I take it?"

She turned at the voice. The barwoman had moved over to her, and was sipping on her own pint glass of water as she watched the patrons. The sleeves of her shirt were rolled up to her biceps, revealing a set of intricate tattoos, the ink a deep blue against the dark of her skin, the shapes seeming to mimic the scrimshaw of a bone charm. The barwoman noticed Billie looking, and gave her a conspiratorial twitch of the head. Billie raised her glass and took a sip before speaking.

"I am."

The barwoman smiled. "I have to admire your dedication." Her accent was broad, familiar to Billie from her childhood. "Like me, I think you've come a long way."

Billie said nothing. She just sipped from her glass of rum.

The barwoman laughed. "Hey, don't get me wrong, I

know how it can be. Work is work. Trust me, I know! But you're the earliest arrival. Most don't get in until the day before. The next sign-up is not for two days—so you're early, which means you're keen, or that the journey north was faster than it usually is." She took a swig of her water and leaned on the bar next to Billie. "They'll like that. And you've made a good decision. Leviathan pay very well, so I've been told. Very well indeed."

Billie sipped her drink. "You've not been tempted yourself?"

The barwoman laughed again. "They don't pay *that* well! But I was lucky in other ways. My husband was a local—he was killed in the war but our pub survived, and now it does a fine business catering to the likes of yourself." She shook her head and grinned. "So no, I'm not tempted. You earn your coin over the wall, and you come back and spend it here, and we'll both be happy. Another?"

Billie drained her glass and accepted the offer. "Maybe you can help me out," she said, as the barwoman refilled her glass from a bottle of Karnacan spiced blue rum. "What can you tell me about the causeway?"

"Well, what is there to know? It'll make history, it will. The Leviathan Causeway, the first direct link between Morley and Gristol, right? And then maybe even beyond. Link every isle in the Empire, one day." The barwoman slid Billie's glass along the bar. "Maybe even get as far as Karnaca, eh?"

Billie picked up the glass and took a large sip as she processed what the barwoman was saying.

A direct link between Morley and Gristol—and beyond? It was true that Alba was more or less the closest point to the neighboring isle, but still, the distance the bridge would have to cover was enormous. And, despite the intense activity around it, it clearly had a very long way to go.

The barwoman served a trio of new customers, then returned to Billie's corner.

"Of course, then the rift appeared. Not that it stopped Leviathan. If anything, they've been working a whole lot harder, ever since."

Billie nodded. "When was that?"

"Oh, had to be a year ago now."

"Seems like the rift would be a problem. It cuts right across the causeway."

The barwoman sighed. "Aye, well, there's a mystery for you—"

She looked up as the tavern's door opened, and a large group of workers filed in, crowding the already full bar even more. The barwoman turned to Billie and winked. "Better get back to it," she said, before moving away to serve her customers. "Good luck!"

Billie raised her glass again, then went back to watching the patrons.

A few minutes later, she had selected her target.

Finishing her drink, Billie slid out of the tavern and into the dark, unlit street. She found a spot with a clear view of the door.

She waited. People came and went.

Billie waited some more.

A half-hour later, the door opened, and a worker staggered out. He was a youngish man, well built but slight. He wore a long gray hooded cape, the garment wrapped around his shoulders and buttoned down the front, reaching down to his knees. He got his bearings, took a deep draw of the cool night air, and then headed down the cobbled street.

Billie followed, closing the distance with every step, until they were both away from the light spilling from the Golden Tulip, swallowed by the darkness of the ruined city.

11

LEVIATHAN CAUSEWAY, ALBA

17th Day, Month of Darkness, 1853

As Billie approached the iron gates at a steady pace, she pulled the hood of her recently acquired cape over her head with one hand while the other curled around the stiff rectangle of card she had also borrowed from the worker, whose unconscious form she had left snoring behind a storage shack a few blocks from the Golden Tulip.

She'd picked well. The cape was an excellent disguise, and the punch card pass had SECTOR 2 stamped across the top. With a little luck, both would let her through the gate.

She'd watched the gate a while, hidden behind a stack of wooden pallets, just to get the lay of the land. As she had suspected from the waves of workers who had come and gone at the pub, construction appeared to run on a series of multiple, overlapping shifts that continued around the clock. She had only needed to wait a few minutes before the gate opened and a stream of workers poured out, while a similar line filed in, clocking in with their punch cards at a machine that stood just inside the gate, a black-uniformed Leviathan guard watching them without much interest.

As soon as the next shift change started, Billie had come out into the open and joined the end of the new line. Now she moved through the gates, offering her punch card pass to be read by the machine. Within moments she was inside the construction zone proper.

It was only now that the true scale of the operation became clear. Because beyond the iron wall, the city of Alba ceased to exist.

Billie stood at the head of a road that curved down a gentle slope before disappearing from sight. From here, she could see that the entire construction zone surrounding the causeway was a giant crater-like quarry, the sides of which were cut into the earth in a series of terraces. The entire area was floodlit by dozens—*hundreds*—of enormous arc lamps, and in their harsh white light Billie watched as a steady stream of workers moved like swarms of insects along pathways that zigzagged up the sides of the crater, the roadways all clustered with more of the prefab buildings. Billie couldn't see the floor of the crater itself from here, but the sides of the quarry she could see were at least a couple of hundred feet high. From the top of the road, a mass of scaffolds and gantries rose, surrounding the base of the causeway. The entire place was rendered monochromatic by a thick layer of heavy gray dust that seemed to coat everything beyond the iron wall. At the center of the crater stood the Royal Morley Observatory, its central tower extending from a cluster of lower buildings, the golden dome reaching not even a quarter of the way up to the lower part of the causeway, despite the fact that the complex was now perched on the summit of a small hill, the quarry apparently having been dug out around it. That explained what Billie had seen in the Hollow, anyway.

Billie headed down the road, just another worker reporting for their shift. Nobody paid her any attention in her cape, and she glanced around from under the hood, noting that the black-uniformed Leviathan guards were outnumbered by the construction workers by maybe a hundred to one, perhaps more. All the while, the Sliver burned in her head, pulling her onwards as though she had a strong tailwind behind her.

Because the causeway was not the most remarkable thing about the site. The huge, circular quarry that Billie was descending into was only half there. Straddling the center of the site, cutting the massive causeway itself clean in half, was the Void rift. It spanned the entire space, and as Billie got a better view, she saw that it touched the quarry floor—or at least, it appeared to, as the lower part of it was hidden behind another black iron wall like the one at the gate. People were working right at the edge, loading the block-and-tackle platforms that carried materials high up into the web of ironwork hundreds of feet above.

It was remarkable. Impossible. And, Billie thought as she got closer, pointless. The causeway was huge but it would never reach Gristol, let alone anywhere else—and half of it was inaccessible, disappeared forever in the rift. But despite this, she knew she was in the right place. Dribner's data had showed that someone was experimenting with the rift, in an apparently deliberate attempt to destabilize it—and they were doing it here.

Billie walked on.

It took Billie a full half-hour to reach the floor of the quarry on foot. She realized later that there were a series of rail lines laid into the terraces of the quarry, transporting workers and materials down from the gates. But she used the time to observe, to learn. As she drew closer to the main construction zone, it grew steadily noisier, and busier, and dirtier. The gray dust coated everything, and the once-regular prefab buildings that were clustered all down the road and around the construction zone had become lopsided, even ramshackle, as though mere proximity to the rift had somehow caused them to decay. The workers were covered in the dust as well—in every face, Billie saw raw red eyes and the shine of wet mouths. In fact, the only people who didn't seem to be affected were the Leviathan guards. Their trim black uniforms seemed somehow immune to the dust and dirt as they patrolled in pairs or threes. They swaggered as if they were there to supervise the work, although Billie didn't see any of them give any kind of instruction or direction, and there were foremen aplenty busy with that task, their heads in papers and blueprints stretched out across long trestle tables, voices raised and fingers pointing as they conducted the operation like an orchestra.

The rift stretched right across the site, shielded behind a black iron wall about fifteen feet high. The wall was made up of portable L-shaped panels turned with their flat faces to the rift, the "feet" of the panels serving as a useful raised platform to store smaller materials—toolboxes, small timber, coils of chain and rope. Looking up, Billie was now standing directly beneath the causeway itself. It was a complex construction of girders, a vast latticework of iron and steel like any rail car bridge, only magnified—*amplified*—a thousandfold.

As she looked up, something caught her eye. It was a bird, swooping low. Billie blinked, the outline of the thing flashing red, before she realized that there was nothing there. Billie glanced around in confusion, and then saw she was being watched, not by the workers, but by a pair of Leviathan guards. They were talking to each other as they watched her.

Billie regained her composure and, making sure her

pace was steady, turned on her heel and headed for one of the nearby buildings.

The prefab hut was a supervisor's office. There was a desk and a chair, a set of file cabinets, and little else. As Billie crossed the wooden floor, her boots echoed loudly on the thin boards, which moved under her weight. The walls were just as insubstantial; the sound of her movements was easily drowned out by the noise of construction outside. Working in the office must have been a real headache for the poor foreman assigned to it. Billie only hoped he didn't come back soon, because something caught her eye that looked like it was worth spending some time studying.

A large, flat board made of a single table-sized panel of wood on a simple wheeled stand was pushed up against the back wall, and on the board was pinned what looked like a map of the construction zone. *Finally,* thought Billie—now she would be able to get some idea of the layout of the site, perhaps enough to discover some kind of clue as to the place she should be looking for. The construction site was interesting, but not particularly useful—she would learn little by just wandering around, and already she thought her luck was almost due to run out. She couldn't talk to the workers without arousing suspicion that she wasn't one of them, and the longer she loitered in the zone, the greater the risk that the black-uniformed Leviathan guards would eventually challenge her.

If she wanted to find out what was going on, she needed to get to the heart of the operation, and quickly.

Billie moved over to the board, and cast an eye over the map. It seemed more diagrammatic than strictly accurate, and showed the construction zone as one large, complete circle, although the bottom half of the plan—the area beyond the Void rift itself—was entirely blank. In contrast, the upper half was crowded with detail, every building and path apparently shown and conveniently labeled.

She peered closer, trying to read the tiny labels, tracing her route from Sector 2 Gate A down the main road and around the edge of the main quarry. If she was reading the map correctly, she was now in Foreman Hut AA23, located at the Void rift barrier just to the west of the site's center.

And it was the center that looked the most interesting. Here, the map showed a cluster of what appeared to be more substantial buildings than the prefab offices. They looked like they were built up against the barrier wall itself at the top of a rise, the map showing a series of irregular circles around the buildings to indicate increasing elevation. It was the hill, at the top of which stood what used to be the Royal Morley Observatory—"used to be," because the building's use had clearly changed. On the map, the tower was represented by a large circle, surrounded by smaller semi-circles on the cardinal points. These were labeled as laboratories one through four.

And in the center, one word: CONTROL.

Billie started to make a note of the route from the hut, but she jerked around as she heard voices raised over the noise of construction, voices that stopped right outside the hut.

The display board was almost floor to ceiling; Billie ducked behind it and watched through the gap between the bottom of the board and the floor as the door of the prefab was kicked open. It banged against the thin wall and ricocheted back before being arrested by the outstretched arm of a Leviathan Company guard. His other arm was looped under the armpit of a dust-caked worker, who was being dragged in by a second guard on his other side. As soon as the trio were through the doorway, the guards flung the worker onto the floor, then the one on the right turned and slammed the door shut.

The worker lay on the floor, panting, a thick tendril of mucous unspooling from his mouth to the rough wooden boards. He tried to push himself up, but the booted foot of one of the guards shoved him back. The man's jaw clicked as it connected with the floor, and bright blood spattered the boards in front of his face.

Billie flattened herself against the floor to get a better view.

With his colleague's boot still pressing down on the worker's back, the second guard folded his arms and began to pace the small office.

"This employment tribunal meeting is now in session," said the guard. His companion grunted in amusement, then he bent down and hissed at the worker, who had mumbled something. He grabbed the worker by the hair and yanked his head up.

"What did you say?"

The worker spat blood onto the floor. "I said that an employment tribunal is composed of *three* officers."

"That so?"

Somehow, the worker managed to nod while in the guard's grip. "And then I said your mother is a rat whore who should never have left the sewers."

The guard shoved the worker's head back to the floor; his chin bounced on the boards again and he grunted in pain, before the guard's boot connected with his stomach, once, twice. The worker groaned, curled up in agony on the boards, blood and spit bubbling from his mouth as he fought to catch his breath.

"Mr. Hearne," said the pacing guard, pausing only to glance down at the prostrate form of the man for a moment before resuming his circuit of the office. "I have to say, I admire your persistence. We all do, really. There's something admirable, even remarkable, in the way you just won't *ever give up*." He came to a stop by Hearne, and bent down, his arms still folded, as he peered at the man. "It's gone right to the top, too. Oh yes, believe it. Even Severin himself has taken notice." He paused. "Thing is," he said, "Severin is a busy man. *Very* busy man. He's got a lot on his plate, as I'm sure you know." At this he stretched out with both arms and looked around the office; behind the board, Billie shrank back instinctively as she watched. "This whole place belongs to Severin. His design, his vision, his work." The guard spun back around. He pointed at Hearne, who had managed to turn himself around under the other guard's boot, so he was looking up at his tormentor. "His *workers*. That includes you, Mr. Hearne. And it seems you've forgotten it again." He made a clicking sound with his tongue against his teeth, and looked at his colleague. "What are we going to do with the remarkable Mr. Hearne now, Blanco, eh?"

The other guard, Blanco, juggled his shoulders; Hearne moaned as the pressure increased under Blanco's boot. "It's a puzzle, mate, a puzzle all right. Nothing works, does it?"

The first guard was quick to agree. "You are right there, mucker. Nothing works for Mr. Hearne. We turn him out, he'll just be at it again." He folded his arms and cocked his head. "I think we've reached a certain point now, don't you, Blanco?"

Blanco grinned. "Sometimes accidents happen, even to the best of us. Or maybe we can disappear him. He'll be just one of many. Nobody will bat an eyelid, they won't."

"You're right there, mucker. You are so right there."

Hearne squirmed under Blanco's boot, but the two guards just laughed. The worker managed to twist again, his fingernails scrabbling against the boards; as he craned his neck out, his eyes went wide, and his ragged breath caught in his throat.

Billie fixed the man with a steely look, and, ever so gently, shook her head. From his angle on the floor, Hearne had a clear view of Billie crouched behind the display board, her face almost at the same level as his. She held her breath, but after a moment, the man seemed to relax, and he blinked, quite deliberately, indicating his understanding.

The two guards had been talking; now, Hearne interrupted them, his voice loud, echoing with surprising volume from the hard surfaces of the prefab office.

"I want to see him."

The two guards fell silent. Blanco lifted his boot from Hearne's chest, and the man convulsed, briefly, his hands squeezing at his chest as the pressure was suddenly relieved. Billie watched two pairs of booted feet moving together, until the guards were both standing in front of their prisoner.

"Take me to Severin," said Hearne. "He may be a son of a witch, but he is an engineer, at least. He'll see reason."

There was silence for a moment. Then the guard who wasn't Blanco laughed.

"Oh, trust me," he said, "you don't want to see Severin."

Hearne pushed himself up into a sitting position, so he was now mostly out of Billie's sight. "You said that even he had taken an interest in what I was doing. So, fine. Take me to him. Let me talk to him. Let me take the workers' concerns directly to Control."

The first guard chuckled again. "See, Blanco? What did

I tell you? Admirable, that is. There's something there."

"Bravery," said Blanco.

The other hissed. "Ooh, no, I wouldn't go that far, mucker. I'd be more inclined to say… foolishness."

Hearne stirred on the floor again. "Severin. Take me to him."

"No, mate, that's not going to happen," said the first guard. "See, it's like I said. All of this is Severin's. The whole project. So Severin is a busy man. He's got a lot to oversee. And, let me tell you right now, the very last thing he needs is some self-appointed representative—"

"I am not self-appointed," said Hearne. "I was elected by the union—"

Blanco shot forward; Billie couldn't see the punch, but she heard the guard's fist connect with Hearne's cheek, the worker flying backward across the floor, the back of his head thudding onto the boards with a sickening crack. He lolled on the floor, rolling his head back, and Billie saw the blood from the man's smashed nose now joining the blood trickling from his mouth.

"You will hold your tongue in the presence of the Leviathan Company!" yelled the first guard. "The union of workers is a criminal fraternity, and *you* are the leader." He stepped forward. Billie listened to the creak of his boot leather, the rasp of the dry, dusty floorboards under those boots, and the meaty slap as the guard began pounding his fist into his other palm.

"Tell you what. You want us to take you to Severin, eh?" asked the guard. "Okay, we'll do that. Just answer me one question."

The snick, unmistakable, of metal on metal, a faint ringing in the air. The guard had drawn a knife.

Blanco bent down over Hearne. Billie couldn't see his face yet, but she could see the glint of steel as he placed the tip of his blade into the hollow of the worker's throat.

"How many pieces do you want to be in?"

The guard drew the blade back, then paused.

It was now, or never.

Billie pushed up with her legs, powering forward. She crashed through the display board, splitting it clean in two. Blanco, standing further back, saw her first, and was already turning to run for the door when Billie tackled him, throwing her entire weight behind her raised forearm, aiming squarely for the man's larynx. The arm connected, something audibly popped, and Blanco collapsed. Billie landed astride him on her knees, but without pause she stood, spun around, and kicked out. As she had anticipated, the first guard, his reactions slow thanks to the element of surprise, was still raising himself from the awkward position he had been in, leaning over Hearne. He still had his dagger clutched in one hand, but wasn't ready for any kind of attack.

Billie's foot took him in the side of his head just as he was standing. He yelled out, his right arm swinging randomly, the dagger still held only loosely. Billie blocked the arm, and chopped down on the hand, sending the knife to the floor. With Blanco choking behind her, Billie rushed forward, pressing the assault, shoving the first guard back into the shattered display board, tripping him over the heavy base of its wheeled frame. The guard hit the floor flat on his back, but immediately kicked his legs, trying to untangle himself from the frame. Billie stepped over the frame and wrapped an arm around his neck; then, with one hand on the top of his head, she twisted sharply, separating the man's cervical vertebrae. The guard's now lifeless form was an instant dead weight in her arms, and as Billie stood she let him drop with a thud to the floor. As she turned, she saw Blanco staggering toward her, his face purple-red as he fought to breathe through his ruined throat. Billie took a step backward, ready to dispatch him, when the guard froze, then juddered on his feet for a few moments before toppling sideways, landing heavily in front of the desk.

Standing behind him was Hearne, holding the first guard's dagger in his hand, the blade covered in blood right to the hilt, more of it splattered over the front of the worker's gray tunic.

Hearne sighed and dropped the dagger, then he fell to his knees and sat there, heaving for air. Billie moved to his side.

"Are you all right?"

Hearne shook his head, his bloodied hands clutching at his chest. "Yes and no. I mean, they've done worse. I've *seen* them do worse. But I'll live." He looked up and smiled. "Thanks to you." He sat back on his haunches, his eyes roving up and down Billie. In the commotion, her borrowed cape had ridden up around her neck, revealing her red leather jacket beneath. She straightened the cape, restoring the disguise, but Hearne was still looking at her with narrowed eyes.

"Who are you?" he asked, the suspicion heavy in his voice. "Which sector are you assigned to?"

"It's okay. I'm not one of them," Billie reassured him.

Hearne winced at her. "So I gathered. And I'm grateful, believe me. I didn't think they'd ever go as far as killing me, but it seemed that their patience had finally run out." He winced again, then, apparently seeing the blood on his hands for the first time, he began to wipe them on his dusty jacket.

Billie turned to look down at the bodies of the two guards. She couldn't hear anyone else approaching the hut. The fight had been far from quiet, yet the noise of the construction outside must have drowned out the commotion. And if the two guards had planned on beating Hearne to death anyway, clearly they hadn't expected anyone to come looking, no matter how much noise they made.

"Don't worry," said Hearne, noticing her look toward the door. "This is a large site, and as you heard, accidents happen, and people go missing, frequently. This foreman's office is out of use. We can leave the bodies here. I'll get someone to come in and make them disappear."

"You're a leader, here? Among the workers?"

Hearne nodded. "Union leader. Some of us have been trying to organize for months now, right across the site. But as soon as Leviathan got wind of it, they banned all gatherings. So, we kept it quiet, organizing ourselves in the shadows. We were okay for a while there, but recently Leviathan started searching for us again. Hunting us down, eliminating us."

Billie frowned. "And then they finally came for you?"

Hearne laughed; the laugh quickly turned into a cough. "Like I said, looks like my luck ran out. Severin can only be pushed so far, I suppose." He tapped his chest and winced again. "See, I'm the only one they couldn't touch, till now. Severin could pretend all he liked that the union didn't exist, while his men made sure those who joined it disappeared. But me? I was untouchable. If anything happened to me, that would risk everything—the other workers wouldn't have been able to ignore it. It would have been an admission from Leviathan that the union existed and that they were frightened of it." Hearne paused. "Well, at least until now." He shrugged.

"This Severin? He's in charge?" asked Billie.

"Yes," said Hearne. "Miles Severin is the boss. The guards were right—this whole project is his undertaking. His leadership, his direct command. He came up with the idea for the Leviathan Causeway, spent years petitioning the Queen and King of Morley to commission its construction."

"Before the Three-Day War?"

"Oh, years before. But nothing ever got off the ground. It was the war that finally did it. Alba had been reduced to… well, you've seen what Alba has been reduced to. The city had to be reconstructed. Severin adjusted his pitch to include that, and the Queen and King accepted. Work began almost at once. All that you see around you is the result of a single year of construction." Hearne cocked his head. "That's something I have to give Severin credit for. He's a master planner."

"And then the Void rift appeared?"

Hearne looked puzzled, then his eyes lit up. "Oh, you mean the Barrier? Huh, Void rift. Haven't heard it called that before. But yes, it appeared quite suddenly. The causeway's lower half was cut off by the Barrier. It's almost completely inaccessible now, other than by climbing the scaffolding."

"And yet work continues?"

"Oh yes. If anything, Severin stepped up the pace. He didn't appear to be concerned by the change—but then, Severin isn't a man who shows his feelings. But he said the causeway was undamaged—on this side, anyway—and work went on. He built the wall at the bottom of the Barrier, and I believe he turned at least some of his laboratories over to studying the phenomenon. He held a big meeting—actually, it might have been the first time he had gathered the entire workforce together. At that time, there was room enough on the west side of the zone for everyone to gather—there were only a few hundred of us workers at that point. Afterward, Severin expanded the operation to the thousands—that's when some of us tried to get the union together, because the Leviathan Company wasn't just hiring people who came to Morley of their own free will. They were *shipping* people in—recruiting them from all over the Empire, selling them the project. Of course, once we heard about the conditions they had imposed on these workers, it was clear it was nothing but indentured servitude..."

Billie shook her head. She wasn't concerned with the state of affairs among the workers—no matter how brutal Severin and his mysterious company apparently were. No, she needed to investigate their relationship with the rift, because something wasn't adding up.

According to what Hearne had just said, the construction had begun prior to the rift appearing. Strangely—coincidentally?—when it *had* appeared, it split the project exactly in half, without, apparently, disrupting the project. More than that, the work had accelerated, Leviathan bringing in even more workers, expanding the operation significantly.

But was that despite the rift? Or... *because of* the rift?

It almost sounded like Severin had expected the rift to appear, just as construction had started. It couldn't be a coincidence.

Hearne made to lift himself off the floor, wincing all the while. Billie helped him up, then, with the man leaning on the desk, she moved behind it and righted the overturned chair, helping Hearne to lower himself into it. Stepping past Blanco's body, she cast her gaze over the shattered remains of the display board. The map that had been affixed to it had been torn into four large pieces, but the paper was thick and each section was more or less intact and quite readable. Billie found the piece she wanted, and she pulled it clear of the debris. Moving to the desk, she flattened it out. Hearne, watching her, caught on and grabbed the other side of it, helping to hold it down as Billie pointed.

"This is the central administration block?" she asked, tapping the collection of squares on the hill that was labeled CONTROL.

Hearne nodded. "Leviathan Company site headquarters. Severin's private office is here, along with the master site office, control room, and laboratories. It's easy enough to find; you can see the tower from everywhere. And we are here." Hearne traced his finger from the complex, along the barrier, to the torn edge of the map. He kept going, finally tapping the bare desk about three inches from the paper.

"Looks easy enough."

"Oh, you'll be able to find it, all right," said Hearne, "but the path isn't necessarily an easy one. This close to the Barrier, any worker not in their assigned sector is likely to be stopped and searched by Leviathan guards." He chuckled to himself, then fought to suppress the cough his laugh quickly developed into. "That's how they caught me. I was going to meet one of the representatives from a different zone, and I got sloppy."

Billie stood up and folded her arms. Then she turned and looked down at the bodies of the two guards. She nudged Blanco's leg with the toe of her boot. He looked about the right size.

"I'll take a uniform," she said. "They wouldn't stop a guard, would they?"

Hearne shrugged. "Probably not. There are hundreds of Leviathan men and women all over the site. You'd certainly have a better chance of reaching Control as one of them. Although I'd still advise discretion."

"Don't worry about that," said Billie. "I can be careful."

Then she crouched on the ground and began to remove

Blanco's uniform. There was a little blood at the shoulder, but it was hardly visible against the black fabric, and with a little judicious application of the ubiquitous gray dust, it would be easily disguised.

"There is one thing you can tell me," said Billie, as she undressed the guard's cooling body.

"Yes?"

"What's the causeway for? I mean, *really* for? I know it's supposed to link Morley and Gristol, but the distance involved is enormous. The causeway is big, but it'll still take decades to span the continents."

Hearne laughed. "You underestimate Severin's resolve."

Billie paused, looked at Hearne, then continued her work. She had reached Blanco's belt, which was five inches wide and made of very thick, very heavy tooled leather—to support the weight, clearly, of the two large, square pouches that sat on the left side.

Hearne continued. "The great Leviathan Causeway is to be a wonder of the modern world—not just a link to Gristol, but the first part of a great transcontinental rail car system, a network so vast that, when completed, it will link every part of the Empire together. The interminable journeys by sea will be a thing of the past." He paused. "I have to admit, Severin's plan is impressive, even if his methods are suspect. Just think of it—fast travel, to any part of the Isles. Think of it!"

Billie recalled not only her long sea journey from Dunwall to Alba, but also her years of travel around the Isles. Condensing the huge distances that separated the four corners of the Empire to journeys that would take far less time was an incredible thought, and she said as much.

"Exactly!" said Hearne. Billie looked at him, and he smiled. "It would be a revolution. And it wouldn't just affect travel and trade. It will change everything.

Economics. Politics. Everything. And all under the control of the Leviathan Company. You can see the position it would put Morley in. The whole balance of power in the Empire would shift."

Billie whistled between her teeth. "No wonder the Queen and King bought his plan. They'd become more powerful than the Empress herself."

Hearne nodded. "And now perhaps you can see why Severin was so concerned with continuing the project after the Barrier appeared. The stakes are too high to stop."

Billie unbuttoned her cape and slipped it off, then began to put Blanco's uniform on over the top of her own clothes. The guard had been her height but much broader, so overall the fit wasn't bad, although it wasn't comfortable. With some careful arrangement of her hair under the man's garrison cap, even the eyepatch covering the Sliver of the Eye of the Dead God was somewhat less noticeable—at least, according to Hearne's appraisal. As she adjusted Blanco's belt, pulling the two pouches into a more comfortable position over her hip, there was a tiny *crack* across her fingertips, a static discharge, she guessed, from the uniform having been rubbed against the floorboards as she pulled it off the dead body.

Hearne heaved himself to his feet, and looked Billie up and down. "That should do it," he said. "Just keep your head down. There's nothing more I can do for you. I don't know who you are or what you're hoping to find, but I wish you luck, all the same."

"Thank you," said Billie. "You've been very helpful. What will you do now?"

"Carry on, of course," he said. "I still have to meet with the other representatives. And arrange a cleanup." He gestured to the bodies. "I have to say, I'm rather glad I ran into you today."

He moved to the door and carefully pulled it open, peering out through the gap. "It looks clear. You should go."

Billie nodded her farewell, and stepped out of the hut. Adjusting her tunic, she checked both directions, noting the workers and the guards as they went about their business. Nobody seemed to have noticed her coming out of the prefab.

She turned left and headed west, following the Barrier, toward Control.

12

LEVIATHAN CAUSEWAY, ALBA
17th Day, Month of Darkness, 1853

Hearne had been right; the path to the control complex was a simple one—all Billie had to do was head toward the complex that sat looming over the site, at the top of its carved-out hill. She didn't know what had occupied the site of the great crater before it had been turned into the causeway construction zone, but, apart from the giant bridge to nowhere soaring high above, the control complex itself seemed to be the only permanent structure, the last remnant here of the city of Alba. If it had been chosen as the Leviathan Company headquarters deliberately, then it was an admirable decision. The Royal Morley Observatory, its golden dome dulled by the dust, was in an excellent position, commanding a view of the entire construction zone around it. What better place for Miles Severin to look out over his domain?

Around the base of the artificial hill, more prefab huts clustered, and the whole area was a hive of activity, with workers and Leviathan guards alike busy with their assigned tasks. High above, the lattice of the causeway arched, nearly every surface covered by the insect-like forms of the workers. There was a pathway cut into the hill, spiraling up to what would have been ground level, back when the Observatory had just been one landmark in the once-fine city.

Billie followed the path, eventually reaching the complex, a large, low building of pale stone covered in decorative architraves and arches, bas reliefs charting the stars and constellations rendered in gilt, incongruous after the functional, temporary buildings of the construction zone. The main entrance was a large set of iron double doors, intricately engraved, the lines and patterns inlaid with more gilt, which shone brightly under the ever-present arc lamps despite the dust. As Billie approached, she watched black-uniformed Leviathan guards come and go without pause. It seemed that there wasn't any kind of guard or checkpoint inside. That was logical, given that nobody was here who wasn't supposed to be. For those employed by the company, the door was, quite literally, open.

Billie picked up her pace and, keeping her head down, walked into the building. She came immediately into a large atrium, the stone walls a mix of white and gilt. Several corridors led off from the atrium, and stairs went up on two sides.

Billie had brought the section of the map from the site office with her, hidden inside her tunic, but there was no point consulting it now—not only would it draw attention, but the map itself had been largely schematic. The central control room and surrounding laboratories had been shown as being part of the former Royal Observatory's main tower. She needed to find a way up.

Billie picked the stairs on her left.

As she had suspected, the old building was a labyrinth of corridors and offices, although Billie found this very much to her advantage as she made her way deeper into the complex. The place was buzzing with staff—men and women, all wearing the same black uniform as her own. From every office came rumblings of conversation and discussion, the clack of typewriters, the whirr of audiograph recorders being dictated to and being played back. The corridors were thick with people.

It was the perfect cover. Nobody paid Billie any attention.

But she also wasn't getting anywhere. She was somewhere in the administration sector, that much was obvious—and precisely where she *didn't* want to be. What she wanted to see were the laboratories and the control room. There she could find out what Severin and his company were up to with the Void rift, what experiments they were carrying out to destabilize the fragile barrier between this world and the next. And, if she could find out what they were doing, and how—and maybe even *why*—then she would be able to either stop their experiments, or at the very least sabotage them, while gathering as much information as she could to take back to Dribner. Perhaps then the Academy would listen to them. Emily would, anyway. She trusted Billie, and she'd either be back from her trip or Billie would have enough evidence to get the Imperial court to recall her.

Billie kept moving, looking out for any indication she was heading in the right direction. The offices were all signposted, but none of the words meant anything to her until she reached a corridor that ended in a large set of glass double doors, beyond which Billie could see a wide staircase. Above the doors was a large sign in an elaborate script, the letters fat and curled, in typical Morley style, to look as if they were made of flowers and plants.

MAIN OBSERVATORY
OBSERVATORY WORKSHOPS

This was it. Billie reached for the doors, then heard sounds behind her—footsteps and voices. People coming, at least three, maybe four, deep in conversation.

While she had passed by dozens of people in the control complex, she had been just one of many, hidden by the crowds of black uniforms. Here, she was alone. She would be noticed, probably questioned—and that was something she couldn't risk.

Looking through the doors, she could see that the stair lobby beyond was large, the stairs themselves more of the intricate, complex ironwork in the typically ostentatious style of Morley. There was plenty of room beneath the stairs to hide, and plenty of shadow to vanish into.

Billie slipped through the doors and ducked under the stairs. A moment later, the doors opened again, and four people passed through. Billie watched as the first man, a broad-chested guard with a wiry gray beard, held the door open for his companions—two women, one with long brown hair and dark skin, the other pale and blonde, her hair cut into a bob. The fourth member of the party was a very short, thin man with red hair brushed sideways across his scalp, and a pair of silver-framed glasses with large square lenses balanced on his nose.

"I agree with the urgency of the situation, sir," said the pale woman as the bearded man released the door, allowing it to swing silently closed on well-oiled hinges. "But if we are to proceed to the next phase, we need to double our yield of voidrite if we are to have sufficient fuel."

The red-headed man paused at the base of the stairs, one hand on the rail, one foot on the bottom step. He was staring ahead; Billie pulled herself back into deeper shadow, but the man wasn't looking at her. His mouth twitched, and his eyes narrowed behind his glasses. When he spoke he didn't turn around. His voice was a steady monotone, devoid of any expression or inflection that might reveal what he was thinking.

"Then see to it, Uvanov. Voidrite yield is your own personal responsibility."

Uvanov lowered her gaze to the floor.

"Yes, Mr. Severin."

Severin spun around to face his subordinate. "Please do not make me regret my decision to entrust that responsibility to you."

Uvanov didn't look up.

"No, sir. Of course not, sir."

Severin took a step closer. As Billie watched, the other two tensed as their boss confronted his subordinate.

"Remember, Uvanov, that we are at war."

"Yes, Mr. Severin."

"And war requires sacrifices, Uvanov." Severin glanced at the other two. "From all of us. We stand at the pivot point of history. The fate of the world lies in our hands. Do not forget what all of this is for."

Then Uvanov looked up. She held her chin high.

"No, Mr. Severin. I apologize, sir."

Severin snapped his gaze back to Uvanov. His voice remained unchanged in tone or volume.

"We will proceed to the next phase. Increase the yield."

Uvanov gave a sharp nod and snapped the heels of her boots together.

"Yes, Mr. Severin."

Severin turned around and stood on the first stair. Then he stopped.

"Threefold, Uvanov."

Behind her boss's back, Billie saw Uvanov's throat bob as she swallowed, and then she looked at her companion. The dark woman shook her head, very slowly.

"We will require another intake of workers into the Hollow," said Uvanov.

"Then see to it," said Severin.

Uvanov snapped her heels together again. "At once, sir."

"Come," said Severin. "We are expected."

With that, he skipped up the steps. After a pause, his two subordinates and the guard followed. Billie waited until their footsteps faded, then swung out from under the stairs. She looked up, in the direction they had gone.

So, that was Severin, the mastermind behind the Leviathan Causeway.

Billie didn't understand what they had been talking about—Severin had said they were at war, and that the fate of the world was in their hands? Billie didn't like the sound of that at all.

But there was one word that echoed around her mind.

Hollow. Uvanov had said the word *hollow*.

Billie went up the stairs, padding softly on her toes.

She had to discover what was going on.

13

CONTROL COMPLEX,
LEVIATHAN CAUSEWAY, ALBA
17th Day, Month of Darkness, 1853

The stairs narrowed as they went up into the main column of the Royal Observatory tower, then twisted and became a tight, circular spiral; Billie caught up with Severin and the others, and kept herself a couple of turns below them, close enough to listen—not that she learned anything. Severin spoke only in single words as he listened to reports given by Uvanov and the other woman. Sector 5 was ahead of schedule. Sector 3 reported the loss of two workers, having apparently fallen from the causeway. The list went on—nothing in any detail, just a fairly standard, if light, overview of the day's progress. At the top of the stairs, the four passed through another set of glass doors. Billie edged along the wall, and, keeping low, leaned around to peer through the glass. She watched as Severin led his group through an arch-topped entrance at the far side of a circular atrium, beyond which she could see the curve of another, smaller staircase. According to the sign above the archway, this led to the MAIN DOME. There were four other doors leading from the atrium, spaced around the curved walls, each signposted as a workshop.

She'd found Control.

Billie waited by the doors, watching and listening, but there were no sounds from beyond. It seemed that she and Severin's group were the only ones in the tower, and the Leviathan guards weren't coming out from the control room anytime soon.

Billie stood, slipped through the glass doors, and padded over to the archway opposite. There she waited for a moment, glancing around, straining her ears, but there was no sound from the four workshops.

Nor was there any sound from above.

Billie headed up the stairs.

At the top was another archway, this one blocked by a wooden door banded in iron that looked more decorative than practical. There was a large keyhole. Billie pressed her ear to the door, but heard nothing. Then she ducked down to the keyhole and looked through. It afforded a clear view of the circular chamber beyond.

Billie's breath caught in her throat. She stood, counted for a beat, weighing up her options. Then she grabbed the handle and pushed the door open.

The room beyond was large and circular, the chamber that crowned the tower. The domed ceiling was, like the exterior, covered in gold leaf, but here it was further embellished by a map of the night sky, inlaid with glittering gems. The walls of the chamber curved around from the entrance, forming two perfect arcs. Opposite the main door, a large slot was cut into the wall, the opening starting near the floor and curving up into the dome, almost reaching the apex. It was clearly where the observatory's telescope had been fitted; indeed, the floor at the center of the room was cut with a series of channels and divots, a clear indication of where the mechanism of the scope had originally been bolted.

The telescope was gone. There were no other exits

from the dome, no windows aside from the slot. Through the slot she could see the Void rift, and Billie felt the Sliver grow hot and begin to tug her bodily toward the shimmering wall of blue and red light.

The room was also entirely empty. Of Severin, Uvanov, and the two others, there was no sign.

Billie was alone.

Billie backtracked into the central atrium of the Observatory tower, moving carefully, silently, listening for any movements, any sounds of life at all. But no, it was as she thought—she was alone in the tower. The telescope room was empty, as were the four workshops—now. Nobody else had come up the stairs since she had followed Severin's group, and certainly nobody had left.

Severin and his subordinates had just vanished into thin air.

Billie turned and trotted back up the steps and into the telescope room. She stood in the doorway and looked around, casting her gaze over every surface of the chamber. White walls. Gold dome with bejeweled sky. Pale stone floor. The marks of the old telescope fitting. The slot in the wall. The Void rift beyond.

That was it. There was no furniture. There were no doors. No windows. Billie made a circuit of the room, running her hand over the smooth walls, just in case there was a secret panel or door—not that there was anywhere to go or to hide.

Nothing.

When she reached the slot in the wall, she leaned out, as far as she could, ignoring the pressure building inside her head. Directly in front was nothing but the shifting wall of the rift, stretching out in both directions. If she leaned out and down, she could see the iron wall at the base, keeping the workers away from the lower portion of the rift. On either side of the observatory hill were the legs of the causeway, the mammoth construction straddling the control complex. Looking up, she could see the causeway arching hundreds of feet above the observatory's golden dome, emerging from the rift like the prow of a ship cresting some gargantuan ocean wave.

There was certainly no way out via the slot in the wall. The room was empty. Billie was alone. Severin, Uvanov, and their companions had gone.

Billie clicked her tongue in irritation, and considered her options. The room was empty; she had to accept that. But equally strange was the fact that the telescope room was, supposedly, the master control room. And yet, there was nothing in it. If Severin was using his corporation to conduct experiments on the rift as well as to build the causeway—destabilizing the rift itself—then he certainly wasn't doing it here.

Billie slipped out of the chamber and returned to the lower level. She looked around. Four observatory workshops—now used as four research laboratories for the Leviathan Corporation.

Billie headed for the first door. It was unlocked, the handle turning smoothly, silently. She stepped inside.

The room beyond was circular, much like the telescope room, although the space was smaller and the walls only formed a partial arc, the wall connecting the workshop to the atrium being flat.

But it was certainly a laboratory, complete with workbenches and high stools. The surfaces were covered with a dizzying array of glassware, held in a complex framework of shining copper. The room was lined with cupboards and workbenches. Again, there were no windows. There was a door to Billie's left, the wood elegantly curved to match the turn of the wall itself. Next to the door was a stack of packing crates, their straw stuffing poking out from underneath lids that had been levered open and then left resting slightly ajar. There were more crates on the other side of the room, a pyramid of three next to the main workbench. The uppermost crate was empty, the lid leaning at an angle against the legs of the workbench. The objects that had been packed were lined up beneath an array of equipment.

A pulse of adrenaline coursed through her body. Her human eye went wide, while the Sliver of the Eye of the Dead God hummed in her head, her vision sparking blue and red and yellow, creating an aura as she looked over the artifacts lined up on the bench.

Billie moved over to the workbench, scanning the objects. They were runes. There were three on the bench, another three nestled in straw in the open crate. They were roughly circular, about an inch and a half thick, their ivory forms wrapped in thin strands of silver and leather. Where the yellow-white surfaces were exposed, she could see they were covered with scrimshaw. One was placed under a magnifying lens on an articulated arm. There was an open leather wrap of tools beside it that looked more suited to the workshop of a watchmaker or master jeweler.

Billie shoved the top crate to one side, allowing access to the box beneath. The lid of this one has been partially levered; she gripped the edges and pulled. The loosened nails slid free with ease, and, ignoring the noise it made, she let the lid clatter to the floor.

More runes. Three on the top layer, and it looked like there was room for at least another six in the box—nine per crate, and Billie counted six crates in the room, plus the opened one.

More than sixty runes.

Billie shook her head, trying to understand. She went back to the bench, and, moving the magnifying lens on its arm, peered down at the artifact that someone had clearly been inspecting. Under the lens, the carved whale ivory of the rune was brought into sharp relief. Billie could see the grain of the ivory, and the blackened lines of the scrimshaw, magnified in enough detail to see the marks of the knife that had carved it, who knew how many years ago.

She stepped back, took a breath, and looked over the workshop again. There was a stack of bound papers on the next bench; walking around, she pulled the top notebook toward her and flipped it open. Inside, written in a tight hand, were notes on one of the runes, the comments filled out into a pre-printed form headed LEVIATHAN COMPANY. On the facing page was a life-size sketch of the rune in question.

Billie flipped through the notebook. Each pair of pages was the same—a completed form, a sketch of the rune that was being described. She flipped through the rest of it—dozens of pages, dozens of runes, each one different, each one described in detail.

Billie reached the end and tossed the notebook back onto the bench. There was a shelf of more journals on the wall above the bench. Picking a book at random, she found it was another volume of notes—another catalogue of runes. Trying a third, she found the catalogue continued, the numbers apparently sequential from the preceding volume.

It was staggering. The Leviathan Company, for some reason, had a huge cache of runes—hundreds, easily. She hadn't even considered before that so many even existed. Where Leviathan had acquired them, Billie could only speculate, although the fact that they had them was perhaps less surprising now than it would have been just a few years ago. With the dissolution of the Abbey of the Everyman, and the destruction of the Oracular Order, the Overseers and the Sisterhood no longer had a monopoly on heretical artifacts. It was likely that both institutions had accumulated a vast number of magical objects in an attempt to keep them out of the hands of others. But now they were gone, who knew what had managed to get out into the world before the Imperial authorities had clamped down on it, gathering the objects for themselves?

And there was the Norcross collection, which had been one of the things that had brought her to Alba in the first place. If Professor Dribner was right, some of that collection—the part that hadn't been salvaged by Sokolov—had ended up here, in Morley.

Billie slowly paced the room. Well, Dribner might be right on that point. Either the Norcross cache had indeed been taken to Morley—by the Leviathan Company—or they had collected artifacts from the ravaged Abbey and Sisterhood… or both.

But for what purpose, Billie had absolutely no idea.

Her pacing brought her to the curved door. Billie paused, listening at the wood, just in case. But all was silent beyond. She opened the door.

The second room was the same size and shape as the first, but this one was not being used as a laboratory. Here, the workbenches and equipment were missing, and the whole space was taken up with more packing crates, stacked on heavy-duty metal shelving that had been bolted into the walls, the black iron pins cracking the white finish of the observatory walls.

Billie gave up trying to count the crates—there were dozens in the room, all sealed. She gave one an experimental tug, but it was nailed firmly shut. The crates were all stenciled with the word LEVIATHAN, but aside from that, there were no other markings, no suggestion of the contents.

Billie took a deep breath, and focused. Lowering her chin, she let her vision blur, her attention shifting from one world to the next. The Sliver of the Eye of the Dead God hummed inside her head as she willed it to work, and she felt the pressure grow behind her temples.

Then the world flipped around in front of her, washing out in a bright blue light that threw everything in the room into a series of flickering outlines.

Everything except the contents of the crates. The runes crammed inside glowed yellow, shimmering like coals in a fire. The entire room was filled with them, *hundreds* of them, packed away, awaiting examination and cataloguing.

Billie let out her breath, and let go of the power. Her vision shook and flipped back to normal, and she was surrounded by the packing crates again.

She stood for a moment, waiting for the pain to ease. She was getting close, she knew it. Because if Severin was doing something to the rift, something that was destabilizing it, then it made sense that he was using runes. They were a source of great magical power, after all, and now that the Outsider had fallen and that power had changed… well, who knew what a rune was capable of. The way they were being studied, catalogued, it seemed that the Leviathan Company hoped to find some use for them.

Or perhaps they already had.

There was only one other door in the storeroom. Once again, Billie was cautious before proceeding, listening at the door, looking through the keyhole before opening it. It led back out to the Observatory tower atrium, which was still empty of people. She headed for one of the two doors on the other side of the atrium, and found herself in another laboratory set up like the first, a place where the runes were sorted, studied, catalogued.

In the fourth, and final, workshop, Billie found the great telescope from the main dome—or what was left of it, anyway. The scope had been disassembled, the curved copper panels of its casing propped up against the walls. The two circular mirrors from the telescope, each more than three feet in diameter, had been placed on stands, the reflective sides facing each other, while in the center stood two lenses, each half as wide as the mirrors, again placed on stands, so that all four surfaces were aligned. Billie approached the setup cautiously and peered around the edge of one of the mirrors. The area between was brighter than she had expected, thanks to the alignment of the mirrors. She saw herself reflected into infinity.

She jumped back, and spun around.

She had seen something—some*one*. They had been standing behind her, their image distorted by the curve of the telescope mirror, but still clear before it shattered into gray and blue light.

But the small workshop was empty. She was alone with the device. She stood still, listening, but the only sound she heard was the chaotic rumble of the construction site that surrounded the control complex below.

Billie turned back to the device and, keeping her distance this time, walked around it, examining it. Whatever it was, it wasn't connected to any power supply—there were no cables, no whale oil tanks, and while there were two whale oil terminals set into the far wall, both were empty, the doors open.

But she knew exactly what she had seen—another Void hollow.

Billie took a step back. She had no idea what the device was, and she wished Dribner could see it. Maybe he would understand it. Dribner's own contraption had used lenses and mirrors, although nothing on this scale. Here, while the device was much larger, there was no window available to point it toward the Void rift, which was about two hundred yards away on the other side of the workshop's outer wall.

Billie sighed, and rubbed her temples. She didn't know if she had learned anything useful yet, and one mystery in particular kept coming back to mind—where had Severin and his subordinates gone? They weren't in the telescope room. They weren't in the workshops. There were no other exits.

And yet Billie was quite alone in the tower.

Of course, she had seen people disappear before, although that wasn't *quite* the right way to describe it. Nearly two decades ago, when she had been a whaler, they'd used another word for the power Daud had let them share.

Transversal. The ability to move across space in the blink of an eye, without being seen. To disappear, as it were, from one spot and reappear in another, whether it was a hundred yards down the street or a hundred feet up, balancing on the edge of a rooftop.

Later, when the Outsider had "gifted" her the black-shard arm and the Sliver of the Eye of the Dead God, she had discovered these artifacts that were part of her granted a similar ability. Like the magic of transversal, it had been tied to the Outsider and tied to the Void. When the Outsider had fallen, her power—all of her powers, in fact—had changed, becoming unstable, unreliable, and she had grown reluctant to use them. But although she was starting to get used to the different way the Sliver worked, she hadn't summoned the Twin-bladed Knife in months, and after the last attempt she had woken in a hunter's cabin in a Tyvian forest with no memory of the previous week.

Billie gave the strange machine another glance, then headed back into the first workshop she had visited. She stood in the doorway, surveying the room.

She understood now. The Outsider had fallen, and the Void had become unmoored from the world—but it was still connected to it. It still existed, but its relationship with the world was different. Somehow, that had changed the way magic worked. That change had driven the Overseers and the Sisterhood to moonstruck oblivion, and had affected Billie's black-shard arm and the Sliver.

Severin had found a way to harness that new kind of magic, using the hundreds of runes that had been gathered and the rift itself, two entirely different things that were both connected to the Void—and able to draw power from it.

That explained the sudden disappearance of Severin and his cohorts. Billie didn't know where they had gone, but the runes and the rift certainly provided the mechanism. She thought back to Uvanov's report to her superior. She had mentioned a hollow—a Void hollow.

Billie knew they were reflections of other worlds, shining through the soft spots in the world where the Void touched it. But with the Void unmoored and its connection with the world unstable, the Void hollows would have changed too.

Had Severin found a way to use them? To get *inside* them?

That seemed increasingly likely.

Billie cast her eye over the equipment on the bench, and the runes lined up on it, and noticed a folded leather object at the back of the table. She leaned over and picked it up.

It was a belt, the same kind of heavy-duty, five-inch-wide leather piece that she was wearing now, on her uniform borrowed from the guard Blanco. The belt was missing its large, square pouches—these had been slipped off and were lying on the bench.

Billie saw the shape and size of the pouches—and realized what they were designed to carry. Holding the belt in one hand, with her other she reached down to the one around her waist. She slid her fingertips inside the pocket. There was something there—something solid, but so light she hadn't paid any attention to it when she had put the belt on. As her hand made contact she felt the static spark again. Her fingers curled around it and she pulled out the object that had been strapped to her this whole time. It had been seated firmly in the pouch, which had been custom-made to fit the object perfectly.

It was a rune. Billie held it in her hand. It felt cold, and it was light, like it was made of nothing, like she could just crush it with the slightest pressure of her fingers.

She couldn't help squeezing it. It was solid enough.

Real enough.

She placed it on the bench alongside the discarded belt, and twisted her own belt around as much as she could so the second pouch was over her midriff. She pulled at the pouch buckle, cursing under her breath as the stiff leather refused to yield. Eventually she got the buckle open and yanked the second rune out.

She stared at it for a moment, then tossed it onto the bench alongside the other one. She looked at them, unmoving, her ears filling with the rushing sound of her own blood.

That's why there were so many in the storeroom. Every guard of the Leviathan Corporation was carrying two runes on them. There were hundreds of company employees. They needed hundreds of runes. The other workshop, the one filled with crates—that wasn't a storeroom; that was just a repository, a temporary holding room for runes that had been brought in, checked and catalogued in the laboratory, then packed, ready for distribution to the Leviathan guards. Somewhere out in the construction site, the corporation must have an entire *warehouse* full of the artifacts.

Severin and the others hadn't disappeared. They had traveled—transversed, somehow—using the runes.

She had to follow them. She had to figure out how the runes worked.

Billie raced out of the workshop and up into the telescope room, skidding to a halt in the center of the chamber. It was still empty, as she expected, but… something was different. She wasn't sure quite what, for a moment, and then she realized.

The sounds had changed.

Before, the noise of the construction zone had been a steady rumble, punctuated by hammering, the clanking of the cranes, and the rattle of chains. Now, that had been replaced by something else—a kind of whirring, the sound steady, mechanical, waxing and waning like a rail car passing by at speed. She could also hear whistles, and the tinny, crackling sound of voices amplified through loudspeaker systems. And something else, a rhythmic crunch that, if Billie didn't know any better, sounded like hundreds of boots stamping.

She moved to the slot in the wall and looked out, unable to stop herself gasping in surprise.

The Void rift was gone. She could see the other half of the quarry, with the great causeway curving high overhead and passing down beyond the horizon ahead of her. Here, the causeway was complete—there were no scaffolds, no cranes, no signs of any kind of construction. Below, this half of the quarry floor was a mostly flat, wide-open space boxed on two sides by more of Leviathan's prefab huts. Here, people were marching in formation—hundreds of men, their simple uniforms augmented by black metal breastplates, their heads covered by bucket-like helmets. They were soldiers—all armed, all on parade, following the orders of their commander, who stood on a raised platform at one side of the parade ground, barking orders into a microphone, his words echoing out across the site.

Then the loud whirring sound appeared again, a sudden noise from above. Billie ducked, instinctively. Her jaw dropped as a machine *flew* overhead, passing over the observatory dome, cruising out to the far side of the plaza. There, it paused in midair, turned about its axis, then lowered itself at a snail's pace to land next to what Billie could now see were a half-dozen more machines just like it, lined up on a raised platform. The machines looked like rail cars, the wheels replaced with large angled panels that were narrow and louvered, like huge window shutters. On top of the car section was a large cylinder, like a scaled-up whale oil tank, supported on four tall struts. As Billie watched the machine land, she saw the louvers move, opening and closing, the panels repositioning constantly as a set of three wheels dropped from the bottom of the machine. As it touched down, the vehicle sagged under its own weight, and Billie noticed a squat, square chimney in the center of the roof, directly beneath the huge tank, belch a cloud of yellow smoke that rose up and apparently entered the tank, the underside of the cylinder open in a series of wide slots that ran the length of the machine.

Immediately, more black-uniformed guards ran out from one of the nearby buildings and clustered around the machine, looping the wheels with chains fixed into the ground, while a door slid open in the side and the crew jumped out. While she was watching this, there was another loud whirr from somewhere above, and Billie looked up as another flying machine came in to land. Now Billie knew what she was looking at, she could see how the giant tank was being fed by the yellow smoke from the machine's chimney.

She stepped back from the telescope slot, trying to process what she was seeing.

Flying machines. Machines that flew.

Flying. Machines.

She felt cold and dizzy. She had no idea what was happening down there, but she did know one thing.

She wasn't in Alba anymore.

She was in the Void hollow.

14

THE VOID HOLLOW

17th Day, Month of Darkness, 1853

Billie left the telescope room and headed back down toward the atrium. But halfway around the curve of the stairs, she stopped.

She wasn't alone in the tower anymore. There were people working in the laboratories.

She crept down the remainder of the stairs, her senses alert for anyone who might be coming her way. As she approached the final bend of the staircase, she had a clear view of the atrium and saw it was empty. But the workshop doors were all open. Creeping forward, Billie could see people working on the runes inside the workshop on her right—there were at least four people, but it sounded like more. A couple of them were talking to each other as they worked, comparing some of the notes from one of the many journals, while the other two that were in Billie's line of sight were sitting on the high stools, hunched over their work like master watchmakers, peering down through the multitude of magnifying lenses as they worked on the runes with delicate tools.

Billie pulled back, safely out of sight, and considered her next move. That the source of the Void rift destabilization was here, she was now certain—it was the work the Leviathan Company was doing, with their collection of artifacts.

But Billie knew that the runes themselves were almost beside the point. They were just a tool—whatever Severin and his company were doing, whatever power they had managed to unlock from the artifacts, it was less a question of how, than of *why*.

And what was the Leviathan Causeway itself *really* for?

Billie listened for a few more moments, but the workshop staff continued with their work, with no apparent indication that anyone was leaving anytime soon. Billie turned and went back up the short spiral of stairs into the telescope room. As soon as she entered the chamber, she felt the Sliver grow warm, and the pain behind her eyes started up again as she looked toward the slot in the wall at the swirling red and blue sky. It was impossible to tell if it was day or night; the whole sky looked as though it were a Void rift itself. She moved to the opening in the wall and looked down once more at what should have been the causeway construction zone—or the edge of it, abutting the Alba rift. But what she saw was something entirely different: the vast military base, full of soldiers and strange machines that could fly.

That she was inside a Void hollow was certain—another world, a reflection of her own, created by the shearing apart of the two dimensions. The perfect hiding place for Severin to build a secret army. The man himself had said they were at war, and Billie had found his base of operations.

By now the marching parades had stopped, and the open space that stretched between the control complex and the far wall of the crater was largely devoid of activity. On Billie's left was the row of berthed flying machines—six of them, each chained down, anchored through heavy loops fixed into the stone platform. There were three soldiers working on one of the machines, two of them shoveling what looked like coal from a large sack that sat on a wheeled cart into a large circular drum, which was itself sitting on a square platform that appeared to have descended from the rear of the flying machine on a toothed ratchet mechanism. As Billie watched, the two soldiers stopped shoveling, gestured to each other, then stood back, while the third grabbed hold of a chain hanging from the underside of the machine and began to pull. The platform—and the barrel—slowly began to rise up into the machine. As Billie watched, the Sliver grew increasingly hot, and a yellowish aura appeared around the barrel and the half-empty sack—the same aura she had seen around Woodrow's Void-stone knife, back at the apothecary in Mandragora Street more than a month ago.

It couldn't be—could it?

While the platform was hoisted up into the back of the flying machine, the two men who had been shoveling tossed their tools onto the wheeled cart, and then walked around to the opposite side of the machine. When they didn't appear around the louvered slats that projected from the bottom, Billie realized they must have climbed inside the vehicle, presumably to complete the fueling process.

Billie stood back, arms folded, a frown on her face. It wasn't coal the machine ran on. But it burned something else. She thought back to the overheard conversation between Severin and Uvanov. They had talked about fueling, and yield of what they had called voidrite.

Or, as Billie more simply knew it—Void stone.

So, that was it. The Leviathan Company was preparing for war, building a fleet of flying warships fueled by burning Void stone, hidden inside a vast Void hollow, accessible only to those carrying the requisite runes.

But the question was, was all this activity responsible

for destabilizing the rifts? Had Dribner been wrong about it being deliberate? Billie knew she had more to investigate.

She reached down to the first of the two pouches on her belt, then hissed between her teeth as her fingers closed around nothing. Of course, she had left her own runes in the workshop—in the workshop in the *other* place.

Well, no matter. Without runes she was stuck, but returning to Alba was simply a matter of acquiring some more. Billie put that second on her list of priorities—because first, she wanted to learn as much about Leviathan's plans as she could. There was a chance here to gather more information than she would have thought possible, not just about what the company was doing with the rift, but even its plans for war. If she could learn as much as possible, and bring the particulars back to Dunwall, then surely there was a chance to save the world.

Billie moved back to the slot in the wall. She watched as the soldiers who had been working on refueling the flying machine reappeared, the three of them now pushing their cart away, leaving a trail of yellow flashes bleeding in their wake—an aura that Billie knew only she could see.

If they were using Void stone to fuel their machines, that meant they had access to it—real, *physical* access to the Void that allowed them to harvest—to *mine*—the actual fabric of the place. Perhaps *that* was the cause of the rift destabilization? That sounded like reasonable logic.

Billie had to find the mine.

Billie left the telescope room, made for the atrium. She didn't pause as she walked past the open workshop doors, heading toward the main stairs that led down from the tower of the former Royal Observatory. She kept her pace steady, but her footfalls soft—she might be disguised, but there was still no particular need to draw any unnecessary attention to herself.

It worked. The noise from the workshops continued unabated as she moved past them, through the doors, and down to the main block of the control complex.

Everything was the same as it had been back in… well, Alba. Of course, she was still there, in theory. This place was different, but the same, another version of the city, or at least a part of the city.

Billie didn't let up the pace as she retraced her steps through the corridors. The place was as busy as it had been before, filled with Leviathan guards all going about their business, none of them paying her the slightest bit of attention. That was the advantage of the monumental scale of the operation—she was, literally, lost in the crowd.

And that suited her just fine.

Once she was past the main doors of the control complex, she followed a zigzag path cut into the hill. It was only once she had reached the quarry floor and found a quieter route running between two prefab huts that she took the opportunity to assess her surroundings.

It was, in most ways, exactly like the construction zone in Alba, except there were no workers and, as far as Billie could see—and *hear*—there was no actual construction. The causeway soared above, and it looked complete, the bridge-like structure arcing up from the quarry's horizon to the west, and here, above the camp, it ended in a large, flanged platform, hundreds of feet in the air. Above, the opaque sky swirled with deep blues and reds, blending but never mixing, like oil paint floating on water.

The Sliver tingled in her head, like she was touching the terminal of a full whale oil tank. For a moment—but only a moment—she longed for some Green Lady to dull the sensation.

Then she turned, scanning her surroundings. As she had suspected, there was no Void rift of any kind within the Hollow. The military base occupied the full, unbroken circle of the crater-like quarry, with the Royal Morley Observatory right in the middle.

Billie made for the parade ground, and the landing area for the flying machines she had seen from the tower. Once there, she skirted the edge, sticking to the roadway that ran alongside the prefab huts, keeping to a brisk, determined pace—there were Leviathan guards around, all of whom looked like they were heading somewhere important, although, like her, they all seemed to be wearing the plain black uniforms. Of the more heavily armored soldiers, she saw no sign.

Billie reached the landing platform without being challenged. She ducked around the angled panels of the closest machine, putting it between her and the buildings that skirted the parade ground. She could use its cover to take a closer look—without, she hoped, being noticed.

The flying machines were certainly impressive. The six docked here were identical, and much bigger than she had estimated from her view from the tower, each perhaps half the size of her old ship, the *Dreadful Wale*. Billie walked slowly down two facing rows, the Sliver itching in her head as she watched the yellowish trails rise out of the chimneys and into the slots on the underside of the huge tanks that sat atop the machines. When she reached the vehicle she had seen being refueled, the hazy aura of the Void stone hung around the rear of the machine like a fog, and trailed off faintly in the direction she had watched the soldiers wheel the empty cart. It was the perfect trail for her to follow.

It led her around to the back of the landing platform, where there were three large, windowless buildings with great double doors set into metal tracks in the ground—one of which was open, revealing another six flying machines parked inside, being worked on by more guards. But the trail didn't stop there. Billie followed it carefully, sticking now to the shadows. There were fewer people around this part of the camp—but conversely a higher risk of being caught and questioned.

Behind the hangars, the trail ended at another building, which was as wide as two of the hangers put together, although with a much lower roof. It had no doors, and Billie could see as she approached that it was actually completely open on three sides. Directly in front of her, more of the wheeled carts were lined up against the wall of a loading bay, the floor of the big building as high as the bed of the carts, allowing easy loading of full sacks of Void stone, and unloading of empties. The building itself was a depot, the entire back half of it completely filled, nearly to the ceiling, with Void stone. The entire place shimmered yellow in Billie's vision, the pull of the Sliver like a hand shoving her toward it.

She resisted, and darted for the loading bay, then ducked down behind the wall, her back to the depot. This close to so much Void stone, the Sliver felt like a burning spike being pushed through her head. She closed her human eye, and focused on her breathing for a few seconds. Soon enough, the sensation passed. Keeping low, she turned around and raised herself over the lip of the wall, just enough to get a good look at what was inside the depot.

There were no Leviathan guards here; the loading bay itself was devoid of activity, and the mound of Void stone stood unguarded. Over on Billie's left, the open side of the depot led out to another platform, this one wide and long, and beside it stood the familiar form of an industrial rail car, with three heavy cargo loaders hitched in a train. The loaders were nothing but rectangular metal boxes: two were closed; the third had one side that hinged down completely, showing it to be empty, obviously unloaded before Billie's arrival. As she watched, two guards appeared from farther down the platform and moved to the rear loader. They gestured to each other, then, in unison, they bent down and lifted the side of the cargo car, heaving it closed and securing the door with chains. Then, having given their handiwork a good shake to make sure all was secure, they moved back down the platform and out of Billie's field of view. A few moments later, she heard the familiar buzz as the rails were energized and the rail car started to move.

Talk about good timing. Billie's carriage awaited.

Checking the coast was clear, Billie vaulted over the wall of the loading dock and sprinted across the depot floor, ignoring the almost physical pull of the mountain of mined Void stone and the increasing pressure in her skull.

The rail car was gathering speed by the time she reached the last cargo loader. As the heavy train clanked over a junction in the rails, Billie leapt for the back of the iron box. She grabbed the lip with both hands and paused, her feet balanced against the back of the loader, as the rail car jolted over another track junction. Then, keeping her body as low as possible, in case one of the guards stationed in the rail car looked out of the open rear of the vehicle at the head of the train, she swung herself up over the edge and dropped into the loader. As they clattered onward, she scooted toward the front and risked a peek over the rim.

The two rail car operators were focused on their task, one working the control levers as the other, standing further forward, right at the nose of the vehicle, kept his eyes on the track ahead. Billie could see the track headed straight toward the western wall of the crater in which the camp sat, but beyond that, she couldn't make anything out.

Even empty, the cargo loaders were heavy, built out of thick black iron, and their traveling speed was low. Billie settled into a more comfortable position in the corner of the loader, and watched the scenery pass as they headed toward what she hoped was the mine.

15

THE VOID HOLLOW

17th Day, Month of Darkness, 1853

The journey took the better part of half an hour. As they approached the crater wall, the rail car slowed to pass through a larger junction, next to which was a small collection of more prefabricated huts. Here, two black-uniformed guards stood by a set of track levers. In the rail car, the guard standing at the nose gave his colleagues a signal, and in one synchronized movement, the driver leaned on a huge lever in the cab while the two soldiers trackside did the same at their controls. The rail car shuddered, and the air was filled with the screeching of metal on metal as the heavy vehicle reluctantly changed to the other track, before picking up speed again and heading toward a tunnel mouth cut into the side of the crater.

The pressure inside Billie's head built, the Sliver beginning the now all-too-familiar slow burn as the rail car pulled into the tunnel. It wasn't dark—on the contrary, the tunnel was lit by huge fizzing arc lamps, their mass of cables snaking across almost every inch of the tunnel wall, rendering the underground passage in a harsh, flat white light.

Billie ducked down a little more. While she had managed to get around the base without too much difficulty, in the confined quarters of the mine operation there would be little opportunity for stealth. Getting caught in the back of one of the loaders was not something Billie could afford now.

The tunnel grew warmer the farther they rolled in, and soon the flat white light of the arc lamps became tinted with red and blue. The residue of the Void stone inside Billie's cargo loader began to glow yellow in the magical vision provided by the Sliver, like the stuff was coming alive the closer it got to the main source.

They were reaching the end of the line.

Time to move.

The rail car was rolling slowly now, not much more than a good walking pace. Billie crabbed to the rear of the cargo loader and looked over the rim, checking their speed and looking for obstacles. Breaking a leg—or getting electrified by the live rails—was an easy mistake to make.

She moved to the left side of the loader. The main rail track was electrified, but there was ample room on this side for pedestrian traffic on a wide pavement that had been laid alongside the track. As the tunnel began a gentle curve, Billie judged her moment. She swung one leg over the edge of the loader and then pushed off, throwing her weight forward, aiming straight for the tunnel wall. A moment later she hit it, her outstretched palms stopping her from braining herself against the rough rock walls, and she dropped onto the pathway in a crouch. The rail next to her buzzing with power, she stayed perfectly motionless, watching the rail car disappear around the bend. Still she didn't move, listening instead to the clack of the wheels and the thud of the loaders. Just around the corner it was slowing to a standstill.

So far, so good—but she had to move fast. She stood, alone now in the floodlit tunnel, but without any kind of cover. There were no openings in the tunnel walls, only the path that stretched behind and ahead. If anyone came along, there was absolutely no place she could hide.

Billie moved forward at a pace, thankful at least that the loud buzz from the electric rails was masking the sound of her movements. At the tunnel bend, she pressed herself up against the wall, using whatever slight advantage the curve gave her. As she approached the end of the tunnel, the Sliver burned in her head. The mine was dead ahead, and very close.

A moment later, she began to hear voices over the buzz of the rails. Billie dropped into a crouch and scooted forward, clearing the bend, then stopped as soon as she saw the back end of the cargo loader that had just provided her with transport. There was a heavy clunk, and the buzz from the rails stopped.

Billie ducked down and crabbed forward over the rough path, which ended in a small wall of gray stone blocks roughly cemented together. There she stopped, and surveyed the scene.

The tunnel had come to an end in a small, underground rail yard. Her rail car and the three loaders had stopped in the center of the yard, right underneath another, smaller rail line that crossed the open space via a bridge made of heavy iron lattice. This rail looped around to form an ellipse with two long, flat sides—one suspended over the rail yard, the other passing beneath a large square opening cut into the rock wall just below the roof of the cavern, from which blue and red light flickered. Here, the same dust-covered laborers she'd come across at the main construction zone in Alba could be seen carrying baskets of rock, which they each deposited in turn into wheeled buckets that formed a loop running along the elevated rail, constantly orbiting the rail yard at walking pace. As the loaded buckets came into position over the empty cargo loader, they tipped over, dumping their contents with an ear-splitting roar, before continuing their journey to the opposite side of the cavern. At the wall, where the elevated track curved around, two more workers heaved at the upended bucket, righting it back into position, ready for the next load.

To Billie's surprise, she could only count the two workers on the upper track, and maybe six more, who periodically appeared at the mine entrance with their baskets of rock. The only Leviathan guards in the mine were the two manning the rail car, the pair now standing beside their machine, watching the operation but doing little else.

No, they were doing more than watching—they were guarding. As Billie shifted position to get a better look, she could see the two rail car operators were armed, their pistols trained on the mine workers—men and women, young and old, but all clearly tired, worked to the point of exhaustion. Their clothes were ragged, and coated in thick gray dust, along with their skin, faces, hair.

Billie realized immediately who they were—workers from the causeway, yes, but the ones that had gone missing. Hearne and the two guards who were going to beat him to death had both mentioned the fact that people went missing. That was one mystery solved—Leviathan brought them here, to work in the mine.

The question was, why? The Leviathan Corporation had an entire army hidden in this place; the size of the camp and the number of guards were staggering. And if they could build machines that could fly, couldn't they build mining equipment? Why rely on what appeared to be slave labor?

She had to get a closer look, but she couldn't risk

alerting anyone to her presence. It would have been easy to deal with the two guards, but then they would know she was here. Billie looked around, scanning for options.

Her gaze settled on the elevated rail. If she could get up onto it, the moving train of buckets would hide her as she reached the mine entrance. Once she was up there, she could grab a basket and follow the workers deeper. To help with the disguise, she reached down, scooped up handfuls of the thick gray dust that lined the cavern, and smeared it all over her black uniform. It wasn't perfect, but it would do.

As the first cargo loader slowly filled up, Billie pushed herself off the wall, using the roar of the falling rock to cover her movements. She darted to the cargo loader, using it for cover, then climbed up the side before jumping up, her fingers catching the edge of the elevated rail. She pulled herself up, squeezing next to the buckets, the iron bridge providing a scant few inches of space for footing. With the buckets moving in the opposite direction, Billie skirted along the bridge, finally reaching the cavern wall high above where she had been hiding. She kept going, using the buckets for cover, until she was close to the mine entrance. Here, light blazing from the mine provided a deep shadow for cover, and now Billie could see a steep ramp, cut into the rock wall, allowing access up into the workings itself, a stack of heavy wicker baskets nearby.

Billie took a basket and headed up the ramp.

16

THE VOID MINE

17th Day, Month of Darkness, 1853

Billie needn't have worried about the slave workers ratting her out. As she joined the shuffling line heading into the heart of the Void mine, she saw they were moving as if in a trance, their eyes glazed, showing not a single indication they knew someone else had joined their number.

And this close, she could see they weren't just dirty, their clothes and skin covered with the gray dust from the mine.

They were… changing.

She'd seen it before, of course—or at least, something similar. It had been in the Ritual Hold, high atop Shindaerey Peak in Karnaca, one long year ago. There, the Envisioned, members of the Cult of the Outsider, had gradually been transformed, their long exposure to the Void affecting them like a disease, changing them slowly into beings made of the same silvery metallic rock that formed the Void itself.

It was happening here. All around her, the exposed skin of the miners flashed like polished graphite as one line carried empty baskets to the mine face, the other emerging from the blue-red light with containers fully loaded, their precious cargo—fuel for the flying machines—sparking yellow in Billie's enhanced vision.

Billie heard, rather than saw, the mine face itself, the blazing light too bright to make out any details. But she could hear the slaves at work as they loaded their baskets, and there was another sound, a periodic crunching, which was presumably the sound of the mining machinery itself.

Then she saw them—huge, silhouetted shapes, moving in the light, throwing long, stretched shadows over the slave workers. Billie struggled to understand what she was seeing, until she was close enough, the movements of the miners blocking enough light to hide the workings of the mine face—the one part of the whole underground system that was actually breaching the Void itself.

The slaves were not doing the mining—or rather, the human slaves weren't. Because working in the blazing light were other creatures, the last vestiges of their humanity barely recognizable in their towering forms made of jagged, angled shards of living Void rock.

They were not the Envisioned as Billie had seen them in the Ritual Hold—but they were close to it. Their bodies were elongated, their arms ending in long, thin, wickedly sharp claws. It was with these claws, not tools or machinery, that the creatures were tearing the Void stone out of the blazing maw, before turning with armfuls of the stuff, dumping their loads into an ever-growing pile that sat in the fiercely glowing hole in the world. While they toiled, although without much apparent effort, the humanoid slaves worked in pairs, one shoveling the mined rock into a wicker basket held by their partner. Once full, one helped the other heave the basket up onto their shoulder, and the process was repeated, the slave doing the loading then being the one to carry that load back down the tunnel.

It was back-breaking, bone-wearying work, but the

laborers didn't speak, didn't let up the pace, as they worked in their mysterious trance. And if the miners themselves knew Billie was there, watching them, they didn't show it either.

That the process of transformation was so accelerated here was a clear sign that the area was dangerous. *That* was why the Leviathan Company used slave labor—and looking at the state of the miners, Billie wondered how long they would last at the mine face, reaching into the blazing portal and tearing Void stone from it. Certainly, this would be causing untold damage to the Void. It was clear now that there was no technology responsible—there was no instrumentation or equipment born of natural philosophy, at least other than the device she had seen in the tower back in Alba. And if there was some arcane experimentation spawned from magical ritual, Billie hadn't found it. Instead, what she had found was an open wound, the Void open to the world—well, one version of it, anyway—and being exploited for Severin's war effort.

And there was no way Billie could stop it—at least, not on her own. What could she do? Free the slaves? They were entranced by the Void, not even registering her presence. Go back to the subterranean rail yard and take out the guards? They were just two men. The Leviathan Company numbered in the thousands. Any action she could take would be both pointless and suicidal. All she could do was try to get out, get back to the real world, get back to Dunwall.

The mission was a lot bigger than her. She needed help.

That was when she realized what she was doing. Lost in her reverie, she had walked closer to the mine face, the walls of Void stone close enough to touch. Around her, the transformed miners continued to work, wrenching seams of rock in great clawfuls.

But she didn't see them. All she could see was the light—blue and red and yellow—and all she could feel was the deep, aching cold, penetrated only by the sharp, white-hot point where the Sliver of the Eye of the Dead God sat, embedded in her skull, drawn to the magic of the Void, pulling her toward the mine face—

"You there!"

The voice snapped Billie out of her dream state. She turned around and stumbled, her head throbbing in time with her heartbeat, the sound of pounding drums growing louder and louder in her ears, her vision a haze of color.

A haze that slowly resolved as she regained her senses. In front of her, at the tunnel entrance, stood four Leviathan guards. Over their black uniforms, each wore a long, heavy apron that looked like it was made of rubber, the protective clothing stretching from the neck and only stopping an inch from the ground. Their faces were covered by flat metal masks, large rectangular things with only a small, circular porthole of smoked glass to see out of.

But strangest of all was the bone charm set into the base of each mask, directly below the porthole. Smaller than the circular runes Billie knew the guards had on their belts, the bone charms were irregular pieces of magical scrimshaw, held into a circular cutout in the metal of the masks by two crisscrossed straps. Each of the four guards had a different charm in place.

And each of the four guards also held a pistol, and they were all pointing at Billie.

She raised her arms and glanced around, calculating the odds, plotting her escape. It would be difficult, but not impossible. The slaves and miners ignored the world around them, and the protective clothing the guards were wearing looked heavy and cumbersome. Already she could see two of them adjusting their grips on the pistols, their thick, elbow-length gloves making the task of aiming difficult. If she could take them out, she would have eight runes for herself. More than enough to return to Alba, once she had figured out how they worked.

The guard in front waved his pistol at her. "This is a restricted area," he said, his voice distant and echoing behind the metal mask. "Why aren't you wearing your protective clothing?"

Billie lowered her hands until they rested on the top of her head, and she slowly paced toward the guards.

"Stop right there!" the first guard yelled. Beside him, two of the other masks turned to each other as the first guard held out his other hand. "You're not assigned to Refueling. Show me your pass."

Billie pursed her lips, and glanced down, slowly reaching with both hands toward one of the pouches on her belt.

Then she launched forward, knocking the guard's gun hand away, sending the weapon flying across the chamber, where it clattered against the rock wall and fell into one of the slave's full baskets. The slave didn't notice.

Before the others could react, Billie drove her fist into the guard's middle—with the big metal masks, their heads were well protected and, for the moment, off-target. The thick rubberized apron absorbed a lot of the blow, but Billie put her bodyweight behind it. The guard doubled over with a surprised "Oof," then fell backward.

The other three guards were also surprised, which Billie used to her advantage, their reaction time significantly slowed. One fired his pistol, but too late; Billie had already ducked into a roll, unraveling herself right in front of the man. Again, she knocked the gun arm, easily disarming him, while kicking out sideways, aiming for the knee of the guard beside him. Although the power of her blow was dampened by the apron, Billie heard a satisfying *crack*, and the man fell down onto his other knee, crying out in pain. Even as he fell, she returned her attention to the original target, slamming her fists into his middle. He went down like the first guard had.

Billie spun around, her instincts telling her to be ready for a counter-attack from the first guard she had taken out, but—

He wasn't there. He ought to be recovering, picking himself up off the ground between Billie and the mindlessly working miners.

The ground was empty. The first guard had vanished.

Billie spun on her heel, crouched into a fighting posture, ready to take on the three remaining guards.

One remaining guard. The one in the middle—the one whose knee Billie had shattered—rolled on his side on the ground, his gloved hands clutching at his leg. Billie could hear his moans of pain from behind the mask.

She ran to him, dropping to the ground before grabbing him by the shoulders and pushing him flat onto his back. He cried out in pain again, louder this time, but Billie ignored him. Instead, she placed one knee on the man's breastbone and pushed down hard, as she leaned over the glass portion in the mask. It might have been her imagination, but she could hear the bone charm fizzing in its fixture.

"Where did they go?" she asked. "Back to the city?"

The mask moved, like the man was shaking his head, but Billie couldn't see his face through the smoked glass. She grabbed the bottom edge of it and yanked it upwards, succeeding in pulling it half off his face, the straps caught over his ears, before realizing that it was hinged at the top.

The man's face was pale and damp with perspiration.

He was breathing heavily, spittle coalescing at the corners of his mouth in a bubbly white foam.

"You... you won't get out of here," he said, spluttering, teeth grinding as he struggled with the agony of his destroyed knee. "Whoever you are... you won't get out of here."

Billie relaxed the pressure on the man's chest, and looked down at him. She could take off his protective clothing. Maybe a fresh disguise could get her out.

No. Not good enough. The other three guards had vanished, literally—that power again, some kind of transversal, not granted by the Outsider's Mark, but by the co-opted magic unlocked somehow by Severin's experimentation.

With the man writhing beneath her, Billie tugged at the side of his apron, enough to get her hand around his middle, feeling for the two pouches containing the runes. She found them, her fingers working blindly at the straps.

If she could just get the runes out, maybe she could figure out how to use them, right here, right now. She could get out of the mine—get out of this whole arcane nightmare world.

That was when she was grabbed from behind. But it wasn't by a guard. The arms that encircled her, squeezed her, lifted her off the ground—they were not flesh and blood. They were stone, cold and hard and metallic. Billie gasped at the pressure and looked down, seeing the blade-sharp triangular claws interlock with each other as one of the miners picked her up. Her legs swung uselessly, and despite her struggles, she was held firm, her arms pinned to her sides.

For a moment she flexed the fingers of the black-shard arm, feeling the familiar tug as she began to summon the Twin-bladed Knife into being. But then her magical hand froze, bolts of pain shooting up her arm. The Knife was not willing to be called.

The guard on the floor scrambled backward, but not before reaching up and flipping the front of his mask down. He made it back a couple of yards, and then he wasn't alone.

They didn't walk in, they just… *appeared*. Six guards, all armed, all wearing the protective gear, their forms swirling with glowing red and blue and yellow smoke that Billie knew only she could see. As they raised their weapons, the invisible trails of Void magic evaporated.

Then a seventh appeared, dead center. She was wearing the same gear as the others, but she wasn't armed. She stepped forward, hands clasped behind her back, oblivious to the swirls of energy that Billie could see still clinging to her body, and looked up at Billie, who was held at least three feet off the floor by the towering form of the miner. Then the woman half-turned back to the guards and nodded. At once, two of the guards stepped forward, and as the miner lowered Billie to the floor, they grabbed her arms.

The leader of the group moved closer to her, so close Billie could see her reflection in the smoked porthole of the woman's mask. The bone charm, sitting underneath, seemed to move, the scrimshaw carvings on its exposed ivory surface crawling as Billie tried to focus on them.

"Interesting," said the woman. Billie glanced up, but saw only her own face mirrored back at her.

"Ma'am," said the guard holding Billie's left arm. He shoved that arm forward, holding it up, pulling the sleeve of her jacket back with his free hand. Billie's Void-touched arm was exposed, the shards twisting and turning in the air.

The leader looked down at the arm, staring at it for a

good few seconds. "*Very* interesting," she said.

Now Billie recognized the voice, and the woman's physique, even under the protective apron.

Uvanov. Severin's second-in-command.

"Take her to Control," Uvanov said. "Severin will want to deal with her. Personally."

And then the world went red and blue and yellow, and Billie was carried on an infinite cold wind to somewhere else.

17

CONTROL COMPLEX, LEVIATHAN CAUSEWAY, ALBA

Date unknown, Month of Darkness, 1853

Billie drew in a sharp breath of very cold air. She coughed, and watched as her breath steamed around her face. Her head pounded. The Sliver felt like a burning coal in her face. Her black-shard arm ached to the very bone—bone that wasn't there.

She looked up, her human eye beginning to run with tears, which she tried to blink away as best she could. She was hanging by her arms from the ceiling, her wrists encased in heavy iron manacles that were connected by chains to metal loops in the ceiling. She looked down, swinging her legs, angling her feet to try to touch the ground, but she was hanging just a few inches short.

She swung again, harder. The chains rattled, but held firm, and her actions only made her shoulders ache more.

Billie looked around. The dimly lit room was an irregular shape, but the walls were flat gray, like polished stone. The floor and the ceiling were the same—uniform, featureless save for the electric lighting embedded above. On Billie's left, in a section of wall that angled out like a polyhedron, was a door of black painted metal. There was no handle on this side, nor was there any kind of window or opening.

She tried to relax, letting the weight of her body pull her down a little, but the floor was still out of reach. She realized now that it was the pain in her shoulders that had woken her. The way she was chained, the loops in the ceiling wide enough to pull her into a Y-shape, was designed to cause discomfort—not pain, exactly, but to stress and fatigue her muscles and joints. She knew that after just a few hours in this position, she would be in total agony. A person held long enough in such a position wouldn't last long under interrogation.

But all she could do was wait. There were no sounds from beyond the door at all. Wherever she was, it was well away from the noisy workings of the Leviathan camp, and there was a damp mustiness in the air that made Billie think she was underground again. The way the walls angled around, yet were perfectly flat, suggested the cell had been built within a natural cavern, the artificial walls following the contours of the rock behind.

She waited.

And as she waited, she ran through the last series of events she could remember.

She had been in the mine, held by the creature. And then there was a sensation of falling, and of a sudden rush of cold air. No, not cold—freezing, like plunging into icy water. That had knocked her out, but her stomach lurched again as she recalled the sensation. The last words she remembered Uvanov saying were to take her back to Control.

Her captors had taken her back to Alba, using the runes, although the experience had been different to earlier, when she had accidentally crossed into the Void hollow using the runes taken from the late Mr. Blanco. Perhaps it had been different because she wasn't wearing runes of her own, but had been carried across by the guards.

Whatever the case, it was immaterial. What had happened, had happened.

Her thoughts drifted back to the mine again. She remembered the protective clothing the guards had been wearing to enter the mine face area, and the way each mask had a bone charm slotted into it, the way the guard had asked her why she wasn't wearing her own gear, a fast, breathless hint of fear in his voice—clearly they understood the malign influence of the Void. That was why they were using slaves to mine the rock—the protective gear was unwieldy and would slow the work, and besides, why waste bone charms kitting out the laborers when they could "disappear" them from the causeway construction site in Alba? They had a limitless supply there.

Did that mean the Leviathan Causeway was just… what, a smokescreen for mining Void stone? It couldn't be, Billie reasoned. It was too big an operation. It had to have a purpose—a *true* purpose—although what, she didn't know.

Yet.

She hoped she would get some answers soon. In the meantime, she shifted her position, levering herself up using her arm muscles, feeling her biceps and triceps burn as, elbows locked, chains held taut, she rose up six inches or so. She held herself there, counting the seconds, feeling the pain, glad to have kept herself in top physical condition all these years, despite her intake of Green Lady. Still, there could have been worse habits. Addermire Solution, for instance.

Then she gently lowered herself, until she could let the chains carry her weight. Her shoulders sang in protest, but the sudden relief from her arm muscles more than made up for the discomfort.

And then she went back to her patient wait.

*

The clanking of keys woke her. Billie's head jerked up, the sudden movement causing her to swing on the chains. Immediately, her head cleared, the searing pain shooting from her shoulders and down her back, bringing her to full alertness. That she had fallen asleep, despite the discomfort, was not so remarkable—in her days with the Whalers she had had to occupy positions on watch or surveillance for hours on end that were almost, if not quite, as uncomfortable. But she had no idea how long she had been out, or even how long it had been since they had captured her in the mine.

The door to the cell opened, and two black-uniformed Leviathan guards marched in. The first guard was a woman, pistol in hand, razor-sharp garrison cap at a sharp angle on her head, her blonde hair swept back and fastened in a tight bun. She was followed by another, older woman.

Uvanov.

The guard moved around Billie until she was positioned behind her, out of Billie's eyeline. Billie glanced over her shoulder and caught a glimpse of the pistol trained on her, before the sound of another set of footsteps brought her attention back to the front.

Uvanov stood with her hands behind her back, lips pursed as she peered at Billie, as the third party walked into the cell with slow, deliberate steps. The man looked at Uvanov, then turned a sharp ninety degrees and moved closer to Billie. He looked at her—at the Sliver, Billie realized, suddenly unable to feel whether the eyepatch was in place or not—then removed his thick, square-lensed glasses before he nodded, perhaps to himself, and took a step back toward the others. He put his glasses on slowly, then smoothed down his thin red hair that was drawn flat across his scalp.

"Report," said Severin, his voice flat and emotionless.

Uvanov snapped her heels together, her posture suddenly rigid.

"The prisoner was found at the mine face, wearing this stolen uniform." Uvanov's arm appeared from behind her. Billie saw she was holding a short swagger stick, which she pointed at the bundle of black clothing in the corner. "No artifacts were present."

Severin didn't move. He held his entire body perfectly still, as if he was carved out of the Void rock his creatures were busy mining in the Hollow. His eyes didn't leave Billie's—or rather, his gaze didn't leave the Sliver.

"No runes?"

Behind him, Uvanov shook her head, although Severin couldn't see. "None were found on her. No identification, either. But she must have used them to come through to the Hollow."

Severin cocked his head. "Perhaps. Or perhaps… not." He was still staring at the Sliver. "There were no reports of intruders at the Causeway zone," he said. It was a statement, not a question.

Uvanov's throat bobbed as she gulped, and Billie could see the fear creep over her features.

"We are checking, sir, but—"

"There were no reports of intruders at the Causeway zone," said Severin again. His voice was devoid of any emotion, any feeling whatsoever, and his expression was set.

Uvanov paused, her mouth working for a moment, but she fell silent. She glanced at the floor for just a second before lifting her chin again, and clasping her hands behind her back.

Severin stared at Billie. Seconds passed. Nobody spoke. Billie looked from Severin to Uvanov, then back. Severin was completely motionless, virtually the only movement Billie could see was the pulse in his neck, the blink of his eyes behind the large lenses, and the gentle, almost imperceptible rise and fall of his chest as he breathed.

Billie's shoulders ached, but she ignored it—if nothing else, the ever-increasing discomfort was keeping her alert.

Keeping her angry.

Finally, she could bear it no longer. She lifted her chin at Severin. Still he didn't move, or speak. He was a strange one, of that there was no doubt.

"Aren't you going to ask me any questions?"

Severin just blinked. Uvanov, at least, was showing some signs of life, even if it was just to shift the weight on her feet as she stood behind her leader's shoulder.

Billie looked back at Severin—looked *down* at him. He was a short man anyway, and hanging from the chains as she was put Billie a good few inches or so above him. She took the time to study his face properly this time. He was clean-shaven, maybe fifty years old. His face was sharp, with a fine, delicate bone structure. He didn't have an ounce of fat on him.

Billie thought his face would break rather easily. She promised herself to test that theory the first chance she got.

"This is some strange interrogation technique you have, Severin," said Billie.

Severin's lips parted with a faint but audible *pop*. Finally, some kind of reaction.

"So, you know my name," he said.

Billie nodded. "I know who you are."

Severin's lips twitched, like they were threatening to smile on their own, like he had to fight to quell the urge. "I said you know my name, not who I am," he said.

Billie lifted her chin again. "Don't you want to know who *I* am, and how I got here?"

"Perhaps we are at a misunderstanding," said Severin. Every word was clipped, perfectly enunciated. To Billie he sounded like one of the old aristocrats from Dunwall. "You are now back in Alba. That you were found in the Void hollow means you came into it using runes, taken from one of my men. There is no other way you could have entered, therefore I do not need to ask you that question. The fact that you do not have the runes on your person is meaningless. You had them, you discarded them."

Billie allowed herself a smile. "Why would I discard them?" It wasn't a real question. She was just pushing at Severin, seeing what his reaction was. His responses—as odd as they were—were both interesting and useful.

As a practiced interrogator herself, Billie knew that the subject of the interrogation could learn a lot from their captor.

Severin's lips twitched again. He glanced at the pile of clothes in the corner. "You discarded part of the uniform already. Perhaps you didn't know what the runes were. Whatever the case, it is another irrelevance. You are my prisoner."

Billie stared down him. "I know your name, but you don't know mine. Are you going to ask it?"

"Irrelevant," said Severin. "Your identity, even if I knew it, would have no meaning to me, and therefore would be of no value."

Billie shook her head. "But if you don't know who I am, or where I came from, then you won't know how to prevent more of us coming through to the Hollow. Maybe I'm just the first. Maybe I'm on my own. Maybe I'm a spy, or a saboteur, or maybe I'm both. It's true that I'm your prisoner, but as a prisoner I have value. You could learn a lot from me."

Behind Severin, Uvanov raised an eyebrow. She glanced at the back of her leader's head, and shifted on her feet again.

"She might be right, sir," she said. "We don't know who she is or where she came from. If there is anything that could jeopardize the project, we should know about it. We are reaching a crucial stage, and if anything were to delay the next phase—"

Without turning around, Severin lifted a hand, holding it above his shoulder, palm toward Billie. Uvanov immediately fell silent and looked at the floor again.

"Nothing will delay the next phase," Severin said, "and we will have no more intruders. If the prisoner is a spy or a saboteur as she suggests, then she has failed, because she has been captured. When she does not return to her masters—if she has any—it will be too late for them to act, regardless."

Billie smiled. "You're very confident."

Severin lowered his hand. "At this stage of the project, the next phase has a ninety-nine percent chance of success. Even if any more of you are able to enter the Void hollow, I have an entire army there which will be placed on high alert, immediately."

"You talk like some kind of calculating machine."

Severin smiled, finally. "Thank you for the compliment."

Billie pulled on the chains, making them creak in their ceiling anchors. "So if all of this is an 'irrelevance,' as you call it, then why am I here? If you're not going to question me, then why am I still alive?"

"That status is only temporary, I can assure you," said Severin. "But you are mistaken again. *You* are not an irrelevance. On the contrary, you may be very useful to the operation."

He reached up and grabbed Billie's chin with his gloved hand. Like the rest of him, his hand was small, the fingers thin, the bones within delicate, but there was strength in them. Billie could resist only a moment before she succumbed, allowing the man to turn her head to one side. Standing almost on tiptoe, Severin peered at the Sliver.

"Most interesting," he said, then he let go and took a step back, looking this time at Uvanov. The second-in-command seemed to find her confidence, and she moved forward, pointing at Billie.

"What if there *is* another way into the Hollow?" she asked, moving closer to her prisoner. "What if she didn't use runes, but used… whatever that is in her head?"

She pointed to the Sliver. Billie instinctively turned her head away.

Severin's smile didn't return—maybe he'd used up his daily ration of facial expressions, Billie thought—but his mouth twitched again, betraying his interest, no matter how cold he seemed.

"An interesting supposition," he said. "But one that is contrary to all of our accumulated knowledge. There may be a resurgence in primitive sorceries, but nothing that is of sufficient power."

Uvanov took a step toward her leader. She lowered her voice. "But what if it is *possible*? What if that thing in her head isn't *low* magic? And her arm. That's like nothing we've seen before. She's wielding a higher kind of power, I'm sure of it. Surely that is worth investigating?"

Severin stared at his subordinate for a good four, five seconds, then he gave a short, sharp nod. "Logic accepted," he said. He pointed a gloved finger at Billie's face. "Dissect *that* out of her skull." He glanced at her Void-touched arm, then at the other, then back again, before pointing to the magical limb. "And disconnect *that*. Have both artifacts sent to the workshops for immediate analysis. I will inform my engineers. You have your orders, Uvanov."

The second-in-command snapped her heels together, then marched toward the door.

That was when the door opened. Uvanov came to a rapid halt, almost slipping on the polished floor. Severin spun around to face the newcomers.

They were a trio, two men and a woman, clad in forest-green tunics made out of a rich, deep velvet, over pants that were a brilliant, unsullied white, matching the white leather bandoliers that crisscrossed their chests. The two men wore tall helmets, covered in a heavy red fabric, the peaks and chinstraps more of the shining white. The woman in front wore a round peaked cap. All three had two pistols each, holstered at their hips.

Severin stepped up to the woman. When he spoke, his voice remained perfectly level, perfectly monotonous. "Explain your presence here," he said. "I have not sent for assistance nor authorized any request on my behalf."

The woman frowned, and lifted her chin at Severin.

"I am Chief Constable Tallie Corfield. You will release the prisoner into the custody of the Royal Morley Constabulary."

Billie narrowed her eyes as she watched the exchange. She'd seen members of the constabulary patrolling what was left of Alba when she had arrived, of course, but she hadn't seen them since she'd entered the construction site.

"The constabulary has no legal authority on the premises of the Leviathan Company," said Severin, "under the power of the Royal Warrant granted on the fourth day of the Month of Seeds, 18—"

At this the Chief Constable reached into her tunic, and pulled out a folded sheet of heavy cream paper, sealed with red wax. Severin looked at the item for a couple of seconds before taking it. After studying the seal for a few more moments, he slid a finger under the lip and broke the wax. He began to read, holding the paper close to his face despite his thick-lensed glasses.

Uvanov moved closer to her boss. She glanced at the three constables, then peered at the paper over Severin's shoulder.

"What's going on?" she asked. "What is it?"

Without looking, Severin shot his hand out, thrusting the paper at Uvanov. She took it, and read. Billie watched her lips move as she did so.

After a few moments, Uvanov looked up over the paper at the Chief Constable.

"By Royal Proclamation?"

The Chief Constable nodded, a slight smile playing over her lips.

Billie cleared her throat. Nobody took any notice of her. "Someone want to tell me what's going on?"

The Chief Constable looked at her. "You are coming with us," she said, before gesturing to her two men. They stepped forward, clearly anticipating the transfer of custody.

Severin stood stock still, hands clenched into fists by his sides. He was staring at the Chief Constable, and he seemed to be almost vibrating on the spot with withheld anger.

Uvanov stepped around Severin until she was in his eyeline.

"Sir?" She lifted the paper. "This is by Royal Proclamation. We have to obey."

Severin and Uvanov locked gazes, then finally Severin gave another short nod. Uvanov's shoulders fell, like a weight had been taken off them. She motioned to the company guard, who Billie knew was standing behind her. "Let the prisoner down."

A second later Billie heard the rattle of chains, and there was a clank. The chains holding her to the ceiling suddenly went slack, and she fell to the hard floor, managing at least to roll onto her side to protect her knees.

She looked up to see Severin march out, forcing the constables to make way. Then Uvanov's face loomed in front of her. She frowned.

And then one of the Royal Morley Constables moved forward. He pulled a black cloth out of a pouch on his bandolier, and as he walked toward Billie, he fussed with it, pulling it out, expanding it, until Billie saw he was holding open a black bag.

And then Billie's world went dark.

18

ALBA, MORLEY

Date unknown, Month of Darkness, 1853

The trio of constables walked Billie for what felt like a mile or more, holding her in a solid, uncomfortable grip on each arm.

They went up a set of steps, then along a corridor with a series of turns—right, left, left again. Then they went down a set of steps. Here the ground changed from smooth and even to rough, stony, pitted, and Billie's musty world became just a little bit brighter, the sounds of the causeway construction site suddenly louder.

That they were outside didn't take any kind of deduction, but Billie concentrated nonetheless, trying to determine direction and remember the path they were taking.

That plan went out the window when the constables holding her jerked her to a sudden stop. Billie turned her head, trying to get some kind of sense of her surroundings, but it was no good. The black bag wasn't entirely opaque, but the most she could tell was that it was daylight.

Then something large moved into position in front of her with a heavy rumble, blotting out the dim light that was leaking into her world, accompanied by the sound of hooves on cobbles and the wet snorts of a couple of horses. There was a clatter, followed by another, and then Billie was pushed forward. Her shin caught on something hard and she backed up, then lifted her foot until she found a step. There were only three, and then she was pushed into the coach's compartment before her arms were released. There was a clack again as the door to the compartment was closed, and Billie heard two of the constables moving around the small space beside her.

The horses stamped their feet, and the compartment rocked and started to move. Billie rolled on the floor, hitting her head against one wall. A moment later, two hands hooked under her armpits and pulled her up, until she was sitting on a cushioned bench. Released, she adjusted her position and worked at her cuffed hands, squashed now between her back and the wall of the compartment.

"May as well get yourself comfortable," said one of the constables.

Billie turned to the voice, but there was no longer enough light to penetrate the bag over her head.

"Where are we going?" she asked.

The constable didn't answer.

The journey took about an hour, by Billie's rough estimate. The compartment rocked and rolled with the terrain, while the two constables muttered to each other in a language Billie recognized but didn't understand—Old Morlish, a dialect common to the rural, northern areas of the country. It wasn't a language she expected to hear in Alba, or indeed in any of the cities and townships in the southern half of Morley, but she also knew that the Royal Morley Constabulary, as the national military force, recruited from all regions as a matter of pride and principle, symbolizing one nation unified under their benevolent Queen and King.

Beyond that, Billie knew little of Morley politics, and cared even less.

Eventually, the pace of the horses slowed and, soon enough, the coach came to a stop. The two constables moved around again, rocking the coach on its springs, and there was a bang as the door of the compartment was opened and slammed against the outside. Billie shifted on her seat, rolling her shoulders as her human arm sparked with pins and needles from being stuck behind her. Once more she felt hands on her arms, and now a hand on her head, pushing it down, ensuring she didn't smack herself against the frame of the coach's small door.

Her boots crunched on gravel. The coach door slammed behind her. She heard more people moving, gravel sliding all around her, the horses' heavy snorting breath. They'd reached their destination, and Billie counted maybe three more people, in addition to the two constables and their chief, who must have ridden with the driver.

They led her forward, and the sounds changed: they moved from hard-packed gravel to wood, ancient and as solid as iron, but wood nonetheless. It was a bridge, passing over water—Billie could not only hear the splash from a drain emptying into the main body, but the flicker of fish as they broke the surface. After a few dozen yards, the footing changed again, and they were on smooth flagstones, the echo of their footsteps suggesting there was more stone arching overhead. Billie could feel the cool radiating off them.

The constables were met by more people. Billie assumed they were more of the same, that she had been brought to some kind of station, or maybe even directly to a prison. The constables talked but she learned nothing from their conversation. Yes, they had arrived; no, there hadn't been any trouble; she wanted to see the prisoner immediately, no, immediately, yes, directly, and get a bloody move on.

Billie was led along a stone path. She listened carefully to the footfalls of the group—she was pretty sure there was an open space on her right, and a building on her left. They could be walking along the edge of a courtyard, perhaps. Then she was turned ninety degrees, led down another short path, then up a set of five wide steps. A pause, another muted conversation between constables, then the familiar sound of a large wooden door being opened.

Immediately, warm air wafted out over her, bringing with it the rich floral scent of Morley orchids. Before they led her in, she could hear footsteps on yet another surface. This sound was a crisp, flat tapping. The floor was very hard—marble, perhaps?

They moved inside. The air was rich with the floral scent, and after who knew how many hours of being strung up in the cell and then traveling in the unheated compartment of the coach, the warmth inside was cloying.

Her boots clacked on the floor, then she hit carpet, the sudden absence of footfalls an unnerving surprise in her world of darkness. The hands pulled her to a stop, and a moment later, the black bag was pulled off her head.

Billie blinked in the light, squinting as her human eye adjusted. The Sliver remained quiet, and cold, seeing nothing extraordinary in her surroundings.

Nothing extraordinary in the magical sense, anyway. Because there was certainly nothing ordinary about the woman standing in front of Billie.

She was very tall, and very thin, her jet-black hair falling to her waist. She wore a green pantsuit several shades darker than the color of the constabulary's uniforms, with golden buttons running all the way down the middle from neck to waist. The tunic was sleeveless, and the woman wore thin black gloves that came up past the elbow. Her eyes were green, as was the jewel that sat in the center of her forehead, held in the claws of a raven fashioned out of gold, set with diamonds—the bird held in place by a delicate diadem of copper strands that were irregular and twisted, simulating the natural structure of wood. There was something very familiar about the symbol.

The Chief Constable saluted the woman, then swept her red cap off her head and held it tightly under her arm as she stood to attention.

"Mr. Severin's prisoner, Your Majesty," she said, before giving a short bow. Billie glanced at the Chief Constable, then at the woman. Then, at last, she recognized the raven on the crown. It was the royal symbol of Morley.

Billie raised an eyebrow. She shifted on her feet, and pulled at her arms, but her hands were still manacled behind her back. Seeing the movement, the tall woman smiled and gestured with one black-gloved arm.

"Those will not be necessary," she said.

The Chief Constable snapped another salute, and barked an order at one of her constables. He in turn saluted, and, after extracting a set of keys, undid the binders on Billie's wrists. Billie, grateful at being freed, began rubbing the life back into her human wrist with her magical hand.

"That will be all," said the tall woman.

"Ma'am," said the Chief Constable. With yet another bow, she then backed away, keeping her front to the tall woman, her constables doing the same behind her until they were through the doorway. The tall woman waited until the door was closed, then turned her attention to Billie.

"You must forgive the theatrics," she said, "but there is always a protocol to be followed."

Billie shook her head, and only just managed to stop herself from spitting on the expensive carpet. "Protocol, my ass. You're going to tell me where I am and what you want with me, right now."

The woman laughed. "Spirited, I see." She spread her arms. "You are in the House of the Fourth Chair, the winter palace of the Royal Court of Morley.

"I am Eithne, Queen of Morley. And I have been wanting to speak to you for quite some time."

19

HOUSE OF THE FOURTH CHAIR, NEAR ALBA

Date unknown, Month of Darkness, 1853

Billie looked around the room, a long gallery with a marble floor, over which was laid a narrow, rich carpet. The walls were marble, the ceiling high and arched, with huge windows letting in ample daylight. Every open space along the walls was covered with displays of weaponry—swords, shields, pikes, halberds, pistols, arranged in fans and circles, forming a dizzying display between long, low sofas and chairs upholstered in more of the ubiquitous green fabric.

The Queen watched her.

"Since when do queens want to speak with the likes of *me*?" Billie asked.

"You may call me Eithne," said the Queen. "Only those who serve me call me Queen. And I believe we are very much equals, are we not?"

Billie narrowed her eyes, trying to parse Eithne's words through her mind. The Queen watched, then laughed.

"Billie Lurk, daughter of Asher and Francis, right hand of the Knife of Dunwall, Savior of Emily the Wise."

Billie felt the breath leave her body.

No, that was impossible.

"You know the names of my parents?"

Eithne nodded. "Believe me, Billie Lurk, I know everything there is to know about you. How you loved Deirdre. How you helped defeat Delilah Copperspoon. How you rescued Daud."

Then the smile vanished.

"How the Outsider fell."

Billie ground her teeth together. She flexed the fingers of her Void-touched hand, the magical black stone clicking. She stared at Eithne and the Queen held her gaze.

"Oh, Billie Lurk, how much we have to discuss. And how much time we have to discuss it in."

After leaving the Queen in the long gallery, Billie was taken by a member of the Royal Morley Constabulary through the building. That the constabulary apparently acted as the Queen's personal servants in the House of the Fourth Chair—as well as acting as the general police and security forces in every city, town, and village across the country—was the least of Billie's concerns. As she followed the green-jacketed constable, Billie scarcely noticed her surroundings. The building was made of marble. The carpets were thick. Every wall was covered with an extravagant display of antique weaponry. It was all the same.

Billie was stunned by the Queen's comments. She knew the name of her mother and father—actually, Billie *herself* didn't know who her father was; and while she had no particular reason to believe the name Eithne had given was the correct one, there was no reason she could think of that the Queen would be lying. Besides which, she *had* spoken the name of her mother—Asher. If Eithne knew that, then certainly everything else she had said was true.

Wasn't it?

Deirdre. Billie's heart raced as she thought of her. Truth be told, she had been content to let the memory of Deirdre sleep in her mind. Life had gone on, and as Billie knew all too well, part of life was *death*. If you couldn't accept that, you would lose your mind.

And then there was the Outsider. The Queen said she knew how the Outsider had fallen. How was *that* even possible? The only ones who had been present in the Ritual Hold on that day were herself, the Outsider, and the ghostly echo of Daud. Nobody else knew—could *possibly* know—what had happened there.

Billie blinked out of her reverie as her guide cleared his throat, and she realized they had stopped. The constable was standing to attention by a door, which stood open. With Billie's mind returned to the present, he gestured into the room beyond with an expansive sweep of his arm.

"I trust that these quarters will meet your standards, m'lady. Should you require anything, anything at all, then please do not hesitate to call for a member of the constabulary."

Billie frowned and stepped into the room. It was a sumptuous bedchamber, practically big enough to fit the entire Lucky Merchant tavern into. There were no displays of arms and armor here, but the room was paneled in dark wood, every available space covered with paintings, all of which seemed to be of wildlife.

Billie turned to her guide. He stiffened as she looked at him, his gaze fixed somewhere in the middle distance over her shoulder.

"Why does the Royal Morley Constabulary serve the Queen in her palace? Doesn't she have servants and guards of her own?"

The constable pursed his lips, like he was considering his answer. Then he spoke.

"The constabulary has the pleasure of serving the Queen and King of Morley at their leisure, and has done for the last year, m'lady, since the Crisis."

"The… Crisis?"

"I believe it is called the Three-Day War elsewhere in the Isles."

So that was it. The Queen and King of Morley had been employing the country's military as their own private security force since peace had been restored.

Perhaps Billie didn't blame them.

"If there is nothing else, m'lady?"

Billie snorted. "Oh please, you can lose the m'lady part. I am anything but."

The constable pursed his lips again. "If you will pardon me, m'lady, but any private guest of Queen Eithne is to be accorded all rank and privilege as accorded by official protocol."

Billie shook her head. "Fine, whatever." She turned back to the room. "So what am I supposed to do? Wait for the Queen to call me back into her presence?"

The constable gave a nod. "The very same, m'lady. Now, if that will be all?"

"Yes, whatever." Billie waved her hand and the constable saluted, then headed away down the corridor. Billie stepped out of the chamber and watched his retreating back.

What in all the Isles was she doing here? An honored guest of Queen Eithne? What *did* the Queen want with her? The fact that she had sent her constabulary to the Leviathan Company to retrieve her didn't make any sense either. How had the Queen even known she was there?

Then again, Eithne seemed to know a lot of things about her—some things that even Billie didn't know herself.

She looked up and down the passageway. It was a long gallery, the far wall made up mostly of tall windows that stretched almost from floor to ceiling, looking out onto an immaculate lawn and gardens, at the far end of which was a lake. There were constables positioned at intervals around the garden, either standing rigidly to attention, or marching stiffly between black wooden pillboxes.

To her right was the passageway she had just come down; her guide had left by the same route. To her left, the windowed passage ended at a large, arched door. There was a constable on guard beside it, and when Billie met her eye, the guard stamped her foot and came to attention.

Intrigued, Billie walked down the passage toward the constable, who had her gaze fixed straight ahead. When Billie got within speaking distance, the guard stamped her foot again.

"So..." said Billie, shaking her head, "am I prisoner here or what?"

The guard glanced at Billie, but only fleetingly, her attention returning to the empty passageway almost instantly.

"Do you require assistance, m'lady?"

"Seriously, I wish everyone would cut out the lady shit."

The guard said nothing.

"Okay, fine," said Billie. She rubbed her forehead, looked back down the passage, then turned and gestured to the door.

"Where does this go?"

"East wing, m'lady."

"And I'm free to enter the east wing?"

The guard stamped her foot. "Any private guest of Queen Eithne is to be accorded all rank and privilege as accorded by official—"

Billie waved her hand. "Accorded by official protocol,

all right, I get it." She paused. "So protocol gives me free rein, right?"

Once again, the guard stamped her foot. "Any private guest—"

"Enough already! I heard you the first time."

The guard fell silent.

Billie turned to look out of the big windows. The sun was low, so it was late afternoon at least, although she still didn't know the date. She watched as members of the constabulary patrolled the gardens.

Her guide had said earlier that she was free, until the Queen summoned her. Billie decided to see just exactly what "free" meant.

She headed back along the passageway. In the middle of the windowed wall was a set of ornate gilded metal doors, leading to a small flight of steps that provided access to the garden. The doors opened silently under Billie's hand.

After the far too-warm interior of the House of the Fourth Chair (whatever that meant, Billie had no idea), the cold outside was a pleasant shock. Billie savored the clean air, and looked out across the formal gardens. She saw now that the garden was walled, the boundaries framed on either side by tall red-brick borders, mostly hidden behind elegantly sculpted trees, their branches trained against the brickwork to form a more natural-looking barrier. The gardens themselves were laid out in a geometric pattern of squares and rectangles, with paved paths running between them.

Every flower was an orchid, and, to Billie's untrained eye, seemed to be entirely different to the one next to it. Unlike regular plants, the orchids clung with spidery exposed roots to large logs, which were laid out in groups alongside the paths.

It was an impressive sight, and although Billie had

little interest in horticulture, she had a keen interest in money and a fair knowledge of the black markets of the Empire. The famous orchids of Morley were a key ingredient in several medicinal elixirs, not to mention had been components of both Piero's Spiritual Remedy and Addermire Solution. Billie wondered about the sheer monetary value of the plantings that now lay spread out around her.

She walked directly away from the main building, along the widest path. Constables were on duty at intervals, standing to attention at the points where smaller avenues branched off, their black pillboxes shining in the dying light. Further away, more constables patrolled the brick walls.

At the end of the main path was the shoreline of the lake; across the water, dense woodland crowded the opposite shore, and the body of water curled around to her left, the far side shielded by the trees clustered at the main bend. There was a sunken paved circle at the end of the path, set with a fixed stone table and two long benches, each heavy with rich green moss.

Billie supposed she could swim for it, if needed, but then her eyes caught movement across the water, and she saw a constable begin a patrol from his pillbox, hidden in the shadow of a tree, on the other side.

So much for that idea. Billie turned, and looked back at the winter palace of the Queen and King of Morley.

From this side, the palace was a long, rectangular building, composed of two levels. The upper level was covered almost entirely with a regimented series of tall rectangular windows, while the lower part was mostly hidden behind a row of enormous columns, which broke in the middle for the glass-walled passageway and doors leading to the garden, through which Billie had come.

The style looked more suited to a bank than a palace, but Billie's interest in architecture was almost as strong as her interest in gardening. Rising above the building, not quite dead center from this position, was a huge copper dome, which was now a soft, soapy green, having succumbed to verdigris long ago.

As she cast her eye over the building, she saw a figure in one of the big windows on the upper level—the Queen, although with the light fading it was hard to be sure. She seemed to be watching the garden—watching Billie, perhaps—before she moved out of sight.

Billie sighed, and shook her head. While she was grateful for the rescue from the Leviathan Company, she had no idea why her salvation had been at the behest of the Queen of Morley herself, and any time spent at the palace was time wasted. The journey here hadn't taken *that* long, which meant they were still close to Alba, although Billie had no idea in which direction the city lay. But it was imperative that she get away as soon as possible. She had learned a lot about the causeway site and its strange shadow-world version in the Void hollow, but still didn't have any physical evidence to show what the Leviathan Company was doing.

Her plan was simple. She needed to get back there, collect evidence—runes, bone charms—and take it back to Dribner. He would be able to understand what the company was doing with them, and then together they could get both the Academy of Natural Philosophy and Empress Emily herself to aid them.

It was then that she noticed a constable rushing toward her, having emerged from the glass doors. Billie put her hands on her hips and frowned, but didn't move. Let him come to *her*.

That was when she saw something else—or rather,

felt something. It was subtle, and she almost missed it, but it was only in the stillness of the garden that it became evident.

The Sliver of the Eye of the Dead God was getting warm, the sensation of heat spreading over the side of her face. As soon as she noticed it, she felt the telltale pressure inside her skull, and the faintest buzzing, a vibration, from the arcane object.

She knew exactly what it meant. And it made perfect sense.

There was something Void-touched nearby.

Of course there was. It was in the palace. Because how else did Queen Eithne know so much about her? She must have an object, or artifact, something connected to the Void, channeling its magic.

Billie also suspected that Queen Eithne knew exactly what Severin and the Leviathan Company were doing at the causeway.

The constable reached her at the end of the garden and snapped a salute, his back ramrod straight. Billie could only shake her head at the formality. Being treated like royalty did not sit well with her at all.

"M'lady," began the constable, "Her Majesty Queen Eithne of the Four Chairs, and His Majesty King Briam of the Four Chairs, hereby summon you to an audience, as per official protocol and—"

Billie raised her hand and gave the constable a look that instantly silenced him. As the guard stood shaking in his boots, Billie headed past him, back toward the glass doors. A moment later she stopped, realizing she was alone. She turned, and gestured to the grand building.

"So, are you going to show me where to go, or do I have to find their Royalnesses myself?"

The constable moved his lips first, but it took a

moment longer for him to find the courage to move the rest of himself. He gave a sharp nod and proceeded toward the palace.

Billie followed at a distance, her eyes scanning the building ahead of her.

There was something there. Something inside, hidden.

It seemed that the Queen of Morley was keeping secrets.

20

HOUSE OF THE FOURTH CHAIR, NEAR ALBA

Date unknown, Month of Darkness, 1853

The banquet was as ridiculous as the room in which it was held. For three long, *long* hours, Billie sat at the head of a table longer than the *Dreadful Wale*, on which was laden a staggering amount of food—sweet and savory, hot and cold, delicacies from every corner of the Isles. It was as impressive as it was stupid, because the only company Billie had for the ostentatious meal was Queen Eithne and King Briam, who sat on her right and left, respectively.

Billie was hungry. The last time she had eaten had been in that square in Alba, which felt like a lifetime ago. But the sight of such immoral, obscene decadence robbed her of her appetite. It was only through sheer willpower that she forced herself to eat at least something. Fuel, she told herself, for the work ahead. Nothing more, nothing less.

Also, there had been hardly any *time* to eat, despite the casual, unrushed nature of the meal, given the constant barrage of questions from the King. The Queen only occasionally interjected with a delicate laugh. As they sat at the table, positioned directly beneath the great dome of the palace, constables moved quietly around them, acting both as guards and servants to the royal couple.

Billie found their movements a comforting distraction as she talked, and talked, and talked, while at the same time trying to decide what she made of Morley's royal couple—a couple who had been engaged in a short but devastating war, that had all but destroyed the city just miles from where they now sat in luxury.

The Queen was in an effusive mood. King Briam seemed to be her total opposite. He was polite enough, but cold and distant, not showing a flicker of interest, even as he subjected Billie to his tableside interrogation. He was about the same age as the Queen—that is to say, roughly middle-aged—and, like her, he had jet-black hair swept back under a somewhat more modest diadem. His goatee was sharply cut, the stubble on his cheeks shaved into intricate swirling patterns, which stood out against his pallid complexion. His eyes were blue, and Billie wasn't sure they blinked quite enough. Like her, he picked at his food.

To Billie, the waste was sickening. There was so much poverty, so much suffering, right across the Isles, that to see such pointless luxury made her stomach turn. Especially here, in a palace on the outskirts of a city ruined by an apparently pointless civil war fought between the two people who now sat at Billie's side. A war that had cost the lives of hundreds, and had ruined the lives and livelihoods of countless more.

Of course, it was all a game to them. Because what kind of life, what kind of existence, did the Queen and King really have? Decades of pampering, decades of idleness. To them, war would have been a pleasing distraction from the tedious luxury of their existence. An idle exercise to pass the time.

No sooner had Billie been served her first course—some kind of Karnacan fish swimming in wine—than the

King began bombarding her with questions.

Billie hesitated at first. She looked at Eithne questioningly, and that was the only time King Briam showed any flicker of pleasure on his face. He smiled, glanced over at his wife.

"You will have to forgive me," he said, "I understand Eithne knows far more about you than I do, but I have been distracted of late, with many matters of state to attend to." Then he turned back to Billie. "Besides, my wife may know all there is to know about the famous Billie Lurk, but I, on the other hand, like to learn about our honored guests from their own mouths, so to speak. Knowledge is best learned first-hand, when it is at its purest, most undiluted form."

Billie didn't like the King's smile, nor was she particularly convinced by his speech. It sounded flat, rehearsed, more like something he rolled out to keep the Queen happy.

But Billie finally relented. So far, her stay at the House of the Fourth Chair had been peculiar, but not unpleasant. And for the moment, she wanted to keep the Queen and King on her side. So she played her role, answering the King's questions about Dunwall, skirting the nature of the Whalers as best she could, and only briefly skipping through an account of her years of exile following the betrayal of Daud. She focused instead on her travels, describing the people and places she had seen. This information was safe, and also quite useless to anyone other than an armchair traveler.

Eventually, the King waved his hand. Billie came to a stop, mid-sentence.

"Yes," said Briam, "but tell me, how did you come by the arm, and the artifact you have in place of an eye? They are remarkable curios. I'm not sure I've seen their like in all my studies."

"Studies?" asked Billie.

The King smiled again and picked up his goblet of wine. "Oh, I dabble in natural philosophy, when time allows." He took a sip of his wine, his eyes not leaving Billie's.

Billie watched him, silently. Then the King laughed.

"Oh, come now, don't be shy. We are all equals around this table. Tell us about the hand and the eye."

Billie glanced at the Queen. She still held her knife and fork, but they were resting on the edge of her plate. She was looking at Billie intently—looking at the Sliver.

"Yes, do tell us, my dear," she said, softly.

Billie licked her lips, and sighed. Then she forced an entirely fake smile onto her face. "I really need to get some rest."

The Queen and the King said nothing. The pair of them were almost frozen in place as they looked at Billie. Billie raised an eyebrow as she glanced between them. Then the Queen broke the odd, uncomfortable pause, clattering her cutlery against her plate as she released it.

"Of course!"

The King instantly sprang out of his apparent paralysis. "Of course!" he said, mimicking his wife's tone. It was an unconvincing performance.

"You must rest well," said the Queen. "We have much still to discuss!"

The King smiled coldly at Billie. "Yes," he said, "we have *much* still to discuss."

Billie frowned at the King, then pushed her seat back and bade the strange couple a good night.

When she was out of the Great Hall, she paused by the doors, leaning back against them with her head cocked, listening for any further conversation between her hosts. But all she could hear was the clink of crockery, then a muffled thud, followed by the loud ticking of a clock.

Perhaps one of the serving constables was adjusting one of the many grandfather clocks that occupied the corners and alcoves dotted around the hall.

Billie headed for her room. But rest was far from her mind. The House of the Fourth Chair had a secret, and she was determined to find out what it was.

And what better time to do it than at night?

21

HOUSE OF THE FOURTH CHAIR, NEAR ALBA

Date unknown, Month of Darkness, 1853

Billie lay on top of the cover of her bed, counting seconds, her eyes never leaving the clock on the mantel over the gargantuan fireplace, her ears straining to pick up any noise from outside the chamber. Staying on alert like that came with practiced ease, the bed on which she lay pure luxury compared with some of her experiences working surveillance for the Whalers.

As time wound on, the sounds of the palace gradually quieted as the majority of the constables retired from their duties. True enough, there would be a night shift, but Billie hoped it was a far smaller contingent, their efforts perhaps more concentrated on guarding the *outside* of the building than the *inside*.

Not that there was any threat to the Queen or King, not anymore. The two former enemies were reconciled and had resumed their bizarre, stale existence, confined within the walls of their palace and the boundaries of the protocol that kept the strange kingdom of Morley together.

Billie rose from the bed as the mantel clock struck three. She listened at the door before opening it. The passageway beyond was lit by a bright, full moon, the silvery light streaming in through the glass wall. She glanced up and down the corridor. She was in luck—there was no constable on duty by the entrance to the west wing.

Billie closed the door of her room and headed down the passage. When she got to the west wing entrance, she paused, closed her human eye, and focused her mind.

There. She felt it at once, the gentle hum inside her head as the Sliver came alive, seeing both the real world and the magical one adjacent. As the signature pressure began to build between her temples, Billie concentrated, and looked around her.

The red-blue-yellow trail of the Void was immediately evident—weak behind her, strong ahead. Pulling on her reserves of mental strength, Billie stared at the door, her teeth grinding as she stoked the embers of power that remained in the Sliver. It might not have been able to grant her the abilities she once wielded with ease—like the power of foresight, the ability granted by the Sliver that allowed her to see around corners, beyond walls, through any solid object, which she really wished she could call on now. But as she concentrated, the moonlit passage in front of her faded into deeper shades of blue, until she could see only the skeleton of the building—including the passageway *beyond* the door in front of her.

There. The trail was faint, but clear, a yellowish blur, like a narrow stream of water, running ahead of her, twisting and turning as it traveled from passageway to passageway, corridor to corridor, room to room. Billie wasn't quite sure how or why she was seeing it like that. She had been expecting to see, perhaps, the distant glow of a Void-touched artifact, buried somewhere in the building. This was something else. It was a trail, very clearly—the wake left by someone who had had direct contact with the Void.

No, Billie realized with a start. More than that—not just contact. This person was Void-touched, like she was, a part of both it and the real world. There was no other explanation for the trail being so strong.

The Queen. It had to be her. She knew so much about Billie, impossible knowledge, including facts that even Billie didn't know about herself. It must have something to do with the Void. It made her even more sure that the Queen must have an artifact that allowed her to see the world and gain knowledge without leaving the palace.

Billie let her concentration slip, and her vision snapped back to reality as the Sliver let go of the arcane world. The passageway was suddenly darker, the moonlight duller, and the door ahead of her very solid. She paused, another thought entering her mind.

Was the disturbance of the Void that Dribner had sent her to find actually occurring *here*, rather than at the Leviathan Company?

Too many questions. Not enough answers.

Billie reached for the door handle. It was unlocked. She stepped through, closed it, then followed her memory of the Void trail.

Time seemed to move slowly. Whenever she passed one of the many clocks that lined the passageways of the House of the Fourth Chair, it seemed like the minutes were stretching to hours. She had been stalking the dark corridors of the palace for ages, and had so far found nothing.

She had been right about one thing—the palace was virtually empty. Billie had stopped at several points as she had tried to get her bearings, taking a moment to check the view from the windows. The ornate orchid gardens were bleached of their color in the moonlight, transforming from elegant, aristocratic constructions into something altogether more sinister, an alien landscape rendered in nothing but shades of gray. Constables patrolled in the night, their own forms monochrome and shadowy, their bright tunics hidden underneath black capes.

But as Billie moved on, she lost track of the yellowish trail left by the Void—or rather, by whoever it was who had contact with the Void. She tried a couple of times to summon the power of foresight again, but it was no use. So instead she concentrated on sensing the presence of the Void rift itself, like she had in Dunwall, and in Alba. That must be what she had felt the previous day, looking back at the palace from the garden, it had to be—the Sliver pulling her to the Void.

There was a rift somewhere in the palace. She knew there was.

But the palace that was a maze. The building wasn't *designed* to confuse, she knew that, but it was the sheer scale of the place that made it easy to get lost in. One grand hallway led to another, the walls crawling with arms and armor, or more paintings of wildlife, like a catalogue of zoological specimens had been torn out of the pages of the Academy of Natural Philosophy and framed for the pleasure of the royals of Morley. Soon enough, Billie lost track of where she was, and several times had left one drawing room only to come back in through the door opposite a few minutes later. It was only by picking one direction and keeping to it—eventually leading to a window, so she could check on her position relative to the outside—that she made any kind of progress. If she could call it that. She wanted to find the rift, but the pull of the Sliver was erratic, waxing and waning with no apparent pattern.

Maybe her excuse for avoiding the King's questions had been right. Maybe she was tired—scratch that, she knew she was. Despite the sumptuous banquet, she hadn't eaten much, and as soon as she thought of it, hunger and thirst began to gnaw at her stomach. She hadn't rested properly since arriving in Alba.

There was nothing left to do but give up—at least for now. So long as the Queen and King were playing host—and so long as, Billie suspected, she gave them the right information when they asked for it—she would have another opportunity to go scouting. Perhaps time spent at the House of the Fourth Chair wasn't entirely wasted, not if this was the source of the Void destabilization.

Now the only question was—which way was her room?

Billie sighed, rubbed her face, and picked a direction.

That was when she saw the movement. The sighting woke her up with a start as adrenaline flooded her system. She blinked her human eye, took a breath, and headed down the passageway, intrigued.

It hadn't been a constable. She hadn't seen any inside the building and, besides, there was no reason for one to be prowling the palace in secret. The way the shadow had vanished almost as soon as it had appeared, like whoever it was had ducked away quickly, fearful of being seen… Billie knew that kind of movement well.

She was being followed. But by whom, she could only guess.

Billie paused at the doorway, then quickly turned into the next room. It was quiet, and empty, and, like the majority of the palace, lit by the turned-down electric lighting that emanated from the frosted, shell-shaped fittings that dotted the walls. The light was dull but diffuse—enough to see by, not enough to cast much shadow. As she stepped into the room, the back of her neck prickled, the hairs standing on end. A lifetime of training, a lifetime of experience, had given her instincts that were keen and sharp, abilities that didn't need any magical arm or eye or gift from the Outsider to be used.

She spun around just in time to see her tail dart out of the room. She caught only a glimpse, but the person was tall, athletic. There was something about them that Billie thought she recognized. Someone from Alba? Perhaps Severin had sent an agent from the Leviathan Company to... what? Spy on her? *Assassinate* her? Severin certainly hadn't appreciated the intrusion of the constables. But if he was trying to play with her, then he had picked the wrong person to mess with.

Billie's fingers curled near her belt. She wished she had a weapon—wished she could take the risk and summon the Twin-bladed Knife, but, once again, she decided this was no time to experiment. Instead, she turned to the nearest wall, and walked over to an elegantly curved alcove set into it, decorated with a rich spread of bladed weapons: stilettos, daggers, short swords. Blades that were straight, blades that were curved, and others of more exotic design.

Billie selected a dagger, lifting it gently from the hooks that held it in place in the center of the perfectly circular display. She balanced it in her hand, feeling the weight, and examined the blade. It wasn't the sharpest, but it was in good condition, and, like everything else in the palace, was well looked after. It would do just fine.

She flipped it in her hand, holding it with the blade flat against her forearm. Then she headed toward the door, padding on her toes, silent, listening for her quarry.

The next room was narrow and boxlike, and there was only a single door, dead ahead. Billie moved forward cautiously, then dropped to her knee so she could peer through the keyhole. The room beyond was bright, but the light seemed angled, somehow, so that she couldn't make anything out clearly.

There was nowhere else her quarry could have gone. Billie adjusted her grip on the borrowed knife, and pushed open the door.

She was back in the Great Hall. The chamber was in darkness, except for a pool of light spotting the middle of the table from a large, portable arc lamp. Under that light, King Briam was hunched over, examining a large spread of papers scattered across the table in front of him.

"Won't you come in, Billie Lurk," he said.

Billie frowned, but relaxed her grip on the knife. As she moved down the length of the table to the King's side, she slipped the blade inside her sleeve, concealing it.

"Your Majesty," she said, wondering if she was supposed to bow, then deciding not to bother. Then she looked over the papers on the table.

They were plans—blueprints and diagrams rendered with mathematical precision, along with other pictures and sketches, depicting various pieces of equipment of a kind similar to the ones Billie had seen in Dribner's laboratory, and in the workshops in the Royal Morley Observatory, although nothing that she specifically recognized. In the middle, however, the main blueprint appeared to be of something architectural, a large angled slab—or at least, half of one, the blueprint ending on one side with a pair of parallel lines. It looked, if anything, like a tabletop tomb.

Next to the King's hand was a stack of notes, and next to the notes was a goblet of wine. He stood tall, his upper body now out of the spotlight. He took up his drink, and glanced at Billie. His eyes glittered in the shadow.

"I told you I… *dabbled*," he said.

Billie didn't like the smile that came next. His teeth shone, his skin deathly pale.

A trick of the light, Billie told herself. She straightened up.

"I'm sorry to disturb your studies," said Billie.

The King said nothing, but watched her as he drank from his goblet.

"Did somebody come through here just now?" asked Billie.

The King narrowed his eyes. "Somebody?"

"Yes," said Billie, and then she paused. What was she going to say? "I thought I heard someone." She put on a smile as fake as the King's. "I must have been dreaming. It feels like I haven't slept in days."

"Indeed," said the King. He was still watching her.

Billie glanced again at the papers on the table. None of it meant anything to her. If the King was an insomniac who indulged his hobby of amateur natural philosophy in the middle of the night, then, well, he was welcome to it.

"Sorry for the intrusion," said Billie. She backed away, then turned and headed to the doors. Once there, she glanced over her shoulder. The King was still watching her.

Billie slipped through the door and closed it after her. Putting the strange encounter out of her mind, she considered her options. She still wanted to find the other person—the intruder, who had somehow vanished into thin air. She would just have to go around the Great Hall, find another route.

As she padded through the small boxy room and out into the main passageway, she thought about who else had the power to appear and disappear at will.

Which was, as far as she knew, *everyone* who worked for the Leviathan Company, all of whom carried runes.

Billie let her borrowed knife slip back into her hand from her sleeve, and continued her nocturnal expedition.

22

HOUSE OF THE FOURTH CHAIR, NEAR ALBA

Date unknown, Month of Darkness, 1853

She picked up the trail immediately after leaving the Great Hall—but it was the trail of the Void rift, not the intruder. Not long after she had wandered down a series of connected rooms and passageways, trying to navigate her away around the hall and avoid the King, the Sliver grew hot, and her vision clouded with red and blue and yellow contrails.

She was getting close. The rift she suspected of being somewhere in the palace was near.

Very near.

The wing of the palace in which Billie found herself was no different from any of the rest of it, just another impossibly large maze of interconnected rooms and corridors. Billie didn't bother tracking her progress—she had no reason now to return to her room, after all, not with the Sliver leading her on like this.

The pull was strong, the direction clear. She followed it for several minutes, looping through corridors, drawing rooms, halls, the world flashing in red and blue around her as she walked, knife held firmly in her grip.

Eventually, she came to a large lobby. On her left a magnificent staircase swept up, flanked on either side by somewhat less ostentatious stairs leading down. The Sliver was drawn to the descending stairs, so Billie followed them.

The stairs were wide, carpeted in a rich red tread, and the walls were paneled in dark wood. Billie followed the trail as the stairs twisted down past a series of landings. After she'd descended some way, the decor changed suddenly. Gone was the carpet; the stairs were now bare, smooth flagstones. Gone, too, was the wood paneling on the walls, which were now the same pale stone as the floor. The ornate, orchid-shaped wall sconces were replaced by austere lanterns.

The gravity of the rift pulled her on, and as Billie turned to peer at the next flight of stairs heading ever downwards, she felt the Sliver vibrating in her skull, like a trapped insect. It was an uncomfortable, slightly nauseating sensation, but she ignored it.

Billie continued. By now she was far below ground level, and had entered the foundations of the House of the Fourth Chair, an area of the winter palace that was clearly far more ancient that the luxurious apartments above. As the stairs narrowed, and the walls of the passageway began to close in, it reminded her of the vaults of the Academy of Natural Philosophy, where Dribner had set up his clandestine laboratory.

Finally, the stairs ended in a heavy black arched door. Already, Billie could see a blue light flickering around it, and through the keyhole; she concentrated, shutting out the vision of the Sliver, viewing the world with only her normal human eye, and she knew at once that she had arrived. The blue light leaking around the door was no magical vision; it was real.

The rift was behind the door.

It was heavy, but well maintained, the hinges silent.

Someone had been using this passageway for access, and recently, too.

The chamber beyond was long, the walls on either side punctuated by a row of high, pointed alcoves; Billie counted a dozen on each side. While the ceiling was low, it was an ornate masterpiece of the stonemason's art, an intricate vault carved out of gleaming white stone that looked so delicate Billie couldn't imagine how it stayed aloft. The main floor of the chamber was plain white flagstones, and down the center ran a series of large raised daises, each intricately carved, each unique, on top of which lay the supine forms of men and women, their features frozen forever, captured perhaps by the same master stonemason responsible for the complex ceiling that arched over the top of them.

It was a crypt, a royal burial place. In the alcoves were more tombs, the effigies of their occupants in tranquil repose on the thick slab tops. The entire chamber was lit, not by electric lighting, but by old-fashioned whale oil lamps set at intervals along the two parades of arches. The lamps smoldered with a sickly moving yellow light, and the immaculate stone of the arches was smudged with soot where the thick flames danced lazily against them.

But that wasn't the only light in the crypt. Far from it, for the yellow light of the lamps was bleached out by the dazzling electric blue of the rift that floated at the far end of the chamber.

Billie approached it with care, all the while aware of the growing pressure inside her skull, of the deep, aching pain that was growing within her as the Sliver of the Eye of the Dead God reacted to the presence of the Void. The rift itself was relatively large—far bigger than the swirling crack in the world that Dribner had set his equipment around back in Dunwall, but still apparently self-contained within the crypt, its ragged fiery edges licking the air a safe distance from the floor, ceiling, and walls. It was taller than it was wide, a rough ellipse, the body of which was a swimming miasma of blue and red. Unlike the other rifts Billie had seen first-hand—even the vast walls of light that cut right across the tundra of Tyvia and divided the great construction crater in Alba—this one looked… different. More active, almost alive.

Alive… and dangerous.

Billie reached the last royal tomb, which stood in the center of the chamber, the flickering portal of the Void rift just a few feet from it. Although her attention was focused on the rift itself, as Billie moved around the tomb, she noticed that the stonework was newer, and while the thick slab top was in place, it was devoid of any effigies. Tracing her fingers around the edge of the tomb's lid, she read the names inscribed upon it, the letters decorated in cobalt and gilt, and knew why.

QUEEN EITHNE, LADY OF THE THIRD AND FOURTH CHAIRS OF MORLEY.
KING BRIAM, FOURTH LORD OF THE FIRST CHAIR AND LORD OF THE SECOND CHAIR OF MORLEY.

The tomb was new—and it was also empty. The Queen and King had prepared for their own demise. Billie snorted. It was probably a requirement, another of their precious protocols, written as law somewhere that they had to plan their own funerals.

Billie paused. Was this the blueprint the King was studying in the Great Hall? That didn't make any sense—his hobby was natural philosophy, not monumental masonry. And besides, the new tomb was similar—but *not* the same—as the object, the plans of which the King had been examining.

A movement caught Billie's eye. She turned around, following the flickering shadow as it vanished from her vision. There was nothing there but the rift.

That was when she saw it. Another person, nothing but a shadowed, featureless silhouette, running. Billie jumped back, knocking into the empty tomb, the knife held firmly in her outstretched hand. But while the figure seemed to be running toward her, it was as though it was on the other side of the chamber, running into the rift from the *other* side, and no sooner did it loom within apparent touching distance that it seemed to dissolve, vanishing in the blink of an eye.

Billie caught her breath and, keeping her distance, moved to the side of the rift to look around it. Beyond, the royal crypt ended in a flat stone wall, adorned with a richly decorated heraldic motif nearly as tall as she was, depicting the symbol of the raven clutching the jewel in its claws, the crest of the current Queen and King.

Billie moved back to the other side of the rift, skirting it with her back to the crypt, watching the swirling vista for any sight of the other person.

It was the intruder—the person who had been following her through the palace. But who were they? Were they an agent of the Leviathan Company, as she had at first thought?

Billie shook her head. Whoever it was, they were using the rift, somehow.

And then the pain struck, a bolt of white-hot agony that seared across her skull. She toppled against the empty tomb, clutching her head, her breath forced from her lungs by the unexpected assault. She could feel the Sliver like a burning coal embedded in her face. But as she looked at the floor, fighting to stop herself from blacking out, the Sliver pulled her head around, forcing her to lift her chin, to look into the Void.

She was powerless to resist. Grinding her teeth, the muscles at the back of her jaw aching, the tendons standing out like cables in her neck, she looked up.

The swirling nexus of the Void had cleared, the fiery edges of the rift now framing a red-blue vista that stretched out impossibly before her, as if she was not in an underground crypt but instead looking out from the top of a tall tower. It was a similar experience to that which she had in Dribner's laboratory, but here it was far more intense, the sensation of looking through the Void infinitely clearer. If this was another Void hollow, it was incredibly clear.

She was looking at a city from on high, the steepled roofs clustered along the banks of a wide, sluggish river instantly recognizable even without the tall clocktower, the formidable square fortress, and the tall box-like warehouses and factories.

Dunwall.

Billie slid down the side of the tomb, her gaze transfixed by the sight before her. The vision was closing in on the city, blocks becoming individual houses, buildings, streets. Then she was overlooking a square. A man was waiting, his back to her, his sword ready. And above, crouched on the lip of a nearby rooftop, another man, hooded, his face concealed by a peculiar mask, watching, tensed, ready to pounce.

Daud!

Billie pushed herself to her feet, ignoring the pulsating pain in her head. She knew what she was looking at—she recognized the scene. It was one of her own memories, that first night she met Daud, watched him strike down his enemies. The night she had followed him back to the Whaler's lair, the night he had offered her a new life. The night she had dreamed about not very long ago.

But something was different. There was a shadow on the rooftop behind Daud, peeling out of the darkness, its form indistinct, its claw-like arms stretching out, impossibly long, reaching for Daud.

That wasn't what had happened. Daud had killed the men in the street then escaped, and the young Billie had followed.

Billie watched in horror as the shadowed form unfurled its blade-like fingers, ready to strike Daud before he could launch himself down onto his targets.

Billie yelled out, and without a second thought, she dived into the rift.

23

DUNWALL
Dates unknown

Billie hit the rooftop hard, the impact knocking the breath out of her but also clearing her head. The sudden easing of the pressure inside her skull made her dizzy, and she rolled on her back, her eye staring up into the cloudy night sky above the city of…

Dunwall. She was back in Dunwall.

She heard a scuffling, a cry of surprise or pain muffled behind the thick rubber and respirator of the Whaler's mask.

She rolled onto her side then scrambled up.

Daud was fighting for his life.

And she had to help him. Because this wasn't how it happened.

Even as she ran toward him, she saw someone else—a girl, lanky, thin, her face hidden behind a hood—recoil from the rooftop opposite as she watched the struggle between Daud and the shadow creature. The girl fell backward, then pushed herself along with her hands and feet, kicking out as she desperately tried to get away.

That was her. *Her*. The teenage Billie Lurk, witnessing what was supposed to be the Knife of Dunwall at his finest as he dispatched the pigs in the street. Instead, she was witnessing the leader of the Whalers struggle against the black, shifting shadow creature from the Void.

Something that had never happened.

There was no point in stealth now. Billie yelled out and raced toward Daud and the Shadow, the pair wrestling on the very edge of the rooftop. Daud was beneath the creature, which had him by the neck, pushing his torso out over the rooftop as it struggled to bring its wickedly sharp talons to his neck. Daud was so far managing to keep the claws at bay, but it was a losing battle. Billie could see the immense strength of the Shadow, and even as she watched, it reconfigured itself, shifting mass across its body as it fought against Daud's supernaturally enhanced strength.

Strength that was about to give out.

Billie launched herself at the Shadow's back, her hands sinking an inch through an opaque, smoke-like form before contacting something solid. The creature roared, the sound like waves crashing on a beach, and pushed back against her.

But Billie had done enough. Daud kicked out, knocking the creature to one side. Billie rolled with the movement, ending up on her back with the Shadow swarming over her. From the corner of her eye, she saw Daud fall backward off the roof, the sudden release from the Shadow's grip too quick to allow him to compensate and prevent his loss of balance. But even as he fell, he vanished in the blink of an eye, reappearing on his feet in the street below. Of the three men he had been stalking, there was no sign.

Daud waited a minute, watching the rooftop, then he turned and ran. A moment later, he was gone.

Billie returned her attention to the Shadow, but the creature seemed to dissipate in her grasp. She sat up, clutching at nothing, then looked up and saw the thing coalesce in a miniature tornado of dust and darkness in the middle of the roof. Behind it, the Void rift blazed open, flooding the roof with blue electric light, and the Shadow stepped into it.

Billie scrambled for purchase on the roof, aware that nothing made sense, aware that she was in the past and yet the events she had just taken part in had not happened, not according to her memory.

Aware that the rift was shimmering, pulsating, like it was about to close.

She pushed off from the slate tiles with the heels of her hands, and ran for the wound in the world. As she got closer, she saw through it, back to the crypt… but, once again, something was different. The empty tomb was gone, replaced by a jagged, black monolith, like a fallen tor of glassy stone that had been cracked in half and toppled, and on it, the shadow creature, clinging like some perverse, twisted insect made of swirling dust.

Grunting with the effort, Billie surged forward, arcs of pain singing inside her head, the Sliver alive with a power it hadn't wielded for years. She felt the cool touch of the rift on her skin, and then everything went black.

Billie awoke with a start, and whooped a deep breath. The day was bright, and she was lying on something spongy and fragrant. She lifted herself into a sitting position, her hands sinking into the soft earth beneath her. When she looked up, she saw she was in a private garden, hidden away behind a low curved wall. She could hear the lapping of water, and turning, she looked over the wall behind her. The river churned far below, the water salted with diamond shards of light as the rising sun began to beat down upon its softly undulating surface.

It was the Wrenhaven River—she was still in Dunwall. How much time had passed, Billie didn't know; she felt groggy, the Sliver a pulsing ache in her head that beat in time with her heart. She stood up and moved to the low wall in front of her, one hand massaging her temple.

Then she stopped, and ducked down behind the wall. She counted a few beats, then risked a look over it.

Ahead of her was a large gazebo with a dome roof. Standing there was a woman dressed in a black trouser suit, her hair pinned high on her head. She paced, her arms folded, a piece of parchment clutched between the fingers of one hand. She was not alone. A tall man in traveling leathers stood by her. He was gesticulating, his hands animated, his head bobbing as he spoke at length.

Billie realized she couldn't hear him. The whole world was silent, save for the lapping of the river several hundred yards behind and below her.

The woman—it was the Empress. But not Emily. No. Her… *mother*? Jessamine. And the man, that was Corvo Attano, Royal Protector.

Billie's heart raced. She knew what was about to happen. She knew every moment, every beat of what was to come next.

And she watched it happen. They appeared suddenly, the air swirling in inky black swatches behind them. Whalers, faces hidden behind the respirator masks, knives raised, ready for the kill.

Billie hesitated. Was this just a dream? Or a nightmare? Was the Void showing her the past… or was it placing her *in* it, somehow? She thought back to the rooftop, Daud waiting, crouched, ready for action.

And then she remembered the Shadow. No, that was no dream. Her heart kicked, adrenaline flooding her system, as she lifted herself up onto her haunches, scanning around for any sign of the creature. She had no idea what the thing was, but one thing was clear—it was interfering with history.

Billie had managed to save Daud, but even so, that action had changed history. Had the young Billie still followed Daud to his hideout? Had Daud still made his offer?

And here, now, at the assassination of Empress Jessamine Kaldwin. What was different about it? What was going to happen next? Was it going to be as it was in history? *Her* history, Billie realized with a start.

What if there was more than one history? Which one was the right one?

There was no sign of the Shadow, and Billie could only watch as the Whalers did their job. The black-clad Empress was felled by Daud's blade, while Corvo was held fast by the other members of the gang. Then the young Emily Kaldwin, clad in white, tiny compared to the bulky, muscular gangsters around her, appeared from behind one of the gazebo columns and was grabbed by a Whaler.

This was it. They would take her, keep her hostage while Corvo was framed for the murder of her mother. Billie knew her history—and she felt this moment perhaps more than others. This was a pivot point, on which the course of history turned—not just of the world, but of her own life.

She sensed, rather than saw, movement near her, and turned as the Shadow poured itself over the wall behind her, the air in front of it already sparking blue as the rift began to open.

And history was changed once more.

The Empress was dead. But so was Emily, her thin frame lying crumpled beside her mother's body, her white trouser suit stained heavily with bright, arterial blood. Daud turned to Corvo, who was still on his knees, each arm held by a Whaler. If Daud said something, Billie couldn't hear it, and his mouth was hidden behind the respirator. A moment later, Daud slit the throat of the Royal Protector, and, with a gesture to his men, they released him. Corvo's body toppled sideways under the gazebo, and a moment later the Whalers were gone.

This wasn't what happened. This couldn't be what happened. Daud had never killed Emily or Corvo. Emily was leverage, Corvo a pawn.

Billie spun around, the rift looming ahead of her, the Shadow disappearing into it. She gritted her teeth and dived headlong across its horizon.

To say the house was grand was an understatement; while it wasn't a patch on the House of the Fourth Chair, it was impressive in other ways. The palace was cold, almost clinical, too big and too empty. This house was, in contrast, equally grand but warm and inviting. *Cluttered* was the word that sprang to Billie's mind as she crept along the passageway that led from the foot of the stairs, heading toward a large arched doorway, through which came the sounds of music and conversation.

She'd woken up in a musty bedroom, the door locked, the clammy, stifling atmosphere clouding her mind until she remembered what had happened.

Daud. Corvo. Emily. Jessamine.

The Shadow.

The Void rift had, once again, not returned her to the royal crypt. Billie wondered if it ever would.

Perhaps... if the Shadow returned there. It was clear now that she was just following behind it, being dragged along in its wake as it moved through time.

Changing things. Changing *history*.

And now it had come to this... house? Well, *house* was the wrong word. It was a mansion, one of the grandest. Billie had no idea where or when she was, except that the place reeked of money. The decor was vaguely familiar in the way that all aristocratic fashions and styles were—the hallway was lined with overstuffed chairs that looked like the last thing they were designed for was comfort, and the walls were papered over with embossed floral prints. The warm air suggested… summer? The Month of Harvest, perhaps, when the sun reached its highest.

The perfect season for a sophisticated soiree.

Billie emerged from the passageway onto a large minstrel's gallery; she hid quickly behind a rich velvet curtain, given that the minstrels in question were hard at work—a string quintet, providing some pleasant, if somewhat soporific, ambience to the gathering in the large hall beneath them.

Billie stood and watched a while. The minstrels were dressed in simple red and white outfits, clearly their theme, but the crowd gathered below—what she could see of them—were in velvets, men and women alike with great puffed sleeves, and flat, circular caps, most of which were adorned with a long feather, the more exotic the better. The clothing was strange, but Billie couldn't quite put a finger on why.

Of the Shadow, there was no sign. The Sliver was quiet in Billie's head, and there was no characteristic red-and-blue trail leading back to the Void rift.

She had to get a closer look. If she was indeed merely following the Shadow through time, then it had come here for a reason. She didn't know where or when she was, or whose house she was in, but it was important. It had to be.

Billie took a step back into the passageway, and smoothed down her clothing. With her red jacket and high boots she cut a formal figure.

Would it be formal enough?

Straightening, she stepped back through the doors and

to the left of the musicians. Two of them glanced up at her as they played, but she nodded, holding a hand up.

"Guard detail," she mouthed. The two musicians glanced at each other, but kept on playing, returning their attention to the sheet music on the stands in front of them.

So far, so good. She moved around the group, and headed over to the far end of the gallery, where the rail met the wall. It was less conspicuous than standing in front of the quintet, after all.

Here, the view down into the hall was much better. It was the ballroom of the mansion, the floor a black-and-white checkerboard, the walls papered in richly patterned green, covered with dozens of portrait paintings of all sizes. High windows—well above Billie's position in the gallery—let in warm, bright sunlight, and high above, the hammerbeam roof was hung with myriad colored ribbons.

It was a celebration, and quite a formal one—and then Billie frowned, as she looked down over the people. She realized why their attire was strange. It was… well, old-fashioned. Billie had seen enough examples in paintings and even in newspapers, but she thought the scene looked at least—what?—twenty, thirty years before she had been born.

Where had the Shadow brought her this time?

Her eye was caught by two men below, dressed not in the rich velvet suits that looked far too hot for the sunny afternoon, but in sharp military uniforms, their jackets bright red, their tricorn hats trimmed with fur and a tall, colored pennant rising from the edge. They marched down the center of the room, the crowd parting with an appreciative murmur, and then did a smart about-face at the end. Stamping their feet, the one on the left drew breath.

"My lords and ladies, pray silence for his Imperial

Majesty, Emperor Alexy Olaskir!"

As one, the crowd turned to face the ballroom's main entrance, which was invisible to Billie as it was directly beneath the minstrel's gallery. The string quintet, meanwhile, all stood and, with a couple of glances at Billie, began a much more strident performance.

The crowd below erupted in applause as a large man in an orange military jacket, which was festooned with badges and medals and crossed with a wide blue sash, strode out from under the gallery, acknowledging the crowd as he headed toward the two soldiers. Once in position, he turned to face the audience; Billie noticed a young woman with long black hair piled high above her head, red waistcoat bright under her black, high-collared jacket, move close to the Emperor, turning her body so she too was facing the audience.

Emperor Alexy Olaskir. Billie racked her brains. When had he ruled the Empire of the Isles? It had been in the late… seventeen-hundreds? Billie wasn't sure, although she had seen his name engraved on a sizeable number of old coin, that was still used as viable currency in some of the more far-flung corners of the Isles. But that explained the clothing. She was in the past again—much further back, now.

As the Emperor spoke, Billie tuned him out, instead searching the room for the Shadow. But there was nothing, and no telltale drag on the Sliver, no flashing colors in her vision. Billie clutched tightly at the wooden rail of the minstrel's gallery. The audience below laughed at something the Emperor said, dragging Billie's attention back down to the room. She looked again at the young woman in the red waistcoat. Billie was sure she recognized her, but from where, she had no idea. This was, after all, at least thirty years before she had been born.

"Although she broke my heart," said the Emperor, to another outburst of laughter, "it is with honor that I have accepted the kind invitation to officiate the wedding." He raised his glass in the air, and turned to the woman in the red waistcoat. "Tomorrow, Vera marries Preston, and the houses of Dubhghoill and Moray are united at last. To the current Lord Moray and the future Lady Moray!"

As the audience repeated the toast and the string quintet started a new, celebratory number, Billie backed away from the gallery rail, allowing the Emperor and his host to vanish from her sight. She shook her head in disbelief.

Vera Dubhghoill. Soon to be Lady Vera Moray.

Better known to Billie as… Granny Rags. This mansion was the home of Lord Moray, and tomorrow she would become his wife.

Which made this the year… 1790? In twenty-seven years, the young woman would be a proud, middle-aged aristocrat, and she would join her husband on an ill-fated voyage to the Pandyssian continent. There she would meet the Outsider, and receive his mark, and Lady Vera Preston would become something else entirely.

Billie shuddered at the memory. She knew Granny Rags had been marked by the Outsider, like Daud. Years later, that same marked hand would become a powerful artifact wielded by Paolo, leader of the Howlers in Karnaca, granting him vitality, long life, and the ability to cheat death.

Now she knew why she was here. In Billie's timeline, the marriage was an established fact, and set Vera Moray on course for her meeting with the Outsider.

The Shadow was going to stop it, somehow.

That was when the screaming began.

24

ESTATE OF LORD PRESTON MORAY, DUNWALL

25th Day, Month of Nets, 1790

Billie raced back to the gallery rail, pushing past the musicians who were fleeing in the opposite direction, half their instruments abandoned, half carried to safety. Below, the ballroom was filled with cries of terror as something attacked.

Billie watched in horror as the black smoke of the Shadow materialized around the Emperor, surrounding him in a spinning vortex of darkness. A moment later, it dissipated, and the Emperor, his face contorted in agony, collapsed to the floor.

His two bodyguards immediately sprang into action, with another four soldiers rushing onto the scene from somewhere beneath the gallery. But their efforts were fruitless. One soldier was tending to the Emperor, checking for any signs of life, while another had grabbed Vera and had shoved her behind him, trying to protect her as the Shadow attacked his colleagues. They fought valiantly, doing their duty to protect His Imperial Majesty, but it was to no avail; moments later, Vera and her protector lay on the checkered tiles next to the body of the Emperor. As the crowd of people crushed each other underfoot in the scramble for the exit, the soldiers fired shots wildly into the air, trying to hit the insubstantial form of the Shadow as it crawled through the air above their heads, diving down periodically to stab its blade-like claws into aristocrats and soldiers alike. But as the ballroom floor cleared, the Shadow spun and coalesced back into physical form, the strange, elongated body with wicked sharp-clawed limbs now stalking toward the soldiers as they protected the fallen Emperor and his dead host.

It was now or never. The Shadow was almost directly below the minstrel's gallery. Maybe Billie couldn't stop it. Maybe her knife would be as ineffective as the bullets from the soldier's gun.

But she was going to try anyway.

She swung her legs over the gallery rail and, arms outstretched, leapt down onto the Shadow. As her boots connected with the thing, great clouds of black dust puffed out, stinging Billie's human eye, cutting the insides of her nostrils like razors.

But she hit something. Somewhere, inside the arcane monstrosity, there was a physical form. As Billie's full weight connected with it square in the back, it collapsed onto the floor beneath her, a great cloud of black dust exploding into the air around them.

Billie swung down, stabbing with the knife—and again, found some limited success as a splash of inky black liquid was sprayed across the white tiles of the floor. The Shadow roared in pain, the sound like the deafening crash of the ocean, and Billie's head exploded in pain. All her muscles tensed at once, and Billie slid off the monster and lay, twitching and powerless, on the tiles. She managed to open her eye, and took a breath as the Shadow, dripping its foul ichor onto her, reared above, claw-hands raised, ready to tear her to pieces.

Paralyzed with pain, Billie could only watch as the Shadow raised one hand, curling its blade-like fingers into a crude fist, while keeping its index finger straight. That finger grew longer, the tip sharper, until it was a long spike. It held it in the air a moment, as if it was examining its new tool with its featureless, mask-like face, and then it lowered it, slowly, slowly, toward Billie's face. A moment later, Billie felt the razor's edge cut the skin below her eye—her right eye.

The thing was going to cut the Sliver out of her head.

Then the Shadow convulsed, and roared again. Hot, acrid liquid—the closest the creature had to blood—spat across her face, and then the pressure was gone as it lifted off her and spun around the room.

There was someone standing in front of her. Her vision hazy and sparking at the edges with the now-familiar red and blue aura, Billie couldn't make out the figure completely. All she saw was a hand stretching down toward her.

Billie reached up and grabbed it, and felt an electric shock kick down her arm, jarring her senses. The person pulled her to her feet with one strong pull, and Billie realized the hand she was holding was hard, and cold, like it was made of…

She looked at the arm. It was a weird composite of freely moving shards, splinters of metal and wood, held together by some unknowable force.

Billie looked into the eyes of her rescuer—or rather, her *eye*. Because while one was human, the other was a glowing red ember in a dull, grayish silver surround.

The Sliver.

Her rescuer flipped the bronze Twin-bladed Knife around in her black-shard hand and the weapon dissolved into nothing.

"Come with me," said the woman.

Then she—Billie, herself, somehow, impossibly—

turned and jogged away. On the other side of the ballroom, beneath the minstrel's gallery, was the swirling, shining form of a Void rift. Billie—the other Billie, the impossible Billie—paused at the threshold, her stern gaze fixed on the Billie being rescued.

Then she turned and walked into the rift.

And Billie followed… herself.

25

HOUSE OF THE FOURTH CHAIR, NEAR ALBA

Date unknown, Month of Darkness, 1853

The crypt beneath the House of the Fourth Chair was cold, shockingly so after the muggy warmth of Lord Preston's mansion in that long-ago summer of 1790. Billie tumbled out of the rift, her knees hitting the hard flagstones. It hurt, and it felt good—the sudden shock, combined with the cold of the subterranean chamber, once more helping to clear her head.

And then she looked up. Her rescuer was standing by the empty tomb, arms folded as she leaned against it, ankles crossed. She watched Billie, her expression set. But Billie's eye was immediately drawn to the weapon that was once again in her rescuer's hand.

The Twin-bladed Knife, the parallel polished blades gleaming, sparking in the blue light from the rift.

Billie squeezed her human eye shut, and the Sliver likewise obliged. Except… she could see it, still, the Knife, a glowing yellow outline in a washed-out, magical view of the room.

Billie snapped herself out of it and stood. She watched her rescuer warily, her mind unable to comprehend what—*who*—she was looking at. She paused, trying to think of the right words, form the right question, but after a few moments she just shook her head. She was exhausted, her fight was gone, and events were spiraling well beyond the reach of her understanding.

The other Billie looked at her and nodded. She uncrossed her arms and pressed the heels of her hands against the tomb behind her.

"I'm sure you're pretty confused about what's happening," she said.

Billie looked at her rescuer. Her face creased into a frown, and then she laughed. She couldn't help herself. She felt tired. So very, very tired.

"You are me and I am you, right?" asked Billie. She paused. "I guess the rifts have done more damage to the world than I realized."

"They have," the other Billie said, "but it's not just the rift. It's you, as well."

"What do you mean?"

The other Billie shifted her position and cocked her head. "Do you remember what the Outsider said? What was it, a year ago? More? From your point of view, I mean. But back then, when he visited us aboard the *Dreadful Wale* that night. When he took away our eye and our arm, replacing them with… this."

The other Billie held up her black-shard arm, turning it in the air. Billie looked down at her own arm—the very same arm.

"He said that the world was wounded around me, and that I carried the scars."

The other Billie pushed herself off the empty tomb. "And that time moves around us differently—that we now exist outside of it, part of this world and yet… apart." She paused. "I came from another time—somewhere ahead of you, although it's hard to tell how far now, as every moment I am here risks changing things. Time is malleable, and the more we push on it, the more it has the potential to change."

Billie narrowed her eyes at her future self. "How did you even get here? Through the rifts?"

"I—we—can control them. You'll learn how, soon."

Billie blinked at that casual revelation. "Okay, so... what are you doing here? What's worth the risk?"

"I saw what happened at the Preston mansion. I saw you—*me*—about to die there. I had to act, to save us. That seemed worth it to me."

Billie chuckled. "Oh, trust me, I appreciate it. So that creature, the Shadow—what is it?"

"It's the Queen of Morley. Or at least, a projection of her."

"*What?*"

The other Billie nodded. "She has an artifact, something Void-touched. I don't know what it is, or even where it is—that's something I've never been able to find. But it's given her power, the ability to see through the rifts into time. Letting her watch you. Watch *us*. That's how she knows so much about us."

Billie shook her head in disbelief—and yet, she believed every word of it. She stared at her future, possible, self. "And this artifact allows her to *project* herself into the rifts, as the Shadow?"

"Yes. It seems to be the only way she can move through time, in an incorporeal form. I—*we*—can travel a little more directly. I've been chasing the Shadow for months. It's taking all my time and energy just to repair the damage that the creature is doing."

Comprehension slowly dawned on her. "It's changing history, isn't it?"

The other Billie pursed her lips, and cocked her head again. "That's one perspective. But for us, it's not the only one. As the Outsider said, we exist outside of time—we warp it with our presence, time bending around us like a rock in a stream. So don't think of it as history. Just think of it as time itself. That creature, whatever it is, is changing *time*."

Billie looked around. The crypt was exactly as she had left it earlier. She assumed that the palace itself was still over their heads, that the strange Queen and King were still pacing the halls somewhere.

"But those things I saw, when I was dragged through the rift by the Shadow's wake—they didn't happen like that. If they did, well… I wouldn't be here. *You* wouldn't be here. None of this would be happening."

"That's true," said the other Billie, "but like I said, I've been fixing it."

Billie frowned. "So the changes are reversible? Time can be fixed?"

"While the Queen can only travel in her shadow projection, yes. But she has a plan to overcome that."

Billie lifted her magical arm, and watched the shards of Void stone turn in the air.

"That's why she brought me here," she said. "She wants the Sliver and the arm. You said I'll learn to control the rifts and how to travel through them. It's to do with the Sliver, and the arm."

The other Billie nodded. "Partly, yes. But combined with the artifact she already has, she'll have full mastery of the rifts. She'll be able to travel through them corporeally, and the changes she makes to time will crystalize, become fixed points on which the world pivots."

"Okay, so, how do we stop her?"

"Not we—*you*."

Billie stood, taking a hesitant step toward her other self. "You can't be serious! You can't leave now. You just said that time itself was in danger. We have to stop the Queen."

But the other Billie shook her head. "Haven't you been listening? The longer we are together, the more time bends around us. We are *rocks* in the *stream*. If I'm here too long, with you, then the divergence will become greater and greater as time pulls further and further away from its true course. More than that, it will become permanent. So I'm sorry, but I can't stay."

Billie stared at herself, unsure what to believe, unsure what to do next. Her other self was… well, she was the same, wasn't she? Her hair was shorter, as it was when she had saved Daud from the Albarca Baths. But it was grayer too. This Billie had come from the future to help her.

But which future? And how much help was she, exactly?

Billie sighed, and folded her arms. "I can't do this on my own. If you haven't been able to find the Queen's artifact, how am I going to find it?" She gestured at the Twin-bladed Knife. "I'm not even sure you are from the right future. I can't use the Knife anymore."

The other Billie hefted the blade in her magical hand. "Yes, you can," she said. "The Knife is part of you, like the arm and the eye—and you still have those, right? It's true, none of them have quite the same powers they had before the Outsider fell. They are part of the Void, not him, and there have been other deities before and there will be new ones to come. But there was something different about him, and when he fell, the Void changed, as did those objects which are connected to it."

Billie frowned. "I've tried to use the Knife a few times, but it never works. It's like it is resisting me, fighting back."

The other Billie looked nonplussed. "The only thing stopping you summoning the blade is your own fear. You think you're different, that your powers have changed, and the Knife knows that." Then she pivoted the grip in her fingers and the blade dissolved. A flick of the wrist, and the Knife was back in her hand. "You need to stop being so afraid. You've changed, but so has the world. The Knife is still part of you. So use it."

Billie rolled her neck, then held out her black-shard arm. The other Billie watched, and nodded.

Billie narrowed her eyes, and called on the Void. For a moment, she realized she *was* afraid—of the pain, of failure, of being out of control of the powers she had been granted.

Then she pushed past that. She gritted her teeth. She drew on the Void.

She *commanded* it.

She felt the grip of the Twin-bladed Knife coalesce in her hand. Immediately, it felt as though her magical arm had been dipped in a warm bath, and the lightness of the large dagger, in reality more like a short sword, was both surprising yet instantly familiar. She turned the blade in the air, watching how the polished golden metal flashed with orange, the reflection of a fire from another time, another place.

Billie couldn't resist a grin. "I have to say… I've missed this feeling. Thanks."

The other Billie joined her past self with a grin. "Rocks in a stream, Billie Lurk. Rocks in a stream."

Billie flipped the Twin-bladed Knife around and it dematerialized in a blur of golden light. She twisted her fingers, and the weapon reappeared.

"Find a way of stopping the Queen," said the other Billie.

"What will you do?" Billie asked her, as the Twin-bladed Knife returned to the Void.

Her future self pointed at the rift. "I've still got a lot to do, trust me. I'll try to hold time together for as long as I can, but it's relative—the faster you act, the better it will be, for the both of us."

"Good luck," said Billie. Her other self nodded in acknowledgement, then stepped through the portal. Billie was alone once more.

It was time to end this. And yes, it was true, she couldn't do it on her own. The key, it seemed, was finding out where the Queen was keeping her artifact. And there was someone else in the palace with a keen interest in philosophy, both natural and *super*natural.

It was time to interrogate King Briam.

26

HOUSE OF THE FOURTH CHAIR, NEAR ALBA

Date unknown, Month of Darkness, 1853

Dawn was breaking as Billie emerged from the crypt back into the main part of the palace. But despite the hour, the building still seemed deserted—even more so, because as she headed toward the Great Hall, there were no constables on duty at all.

That was strange, but Billie wasted no time. She had to find the King, and find out what he knew about what his wife—his former enemy—was plotting in the House of the Fourth Chair. He "dabbled", as he put it, in natural philosophy, and had more than a passing interest in magic. Billie thought back to the papers on the table in the Great Hall. The blueprint that looked more like a tomb than anything else.

A new, empty tomb.

The King would tell her everything he knew, or Billie would exsanguinate him.

Billie raced down the corridor. She was fairly sure the large double doors ahead—set with gilt woodwork, and arched at the top—led back to the Great Hall. That was a start. Perhaps the King was still there, poring over the papers.

But before she reached them, the doors were flung

open. She came to a halt, body turned sideways, ready to react to whatever was coming, the Twin-bladed Knife already singing in her hand.

They marched out, four men, one woman, all of them with pistols raised and trained on her. But they were not wearing the green jackets and red caps of the Royal Morley Constabulary. These newcomers wore plain black uniforms, devoid of any insignia, and had sharply creased garrison caps set at a precise angle on their heads.

The Leviathan Company.

Billie raised her hands, ignoring the shouts of the Leviathan soldiers to drop her weapon. Instead, she focused her attention on the sixth member of their party, who had calmly followed them from the Great Hall, hands clutched behind his back. He stopped in the doorway, unhooked one hand, and smoothed down his thin red hair, as though the furious actions of his people were ruffling him. He took the opportunity to adjust his square glasses, staring expressionlessly at Billie, then turned smartly on his heel, clicking his fingers as he did.

"Bring her," said Severin.

Billie finally surrendered to the wildly gesticulating Leviathan guards. Although between them they had five guns aimed at her, they kept their distance, circling her as she walked forward like she was electric. She kept her hands above her head, the Twin-bladed Knife firmly in her grasp. None of the agents seemed inclined to try to wrestle it off her, for the moment. Billie saw the gaze of one of them—a young black woman with tight, wiry hair tied back under the cap—on the Knife, rather than on her prisoner.

Billie followed Severin through the arched doorway, into the Great Hall. There were more Leviathan agents inside, a whole platoon of them. They were spread out, covering the doorways that previously the Royal Morley Constabulary had guarded.

Billie wondered if something had changed since she had emerged from the Void. Had time been altered, despite the efforts of her future self to undo the damage caused by the Queen's shadowy projection?

Severin came to a halt by the big dining table and, to Billie's surprise, clicked his heels together and raised his hand, giving the salute customary to the constabulary.

"The prisoner, Your Majesty," said Severin, before snapping his heels together again and stepping to one side, revealing to Billie the person sitting at the table.

It was King Briam. He was, as usual, holding a silver goblet in his hand, but there was a clarity to his bright, sparkling eyes, and as he stood, he grinned cruelly, his teeth stained red from the drink. The effect, in combination with his black goatee and sunken, pallid cheeks, was not of a noble king, but a creature from a fireside story, the ghoul who lurked under the bed. The papers were still spread out on the table in front of him. Billie's eye was drawn again to the central blueprint of the tomb-like object.

"Billie Lurk," said the King, rising from his chair and walking slowly toward her. Severin kept behind the King, his hands behind his back, his face as unreadable as ever. "The spanner in the works," the King continued, sipping slowly from his goblet. "Or perhaps a tool to be wielded."

Billie held her breath. Then, with a glance at her captors, she took a step forward. Immediately, her guard escort began screaming at her to stand still, and she did, but not because of the order. They used this technique to instill fear into those who opposed them. Billie was not easy to intimidate, and she had no time to humor them.

"Your Majesty," she said, "you need to listen to me, and listen carefully."

"The prisoner will be silent!" snapped Severin. Again, the voice was strong, strident. It had absolutely no effect on Billie. She lowered her chin, fixing the King with her human eye.

"We need to work together," she said, trying a different tack. "Because there is an evil at work in your house. I need your help to stop it."

The King looked at her, the sick grin still plastered on his face. His eyes flickered between Billie's human eye and the Sliver. He sipped his drink.

"It is still linked to the Void, isn't it?" Briam gestured with his goblet to Billie's face. "A piece of the eye of a lost divinity. A unique artifact. One that will be of great use, I'm sure."

The King glanced at Severin, who gave a nod. "It may be the missing piece you need to complete the experiment."

Briam smiled. "You will learn how to control it?"

"My workshops will analyze it," Severin said. "Once we have derived its magic, we will be able to control it, yes."

Billie shook her head, looking at both them. "You need to *listen* to me. The Queen has an artifact of her own, an object—"

"That allows her to project herself into the Void and across the barrier of time?" said the King. He took a sip of his drink, feigning complete disinterest. "That's partly correct. The Queen is projecting herself into the Void, but the artifact is not hers. It is *mine*."

Billie's heart started to race. Had she got it so wrong?

"I don't understand."

"No," said the King, "I expect you don't." He looked at Severin. "How long will you need?"

Severin's expression didn't flicker. "Forty-eight hours, if it can be spared. Thirty-six may be sufficient."

Billie glanced around at her guards. Five of them—

maybe she could take them out. But the Great Hall was full of dozens more. She met the eye of the female guard, who just…

Nodded at her? Billie froze. The guard didn't repeat the gesture, but she did move an eyebrow. Billie got the message. Did she know her? Billie racked her brains, but didn't come up with anything. She'd traveled widely, dealt with a lot of people in her time, and she knew that the Leviathan Company had recruited from all over the Isles. Was it possible they knew each other?

"We've waited this long," said the King. "Take forty-eight. In the meantime, I want to study *that*."

He held out his hand. Billie frowned at him, then realized what he was referring to. Around her, the guards adjusted their aims.

Billie sighed. She gently—and very, very slowly—lowered her arms. The guards shifted on their feet, ready for anything.

The King smiled as Billie turned the Twin-bladed Knife in her grip, and held it out toward him.

He barked a laugh, and took the handle. As soon as he touched it, Billie saw his eyes go wide, the smile on his face changing into an expression of surprise.

The Knife tended to do that. She could imagine how it felt—as light as air, the grip buzzing with an almost imperceptible vibration, the twin blades themselves shiny and sharp and, if you turned them just so, flashing with red and orange, as if they were reflecting the moving light of a great inferno.

"The weapon of legend," said the King, turning it just as Billie had thought he would, his gaze lost in the reflections. He glanced at Severin. "Perhaps I won't need your army after all, eh?"

Severin said nothing. The King continued to weave the

blade in the air, and then his eyes flicked up to meet Billie's gaze. He raised the Knife until the point was aimed at her throat, and poked it into her neck. Billie lifted her chin as she felt a thin trickle of blood run down her skin.

The King's eyes narrowed. "But you didn't arrive at the House of the Fourth Chair with this, did you? It's a little hard to conceal." He paused and cocked his head. "Where did you get it? Was it hidden in the Void, perhaps?"

Billie focused on the King's face. The blade moved a fraction of an inch down her neck, the twinned tips nicking her skin.

"And now you have lost your voice, it seems," said the King. "A pity, given you were so interested in talking just a moment ago. Never mind."

With that, he pulled the blades away from Billie's neck, then lifted the weapon until it was pointing at the Sliver. "You won't need to take her back to your workshops, Severin," he said. "I'll cut this object out of her head now for you."

Billie tensed, ready to fight for her life.

That was when the big double doors of the Great Hall were flung open, and a tremendous wind rushed into the room. The Leviathan guards turned as one to face the intrusion, soldiers from all over the hall abandoning their posts and moving to cover the main doors with their weapons.

It was no use. Of Billie's guard, the four men were swept into the air by the dusty, particulate form of the Queen's Shadow as it swirled around them, breaking their bones in midair before flinging them to the far corners of the hall. The female guard was already down on the floor, scrabbling backward, safely out of the way of the Shadow's wrath.

Billie knocked the King's arm away, but he managed

to keep hold of the Twin-bladed Knife. She spun around, ready to face what was coming, but was herself thrust aside as the Shadow rushed the table. Billie was flung against the wall and bounced onto the floor, face down. By the time she pushed herself up, it was too late.

She watched as the Shadow grabbed the King and lifted him into the air, one long, sharp claw made of nothing but dust and darkness holding him by the throat, while the other grabbed him by the wrist of the hand holding the Twin-bladed Knife. Billie moved forward, only to be immediately thrown back by another gust of wind. There was a *crack*, and the dining table split down the middle, the two halves collapsing together onto the floor.

The King and the Shadow vanished.

Billie staggered forward, bracing herself at the broken V of the table, looking around. A good three-quarters of the Leviathan soldiers had been done for by the Shadow, and the remainder groaned insensibly as they struggled to right themselves after the sudden, tornado-like onslaught.

The Shadow had the King—and the King had the Knife.

Billie had a very bad feeling about that.

And then there was a click, metal on metal, and Billie felt the cold end of a pistol pushed into the back of her neck.

"Don't move," said Severin from behind her. "And put your hands where I can see them."

Billie slowly held her hands up. She glanced over her shoulder.

"I said don't move!"

Billie pushed her luck, slowly turning to face him. Severin hissed in annoyance, but he stood back, keeping the gun pointed at her. He looked a mess—his thin hair was swept to one side, revealing most of his head to be bald, and one lens of his glasses was cracked, the frame sitting unevenly on his nose. His face was flushed, and he was breathing heavily.

The cool, logical, emotionless Severin was rattled.

Billie shook her head. "Now what?"

A flicker of a frown crossed Severin's features, but he was fighting hard to control his expression. He paused for a moment, apparently contemplating the meaning of Billie's question, trying desperately to claw the situation back under his control. Eventually, he rolled his neck and stood a little taller.

"You are my prisoner," he said.

"It's a little late for that, Severin," said Billie. "I don't know if you noticed, but we've got bigger problems here. Your boss was just taken by the one thing the Leviathan Company has no control over."

Severin grimaced, like he was in pain, but it was clear he was still trying to understand the situation.

"That's not true," he said. "The Queen is the experiment, and the experiment is under the King's guidance—"

"The King's *experiment*," spat Billie, "has just taken over. And now she has a new artifact of her own. My knife."

Billie took a step forward, and Severin took a step back. Around the room, those Leviathan guards who were still alive had managed to get back to their feet and were watching the tense situation, exchanging glances, hands hovering over weapons. But so far, nobody was doing anything. Billie was willing to bet they'd never seen their commander-in-chief in this kind of situation, and his clear display of emotion was something strange and unnerving for them.

Severin's lips moved silently, clearly still trying to reconcile events in his own mind, when there was another *click* as a second pistol's safety catch was deactivated.

"Drop it," said a voice from behind Severin. Billie glanced over. The female guard now had Severin at the end of her pistol. Behind his big glasses, his eyes darted to one side, straining to see what was going on.

The guard looked at Billie. "Martha Cottings, at your service." Then she smiled. "It's good to see you again."

Billie stared at her. The name meant nothing.

Severin sighed, and lowered his weapon. Martha—whoever she was—ducked forward and pulled the gun out of his hand, and stuffed it in her belt. She nodded at Billie.

"Just tell me what to do."

Billie was aware that time was ticking rapidly away. She had to get to the King and Queen—wherever they were.

She turned back to Severin. "I think you know more about what's going on than you're saying."

Severin looked up at her, but he said nothing, his lips firmly pressed together.

"The Leviathan Company is run by the King, isn't it?"

At last he spat out a breath. "I don't have to answer to you," he said.

Billie ignored him. "Do you know where he's been taken?"

At this, Severin glanced at the floor. Billie frowned at the top of his head, racking her brains.

Her future self hadn't been able to locate the Queen's artifact, the arcane object the King had been using to project the shadowed form of the Queen into the Void—until, at least, the Queen had broken out of his control.

Then Billie remembered the vision she'd seen through the rift as the Shadow had pulled her along. The crypt, and the empty tomb. The same, but different. Another Void hollow.

Except…

Billie moved over to the split table. In the middle sat

the King's blueprint of the tomb—of half a tomb.

The crypt, and the empty tomb.

Except it wasn't this crypt. It was the *other* crypt. The one in—

"Hey, hands where I can see them!" Martha shouted. She gestured with her gun at Severin. Billie glanced down and saw the man was reaching for the pouches on his belt.

Reaching for the runes.

Billie grabbed Severin's wrist, and pulled his arm up, but the small man was surprisingly strong and the angle between him and Billie wasn't quite right, giving him the advantage. Grimacing with effort, he went with the movement, throwing Billie momentarily off-balance, allowing himself to yank his hand out of her grasp.

Billie cried out.

Someone fired a gun.

And then the room spun anticlockwise and Billie was plunged into an infinitely cold darkness. A moment later, the spinning stopped.

She looked around. She was still in the Great Hall, but it wasn't the Great Hall in the House of the Fourth Chair. Or rather, it was… just not the one she had been standing in moments before. The huge dining table was perfectly intact, and there were no papers on it.

She was also suddenly alone with Severin.

This was the *other* place. The other version of the world, reflected through the Void, a ghostly afterimage stretched out in the unimaginable, unfathomable interstitial space between the real world and the Void.

The Hollow.

Billie snapped her attention back to Severin. She made to reach for him, but with a snarl he bolted for the main doors.

Billie ran out after him.

27

CRYPT OF THE HOUSE OF THE FOURTH CHAIR, THE VOID HOLLOW

Date unknown, Month of Darkness, 1853

She didn't need to waste time trying to track Severin through the maze of the palace. Billie knew exactly where he was going.

The crypt.

Because whatever the artifact was that the Queen was using, it was there: the empty tomb, or at least the half of it that the King had blueprints of. That had to be it. She had seen it herself, in the vision of the crypt the Sliver of the Eye of the Dead God had shown her. There, the empty tomb was not a tomb but part of another kind of structure, a cracked and split plinth of some kind, with someone lying on it in tranquil repose, looking for all the world as if they were carved out of alabaster, just like all the other royal ancestors in the crypt.

That someone was the Queen. And the tomb—the plinth, whatever it really was—must be the artifact. The fact that it was in the Hollow, not the "real" world, was why Billie's future self hadn't been able to find it, and hadn't been able to discover where the Void Shadow vanished to after returning through the rift.

The Hollow. The strange echo of the real world, a projected image stretched out across the gulf of nothingness that now separated the world from the Void as the Void drifted away, unoccupied by any controlling divinity.

A place Billie was now in—and where she would remain, trapped, unless she could get hold of Severin and his runes.

Billie raced along one passageway after another, eventually reaching the twisting stone stairs that led deep into the ancient foundations of the palace. She could already hear the hurricane roar of the Void Shadow as she approached the door, red and blue and yellow light blazing around the edges and through the keyhole. Of Severin there was no sign.

Billie pushed at the door, but it was firmly shut—not locked, but there was a pressure behind it, like someone was pushing from the opposite side. She summoned her strength, and shoved. The door flew open.

The crypt in the Hollow was similar to the one in the real world, but here, at the far end, the Void rift was an angry blaze of red, a terrible tear in the world that hissed and spat like burning oil. In front of it, the empty tomb was replaced, as in Billie's vision, with an angular mass of black stone, the object clearly having been cut and carved and polished centuries ago, but it was now worn and shapeless, save for a few particularly sharp acute angles. The rear half of it was a rough, jagged edge, like the thing had been split in two.

The Queen's body was lying on the slab, her hands crossed over her chest. Above floated the Void Shadow, its vast black form expanding almost to reach the vaulted ceiling. Black dust fell in ash-like flakes from it, the particles drifting lazily to the floor and starting to coat the Queen's body in a thin film.

The Void Shadow still had the King in its grasp, holding him by the neck in one seemingly insubstantial, mist-like talon. The King was alive, but the kick of his legs in the air was weak, and he had both hands at his throat, trying to ease the pressure and prevent the Void Shadow from throttling him.

In the other cruelly curved claw, the Shadow held the Twin-bladed Knife. It seemed to shine more golden than ever, the blades polished to almost a mirror finish.

Billie approached the Shadow at a crouch, skirting around the occupied tombs that lined up down the middle of the crypt, careful to keep their ancient hulks between her and her enemy.

The Void Shadow was looking at her, watching her, its oval head—nothing but a darker outline within a halo of drifting smoke—pointing in her direction. As Billie blinked, she thought she could see the thing's eyes, two dark spots in an otherwise infinitely black face.

"Billie Lurk," said the Void Shadow, its voice like the howling of the wind. "You are too late to interfere now. You bear witness to the culmination of the King's experiment, and my paramount success."

Billie stopped. She looked up at the arcane creature.

"I don't know what you think you've achieved," she said, "but we—*I*—have fought against it. You know that's the truth. All your journeys through the Void, all the moments you have tried to corrupt, they've never crystalized, have they? Every time you've come back, only to find time unchanged, history left the way it always was. You failed, over and over again. What makes you think you can succeed now?"

The Void Shadow seemed to cock its head as it regarded Billie. Then it lifted the arm holding the Twin-bladed Knife, darkness streaming out behind the limb like a cloak made of night.

"You have brought the means of your world's destruction

to me, Billie Lurk," said the Void Shadow. It lifted the Twin-bladed Knife in the air and turned the points to indicate the black slab on which the Shadow's human body—the Queen—lay. "With the altar and the Knife, the two most powerful artifacts in existence will be reunited once more. There will be no power that can stop me."

With those words, the Void Shadow rose even higher in the air, then flung the King down onto the black slab below it, beside the unconscious body of the Queen. Before Billie could react, the Shadow swarmed down, collecting itself from the corners of the crypt and coalescing into the shadowed form of the Queen herself, the mirrored version of the body lying below. With a howling roar, it stabbed the Twin-bladed Knife down, slashing across the King's chest, continuing across the Queen's body. The King screamed in pain, but his cries were muffled as the Void Shadow condensed down onto the black stone, smothering both bodies lying on it.

Immediately, Billie felt the Sliver blaze into life in her skull, the intense and sudden heat almost unbearable. She staggered backward, clutching her face with her magical hand. But that, too, was ablaze with pain, the impossibly suspended shards of metal and stone almost glowing as they were affected by the Void Shadow. Billie staggered back against one of the other tombs, and looked up, struggling to see with her human eye while the Sliver showed her nothing but red and blue sparks.

The Void Shadow had enveloped the whole monolith, covering the bodies of the Queen and King as they lay on the slab. The entire mass had turned into a convulsing, bubbling shape so dark it was almost impossible to focus on, light disappearing into it.

Quite literally—because as Billie watched, the blaze of the Void rift behind began to distort, wispy trails of energy lazily curling off the edges before being drawn down toward the shapeless mass of the Void Shadow. Within moments, the trails had become thick, bright tendrils of smoky energy, and the entire glowing form of the rift began to be drawn in toward the Shadow.

Billie felt the drag too—on the Sliver, on her arm. She tried to turn her head away, but it felt like the Eye of the Dead God was going to be sucked from its socket, while her arm was pulled with steadily growing force toward the altar as the Void Shadow absorbed everything connected to the Void.

Including Billie.

She fought it with all her strength, but she was weakening. She slid across the floor, dragged by the gravity of the black whirlpool, and only just managed to grab the edge of one of the free-standing tombs to arrest her progress. She pulled with her human hand, trying to fight the pull of the Shadow, but knew she couldn't last for very much longer.

That was when she felt the hands under her armpits, and the weight of someone pulling her away. She slid back, and managed to get enough leverage to angle her boot up against the end of the tomb and push with all her might. Together with the hands helping her, she dragged herself away from the rift, back toward the door. She craned her neck up, and watched as Severin gritted his teeth and heaved, like her, using his feet against the sides of the tombs as the pair slowly pulled themselves back across the floor.

The howling wind picked up, blowing the arcane ash around the crypt in a great tumult, and as Billie managed to crawl another six inches back with Severin's help, there was a deep rumbling that shook the floor under them. There was a sudden slackening of the power pulling her toward the rift, and she and Severin collapsed together by the foot of one of the other tombs. She glanced at him, but he was staring in horror over her shoulder. She turned to see.

The Void Shadow was starting to rise, but it was no longer an insubstantial creature of dust and smoke. The thing had merged with the black stone of the altar, its body now a sharp, almost metallic collection of geometric shapes, its whole being composed of black cubic crystals. Behind it, the Void rift continued to power into the monstrous form, silhouetting the creature in a burning halo of red energy. Framed against the bright light, it lifted its rocky arms into the air and roared, the sound like a collapsing mountain.

"Now I must feed!"

With a blinding flash, the rift exploded, bringing down part of the crypt's ceiling, a giant wedge of masonry and stone that crashed down onto the tomb in front of Billie. Ears ringing, vision clouded by dust and the smeary afterimage of the flash, Billie scrambled back as fragmented brickwork and alabaster showered across the chamber as the tomb was shattered. Then there was another crash; looking over her shoulder, she saw the single door to the crypt was now likewise blocked by huge chunks of debris cast down by the disintegrating ceiling.

Then, nothing.

As her hearing came back to her, Billie realized that the crypt was quiet. The roar of the Shadow was gone, as was the aura of the Void as seen by the Sliver. There was no pull on any part of her body as she lay on her side, against the huddled form of Severin.

Billie pushed herself to her feet. The rift was gone—along with the Shadow. Somehow, a couple of the whale oil lamps that lined the crypt's parade of archways had stayed alight, and the whole chamber was cast in a dull, flickering flamelight. Turning on her heel, Billie's fears were confirmed. The ceiling had come down over the door.

They were trapped.

At her feet, Severin moaned and rolled onto his other side. Billie reached down and grabbed him by the front of his tunic. She lifted him bodily into the air, then shoved him against the angled slab of ceiling masonry that covered the door. He yelled out in fright and pain, his eyes wide behind his cracked glasses, his thin red hair a messed-up halo around his head.

Billie pulled on his tunic, pulling him toward her. She snarled in his face.

"You're going to tell me everything about the Leviathan Causeway and the King's experiment, and you're going to tell me *now*."

28

CRYPT OF THE HOUSE OF THE FOURTH CHAIR, THE VOID HOLLOW

Date unknown, Month of Darkness, 1853

"Please," said Severin, struggling to maintain his calm, monotonous tone, "there is no need for violence."

Billie snarled again and pushed Severin back against the slab. He coughed as the air was knocked out of his lungs, then he whooped a great breath of dust-filled air as Billie dragged him back to her face again.

"Whatever that Shadow has become," whispered Billie, "we need to stop it. And if we're going to stand any chance of doing that, then I need to know what's going on and what I'm up against. If you want to get out of here alive, I suggest you start talking."

Severin looked up into Billie's face, then he glanced down and made an effort to clear his throat. Billie released her grip on his jacket, and he fell back against the slab again. He winced, then ran his fingers through his hair, trying to get it back under control. Billie watched, but he was taking too long, so she slapped him across his face, sending his glasses askew. Severin nodded furiously and held up a hand.

Billie stepped back and folded her arms, as Severin readjusted his broken glasses and took a breath.

"It was after the... *changes*... that it started," said

Severin. "You must know about the dreams and the night terrors. It seemed like almost everyone had them. The Queen was very badly affected. The King tried to find a way of helping her. He is—*was*—a natural philosopher, but one more interested in the mechanisms of magic than the workings of the natural order. A heresy, I know. But he began experimenting with artifacts to try to cure the Queen's affliction—he acquired part of the collection of a man called Norcross. Thousands of artifacts, far too many for him to study on his own. So he called in my organization, asked me to apply my knowledge of engineering to the problem of magic." Severin shrugged. "I had been petitioning the Queen and King to pursue the causeway project for years. The King had taken a particular interest, and had visited my laboratories and workshops. He knew what my company was capable of. As well as engineers, I employed the finest natural philosophers outside of the Academy. So when he needed to conduct a large-scale study of the artifacts, naturally he came to me."

"Naturally," hissed Billie.

"It worked, for a time. Or it appeared to, anyway. The Queen seemed cured, but there was something different about her. We didn't know it at the time, what that change would lead to, but in the meantime the King had us continue our work. In exchange for their patronage of the causeway project, we continued to study the artifacts. We soon learned that some of them—the runes and bone charms—had changed, somehow. As our work continued, we discovered that the nature of magic itself had altered. We didn't know how or why, but it went some way towards explaining what had happened to the Abbey of the Everyman and the Sisters of the Oracular Order.

"It was then that the Void rifts began to appear. That

was fortunate for us, as we had the tools to study them. That was how we discovered this place, the Void hollow, and learned how to enter and leave it using altered runes."

"And here you found the last physical connection to the Void itself, which you turned into a mine."

Severin managed a weak smile. "Indeed. Our instrumentation also told us that the connection was tenuous at best, and would eventually collapse. The cavern was already unstable—the Void was disintegrating, literally. I sent engineers in to take samples, to analyze the Void stone. It was in the course of those experiments that we discovered the properties of it when combusted. We reported this to the King, and suddenly the causeway project was turned into something else entirely."

Billie began to pace the crypt. "The Leviathan Causeway was a civil project," she said. "The start of a new type of rail network, able to link all parts of the Empire with fast travel routes."

Severin nodded. "Controlled by Morley, thus giving this country ultimate control over the entire economy of the Empire. It would have shifted the balance of power from Dunwall to Wynnedown. That has long been an aim of Morley."

"Except the King had you turn it into a war project."

"Yes," said Severin. "The Void stone is volatile. We call it voidrite. It can be used as a fuel source, not only providing exceptional power, but also allowing the engine it drives to negate the effects of gravity."

"Allowing you to build machines that can fly."

"Quite so." Severin adjusted his glasses again. "And the Void hollow provided the perfect staging ground. Here the King could build up his army, while work on the causeway continued. The King had me adjust the design of the causeway, turning it into a launch platform for a fleet of aerial war machines. Once we had built enough, we were to send them along the causeway, through the rift at Alba. Within *hours*, Morley would have taken control of Gristol. The rest of the Empire would have fallen in days. There is nothing else in the Isles that could counter our aerial supremacy."

Billie looked down at her feet as she paced, deep in thought. "Control the skies—"

"—control the world. Indeed."

Billie paused, then shook her head. "So what about the King's experiment? You said he used artifacts your company had adjusted to cure the Queen of her dreams?"

"Initially, yes..." said Severin. He hesitated.

Billie frowned at him. "But?"

Severin sighed. "We found something else in the Void. Another artifact—or the remains of one, anyway. It was—"

"An altar," Billie interrupted, staring hard at him. "*The* altar. You found the altar on which the Outsider was created."

Severin narrowed his eyes. "We found an altar, yes. Our instrumentation suggested it had a magic of its own. We dragged it out of the mine, and the King had it brought to the House of the Fourth Chair, and said he would make it his personal study. He devoted himself to its study, eventually finding a way to tap at least some of its power. He wanted to use that power to help the war effort. But to do that, he needed a subject for his experimentation."

"So he used the Queen."

Severin nodded. "By that stage she had learned of his plans, and gathered her own forces against him. The civil war would have lasted more than three days, had the King not used the altar to gain control of her. From there, he continued to use her as the subject for his experiments. He had discovered the altar would allow the manipulation of the Void rifts. They could be used as travel portals, and if there was a way to open new ones, deliberately, then they would become the perfect way to transport troops. How better to conquer Dunwall than to bombard the city from the air with the Void-fueled warships, then march in an occupying army, instantly, through an artificial rift? The King's forces would be truly unstoppable."

Billie stopped her pacing, and turned to face Severin. He flinched under her gaze.

"But the Queen wasn't entirely under the King's control, was she?" Billie asked.

"I believe that is apparent," said Severin. "I had suspected as much. She was, effectively, a prisoner of the King, free only when he used the altar to project an astral form of her through the Void. He hadn't yet found a way of transporting physical objects through the portals."

"That was why she had me brought to her," said Billie. "She was free in the Void, and had learned about me. She thought she could use me to turn the tables on the King, regain control herself."

Severin frowned. Billie thought for a moment, then knelt down beside him, and explained how she had discovered that the Shadow of the Queen had learned to use the Void rifts to travel through time, and had been attempting to alter the course of history in her favor.

Billie left out the fact that the Shadow had been foiled by her future self on a crusade to repair the damage caused to time.

"But she succeeded," said Severin. "She took you from my custody, and you brought with you another artifact—that knife—that will give her all the power she wants."

Billie shook her head. "Not yet. Remember the last thing the Shadow said—'Now I must feed.'" Billie stood and walked over to the far end of the crypt—or at least, as far as she could go with the collapsed ceiling blocking the rest of the way. But even so, she could see the space where the rift had stood—and where the altar had been positioned in front of it.

The altar was gone. It had been absorbed by the Shadow, along with the rift.

Billie turned back to Severin. He had managed to get to his feet, and was limping toward her. She could see the trail of blood left on the floor by his leg. He hissed in pain, then collapsed against the side of one of the tombs.

"Feed on what?" he managed to ask between gasping breaths.

"The Void," said Billie. "What else? It used the Twin-bladed Knife to absorb the altar and the rift. But now the Shadow needs more—it needs fuel."

"So it's gone back to the mine," said Severin.

Billie looked over the wreckage in front of the crypt door. Then she stood back and sighed.

"We have to get out of here."

"That won't be a problem."

She turned around. Severin reached down to his belt, and patted the two pouches that held his runes.

"Not only can the runes transport us into the Void hollow, they can move us between any point within the confines of it."

"To the causeway," said Billie.

Severin nodded. He held out his hand.

Billie took it.

"Then let's go."

29

LEVIATHAN CAUSEWAY, THE VOID HOLLOW

Date unknown, Month of Darkness, 1853

They materialized inside the Leviathan Company's master control room—the empty telescope room at the Royal Morley Observatory. No sooner did Billie feel the floor solidify beneath her feet than it shook with a violent tremor. Arms whirling, she managed to maintain her balance, while beside her came a cry of pain.

Severin had collapsed onto the floor. The leg of his black uniform was soaked through with blood. Billie knelt down beside him. She ripped open his trouser leg, then tore it free from the uniform, and began to fashion a makeshift bandage to try to staunch the bleeding.

The ground shook again. Billie focused on the task in hand, all the while aware of the heat gathering behind the Sliver, of the pull on her magical arm.

The Void was near.

As was the Void Shadow.

Severin hissed in pain. Billie completed the binding of his leg wound, then fell against him as the tower shook again. Once the tremor subsided, she stood and moved to the telescope slot in the wall.

She looked out onto a battlefield.

The military camp stretched out below, with the

Leviathan Causeway sweeping high above. As the whole site shook once more, Billie could see the swing and the sway of the enormous structure, and watched as tiny matchsticks—each in reality an iron girder as big as a rail car—fell from it as the gargantuan bridge shook, the debris crashing beyond view, throwing up huge clouds of dirt and smoke.

At the far side of the vast crater, part of the rocky wall had been destroyed. The hole was filled with a blazing blue fire as the Void mine deeper in the ground had been breached from the side, the earth tremors coinciding with huge flares from the breach.

Facing the inferno, the Leviathan Company army had taken up position on the vast parade ground. From her high viewpoint, Billie could see troops racing around as officers gave orders. Some of the heavy ground assault vehicles were positioned at the front, giving the foot soldiers some cover, while above hung two huge aerial warships. Billie looked to her left, and saw smoke rising from the landing pad that bordered the parade ground. It looked like most of the rest of the air fleet had been destroyed, as something had torn through it en route to the mine.

Severin appeared at Billie's side, gasping as he grabbed hold of the wall for support. He looked down through the slot, shaking his head.

"We can't fight it," he said. "We're too late."

Billie turned back to the slot and scanned the battlefield. The Leviathan army was in position, weapons ready, but there was nothing for them to fire upon. One of the airships, thick yellow smoke pouring from its engine chimney into the tank above, spun around and lowered itself in front of the breach in the crater wall. Billie realized they were watching, and waiting, for something to happen.

Which was precisely the worst thing they could do. Because if the Void Shadow was inside the mine, consuming Void stone, then it was getting stronger and stronger as the army stood by and waited.

As if on cue, the ground shook yet again, this time an upheaval so great it threw both Billie and Severin to the floor. As the Leviathan boss rolled on the floor in agony, Billie pulled herself back up to the window slot, just in time to see the Void Shadow emerge from the breach.

It was colossal, a flaming being of blue-black cubic stone, like one of the partly converted miners but on a truly gargantuan scale. It pulled itself out of the breach, tearing the crater wall apart with its claws, then unfurled to its full height, which was almost as tall as the causeway itself.

The airship that had moved in for a closer look pivoted in the air and made to escape, but it was too slow. The Void Shadow reached out, its triangular, geometric claws unfolding to skewer the craft through the middle. As it pulled the airship toward itself, attracted by the Void stone fuel in its hopper, the engine was ruptured and the craft exploded.

The Void Shadow roared in pain, and Billie watched as the crystalline talon it had pierced the airship with snapped off, the sharply angled slab of Void mineral crashing down onto the parade ground. The tip buried itself deep in the ground, the talon rising nearly as high as the tower of the Royal Morley Observatory.

The Leviathan Corporation's army opened fire, and the war machines in front bucked as their cannons fired, but they had no effect. The Void Shadow lumbered forward, its roar sounding like the end of the world.

"We're too late," whispered Severin. "We're too late."

Billie watched as the monster swept through the

army, collecting troops and war machines alike in its terrible claws.

"No," said Billie. "I think I know a way to stop it."

Severin sighed, and shook his head. "How?"

Billie turned to him, her expression firm. "Just tell me one thing."

"Yes?"

"Do you know how to fly?"

30

LEVIATHAN CAUSEWAY, THE VOID HOLLOW

Date unknown, Month of Darkness, 1853

The pair made it out of the control complex and scurried across to the far side of the parade ground. Out on the battlefield, while the Leviathan Company army wasn't able to push the Void Shadow back, they were managing to stop it advancing with sheer weight of numbers.

Even so, Billie knew they didn't have much time before the army was defeated, or the troops' courage deserted them. Severin, to his credit, was doing his best to keep up with her. She was supporting him as they ran, but his injured leg was slowing their progress. He was, however, the only one out of the two of them who knew how to operate the flying machines.

The plan was simple: the only thing that had noticeably injured the Void Shadow was the exploding flying machine. That meant the Shadow was vulnerable to the volatile Void fuel. If they could get enough of it airborne and dumped onto the monster, then maybe—*maybe*—that would be enough to stop it.

The landing platform was a carved-up wreck, a huge trench having been gouged down the middle of it, tearing through the parked airships, as the Void Shadow had headed toward the mine, drawn by the same pull that Billie now felt from the Sliver. That the whole place hadn't gone up as the Shadow ruptured the fuel systems and engines of the machines was remarkable, but Billie knew she needed their luck to stretch even further. As she clambered around the wreckage, all the while half-carrying Severin, she could only hope that there was at least one airship still capable of flight.

It was Severin who spotted it. He tugged on Billie's jacket, then pointed across the smoking crevasse that split the landing platform in two.

He was right. One of the airships seemed more or less intact. It was sitting nose-down on top of a collapsed landing gear, but was otherwise apparently undamaged.

They made their way across the crevasse, doubling back to find a more manageable route, finally approaching the airship from the rear. Ahead, Billie could see the army fighting their battle against the Void Shadow—a battle she knew they would ultimately lose.

They had to work fast. With Billie's help, Severin got the rear platform of the airship to lower, then he crawled onto it.

"Get it started," said Billie. "I'll join you as soon as I can."

Severin nodded. "It will take a few minutes. What are you going to do?"

Billie turned and pointed. On the far side of the landing platform, shielded from the devastation wrought by the Void Shadow, were two wheeled carts, on which were loaded sacks of Void stone, ready for loading.

"This craft should already be fully fueled," said Severin.

"It's not fuel we need," said Billie. "It's ammunition. The Void Shadow was damaged when the airship it attacked exploded. If I can get enough Void stone aboard, maybe we can find a way of dumping it onto the creature."

Severin busied himself with the loading platform to lift himself up into the airship. As he began to rise, he shook his head. "These vehicles are not designed as bombers. Even if you could load the troop compartment with Void stone, you'd need to crash the airship straight into it. It would be suicide."

Then the platform hatch closed, and Billie turned and ran to the wheeled carts.

Of course, Severin was right. The only way to destroy that creature was to deliver the unstable Void stone right where it would do the most damage.

And the only way to do that was the fly the airship straight into it.

Billie pushed that thought out of her mind and got to work loading the fuel.

Billie dropped into the co-pilot's chair beside Severin, exhausted from heaving two full loads' worth of fuel up into the airship, using the rear loading platform. She allowed herself a moment to relax her strained muscles as Severin busied himself with the controls. A few minutes later, she felt a strange sensation and realized that the craft was lifting straight up from the ground, the angled nose leveling as the broken gear beneath it clattered away.

She followed Severin's movements as he steered the craft. With a sinking feeling in her stomach that wasn't entirely to do with the sensation of lift, she realized the machine was difficult to control. Severin had a vertical stick control in each hand, which he moved constantly, and Billie saw there were two—no, *three*—pedal controls beneath the console. Severin was doing his best to operate them, but with his injured leg he was forced to use his good one more, crossing it over to operate the other pedals as needed. As a result, the airship lurched in the air, rocking back and forth and also side to side as he flew the craft in a slow, wide circle, out to the far crater wall to keep clear of the battle, before turning and coming back in toward the Void Shadow.

Then the airship came to a stop and swung gently, nose to tail, nose to tail, as if it was suspended on a chain from the underside of the causeway, which Billie realized was directly above them.

"If you have any ideas," said Severin through gritted teeth, as he fought to keep the machine under control, "then now would be the time to let me know."

Billie looked ahead. The Leviathan army had begun to retreat. The bulk of its war machines had been destroyed; without them, the foot soldiers stood no chance at all against the monster. That they had held it back this long was nothing short of amazing. But now their time was most certainly up.

Billie looked over the controls again. It wouldn't need to be a long flight, or a comfortable one. All she would have to do was get the machine to the Void Shadow—preferably at full speed. She would never have to land it.

Or do anything else.

Severin twisted his head around to look at her. The machine bucked in the air as his injured leg failed to maintain the correct pressure on the pedal under his foot. "Well?"

Billie nodded, then she leaned over. The cockpit had two doors on either side that opened upward, like the wings of a bird. The doors curved down, the bottom edge forming part of the cockpit floor. By opening her door a little, Billie could lean down and see directly below the craft. The ground was flat and devoid of debris or any other obstruction. A hundred yards or so away was a series of prefab huts.

She turned back to Severin. "Set her down here."

Severin frowned in confusion. Billie indicated in the direction of the huts.

"*Set her down!* And then get out. There are some huts nearby—they should give you enough cover."

Severin shook his head. "Your course of action is irrational. I am the only one who can fly the vehicle. You won't be able to make a run at the Void Shadow, let alone return to clear air. The magnitude of the Void stone explosion will in all probability be large."

Billie just shrugged. "Take us down and get to safety. I'll handle the rest."

Severin stared at her in silence. Billie met his gaze, and held it. Then, after seconds that felt like they stretched into minutes, Severin finally nodded.

Billie let out a breath. Time was of the essence.

As the airship made a rocky descent, Billie reached over to close her wing door. With a last glance through the gap in the floor, she saw they were now perhaps just six feet from the ground.

That was when Severin yelled and pushed her out of her seat. Billie grabbed for something, anything, but her hands found nothing. A second later she hit the hard ground, the impact knocking the breath from her body. There was a roar, and as she rolled onto her back, she squinted against the hurricane of dust as the airship shot up vertically, gaining one hundred, two hundred yards of altitude before pausing in the sky. Then, nose dipped, thick smoke belching from its chimney, the craft shot forward, gaining speed as it careened toward the Void Shadow.

Billie wasted no time. In her mind, she didn't thank Severin. She didn't regret his action. She didn't wish she'd come up with a better plan. She only had one aim in mind—to get to cover—and one word echoing in her thoughts.

Shit shit shit shit shit!

And then the world exploded.

31

LEVIATHAN CAUSEWAY, THE VOID HOLLOW

Date unknown, Month of Darkness, 1853

She felt the breeze first, a gentle tugging on her hair, on her clothes, then she rolled face down as the breeze became a roaring wind, stirring up great clouds of dust and dirt. She coughed into the ground, and wrapped her hands over her ears, as the world ended around her.

And then there was a heavy, metallic thud, and the wind died along with the roaring. Curled into a protective ball, Billie's head pounded. Her nose was filled with smoke and ash, and every other part of her body hurt.

Then she felt something else. A hand on her shoulder, then another on her back. She heard booted feet running, men and women shouting.

The pressure in her head increased. She uncurled herself, only to find all her strength was gone. She flopped onto her back, and as her vision crowded with black sparks she saw a flying machine had landed nearby. Troops were pouring out of the rear compartment.

And then someone moved into her vision—a woman, her black braided hair falling down to frame her face.

She smiled. "Martha Cottings, at your service."

And then everything went black.

32

DUNWALL

18th Day, Month of Darkness, 1853

Billie looked out over the Wrenhaven River as a patrol boat skimmed the water, throwing up a rainbow spray of color in the morning light. She sat back on the marble bench and closed her human eye, enjoying the peace and quiet. The Sliver of the Eye of the Dead God was asleep, and her black-shard arm felt more like it was made of flesh and blood than it ever had.

It felt good to be back. The journey from Alba to Dunwall had taken just ten hours by airship, and Billie had spent most of that time asleep while the mysterious Martha Cottings plotted their course back to the Imperial capital. Billie still didn't know who the woman was, but she had at least learned what had happened while she'd been knocked out in the Void hollow.

Her plan had worked—and she had Severin to thank for that. The Leviathan boss had flown the airship straight into the Void Shadow's body, and the extra load of Void stone had been enough to cause an explosion that had destroyed the creature entirely, shattering it into tons of black mineral fragments. Billie's luck had held out—the shockwave of the explosion had blown her to safety by the prefab huts, which was where Cottings had found her. While the Leviathan Company army had been all but wiped out in the battle—and the subsequent explosion—their entire force had not been present at the camp. Indeed, the remainder of the army, along with their reserve fleet of airships, had already been on their way back into the Hollow from the House of the Fourth Chair, under the command of Severin's second, Uvanov.

But the plan had worked. The Void Shadow was destroyed, and the Void mine had collapsed, sealing the breach and stabilizing the tenuous link between the world and the Void.

It was true that there was still much to be done. It had only been a day, but Billie felt buoyed by developments. Perhaps there was a way to close the rifts, to stabilize the world? She knew she had a lot to talk about with Dribner, and—

"I thought I would find you here."

Billie opened her eye as Empress Emily Kaldwin entered the private garden overlooking the river. The Empress sat on the marble bench beside her old friend.

Billie smiled. "Thanks for the hospitality."

Emily shrugged. "You don't have to thank me for anything. I'm just sorry I wasn't here when you needed me."

"Don't worry, you didn't get out of it that easily. I'm going to need your help now more than ever."

The pair watched the sun play over the river for a few moments, until Billie heard footsteps approach. She turned, and watched as an officer of the City Watch led two newcomers into the garden. The officer stopped in front of the marble bench and gave the Empress a salute.

"Your Majesty, your guests have arrived."

With a bow, the officer backed away. Billie nodded a greeting at Cottings, while beside her, the gowned figure of Professor Dribner fell to one knee, the tatty fabric pooling out around him as he reached up and held Emily's hand.

"Your most gracious Majesty, Emily the Wise, most noble and beneficent mistress of the Isles, Imperatrix of the, erm, Empire. Empress, erm…"

Billie shook her head. She glanced at Cottings. "What took so long?"

Cottings nudged Dribner gently with her boot. The old man started, and looked up at her with a frown, then he pulled himself to his feet—with Cottings' help.

"I can manage, young lady, I can manage!"

"The Professor here wouldn't open his door," said Cottings, shaking her head. "I had to call in the Porter of the Academy to find a caretaker, who had to find a gardener, who used to know someone who once had a key to the Academy undervault before he retired. And then I had to have him practically arrested to bring him here."

Dribner straightened up and made a show of brushing down his gown. "Well, I'm a busy man, a busy man! You can't expect me to just drop everything for breakfast with the Empress!" He paused, and sniffed, then clutched the edges of his gown. "Although, on further consideration, Ms. Lurk and I do have much to discuss, so I will on this occasion accept the invitation."

Emily lifted an eyebrow, then looked at Billie.

"Are you sure he's the right man?"

"Oh, I'm sure," said Billie. "And trust me, he's the *only* man. Cottings and I have brought a good deal of information about the rifts, and with Dribner's help we should be able to find a way to close them."

Cottings cleared her throat, and gave the Empress a small bow. Emily inclined her head, and Cottings turned to Billie.

"What?" Billie asked, looking between the two of them.

Cottings set down the long case she was carrying,

then opened it. Nestled within the velvet interior was the Twin-bladed Knife. Cottings went to pick it up, then stopped. Withdrawing her hand, she instead turned the case to Billie.

"We found it on the battleground."

Billie reached for it with her magical arm. As soon as she touched it, she felt…

Alive.

Awake.

Connected. Not just to the world, but to the Void. It was still there, just further away, but she was still a part of it.

Just like the Knife.

Billie looked up at Cottings. "You never did tell me how we met."

Cottings smiled. "You've got to go get me," she said. "From years back, when I worked with the Royal Protector."

Billie understood. Of course. Her other self—her future self. She was… her. Here. Now.

This was the moment. She could use the Knife to travel from one damaged moment to the next, fixing the changes caused by the Void Shadow. Changes that had already been fixed by Billie—the other Billie—only not by her. Yet.

It made her head spin just thinking about it. She looked up at her friends.

"Okay, Martha Cottings," she said, lifting the blades, feeling the feather-light weight of the artifact. "Tell me where and when, and I'll go find you."

ABOUT THE AUTHOR

Adam Christopher is a novelist, comic book writer, and award-winning editor. The author of *Seven Wonders*, *The Age Atomic*, and *Hang Wire*, and co-writer of *The Shield* for Dark Circle Comics, Adam has also written novels based on the hit CBS television show *Elementary* for Titan Books. His debut novel, *Empire State*, was *SciFiNow*'s Book of the Year and a *Financial Times* Book of the Year for 2012. Born in New Zealand, Adam has lived in Great Britain since 2006.

Find him online at www.adamchristopher.ac and on Twitter as @ghostfinder.